COFFIN COVE

A gripping murder mystery full of twists

JACKIE ELLIOTT

Coffin Cove Mysteries Book 1

Joffe Books, London
www.joffebooks.com

First published in Great Britain in 2021

Cover art by Nick Castle

ISBN: 978-1-78931-754-1

PROLOGUE

She was dreaming of the river again. She was standing on the bank, feeling the breeze lift her hair and brush it against her cheek. She felt the silt from the riverbed oozing through her toes and the cool water gently lapping around her knees and thighs as she waded further in.

A perfect afternoon. The silvery flashes of shoals of fish moved below the surface, the darting movements casting shadows on the rocks. She laughed and plunged her hands into the water, and then her shoulders, her skirt billowing up around her waist.

In her dream, the sun lowered in the sky, casting ominous shadows. The fish disappeared. There was just darkness below her now. She could see a figure, the outline of a man, on the other side of the river. He was waving, gesturing for her to come over. She pushed her feet against the riverbed and struck out in an effort to swim the few feet to the grassy bank. The current was strong, though, and she struggled to make headway.

The water was cold, swirling around her. She looked up and tried to call out for help, but she couldn't shout loud enough to make the figure hear her. She tried to raise her hand to wave at the man, but he had melted away and now she felt the presence of her father reaching out his hand to pull her to safety. She was close enough to smell whiskey on his breath. She could hear him, he was imploring her, calling to her, and for a moment, she felt his tears splash against her face.

She jerked awake.

It was dark, pitch black. Why was she so cold? She struggled again to move her hand and found that it was clamped behind her back. Her legs were wet, and she couldn't move them either.

She gasped a panicked breath, the spell of the dream gone forever. Her head was pounding, and her left cheek was resting against a hard, wet surface. Her legs were partially covered in water.

She couldn't see, but she could still smell the river — that part was real. She was shaking violently now. She realized that her hands were bound with some kind of rope, chafing and cutting into her flesh as she struggled. Her ankles were also tied together also. She was trussed like an animal.

Where was she? What had happened?

As her eyes became accustomed to the darkness, her head cleared and she remembered.

She opened her mouth to scream and a small reedy sound came out, like in her dream. She tried again and again, as she finally realized where she was.

Then water fully submerged her legs, and she knew that it would not be long before the river crept up her body and engulfed her.

She attempted to move her legs backwards and forwards in a snake-like motion, trying to shuffle up and away from the rising current. She struggled, but despite pushing her body to the limits of her strength, she only managed to bang her head against a rock. She knew then that there was no escape.

"Daddy?" she whispered.

But she knew he wasn't coming.

CHAPTER ONE

The man paused for a moment to breathe in the ocean air. Someone had discarded an old rusty prawn trap on the beach, and a pungent waft of dried seaweed and rotten bait mingled with the fresh night breeze. He was used to that. All he could hear was waves gently lapping against the dock and the occasional thud and groan of boats as they strained against their tie-up lines under the inward tide. All familiar sounds.

Nothing else. No voices. Far away, beyond the government dock on the way to town, there was the occasional rumble of a diesel truck engine, but they faded away into the night.

The man felt sure he was alone. But he paused for a minute or two longer anyway. No rush. He leaned against the wooden rail and fumbled in his back pocket for his cigarettes. His fingers closed around the wad of banknotes before he pulled out his smokes and lit up. His hand was shaking. He needed a drink. But first he needed to get this job done. He felt a small frisson of pride.

He had negotiated well, he thought. People underestimated him all the time. He smirked to himself. *They have no idea.* He had been firm — half up front, he insisted, and half when the job was completed to the client's satisfaction. And satisfaction was guaranteed. *Guaranteed*. Nobody better suited to this job than himself.

He puffed up his chest a little, a half-smile on his face as he played out the fantasy of his "negotiations" in his mind.

A dog barking in the distance brought him back to the present. He stubbed out his cigarette and focused his mind on the task ahead.

The boat was in the usual position. The man had watched its owner expertly dock the boat that afternoon. He had tied up and worked around the deck before disappearing into the galley for an hour or two.

Probably going for a nap, he thought.

As the afternoon light faded, the man watched the boat owner emerge once more onto the deck, lock the galley door, and then hop out of the boat and head up the dock towards the town.

The man had been waiting. The early spring evenings were getting lighter, so he had to wait for the sweet spot — dark enough for him to move around unobserved, but not too late to be disturbed by the returning boat owner.

Now. He moved quickly along the dock. At low tide the metal walkway was steep and hard to navigate in the dark, so the man was relieved for the high tide.

When he reached the boat, he took one last look around before hopping over the stern onto the deck. He hadn't been able to see if the owner had left his keys, but it was a well-known fact: go onto any boat and you'll find the keys an arm's length from the galley door.

He stood in front of the locked galley door and stretched up to feel along the narrow ledge at the top. Nothing. He then stretched his arms out wide, feeling in the dark for small spaces that would conceal keys.

But still nothing. The man fumbled around again, panic rising. Where would they be?

Relax and think.

The boat owner was taller. Of course! The man rose as high as he could on tiptoes and stretched up again. Sure enough, his fingers found a small gap behind a light above the galley door and a small bunch of keys on a chain.

He laughed to himself with relief and then delight as he saw that there was a tiny bronze key, a well-worn door key, and what looked like ignition keys.

Fucking idiot, the man almost laughed. This would be easy now.

The galley door popped open, and he stuffed the keys in his pocket. He'd need those again later. The man stood for a second, waiting for his eyes to adjust to the darkness. It was cloudy, with no moonlight to help him, but he didn't mind.

He got to work quickly. He knew that galleys had a multitude of storage areas tucked away, making the best use of small spaces. He ignored the small cupboards and instead pulled up the cushions behind the galley table and opened the long narrow cupboards above the windows. Nothing. He eased himself into the stateroom in the boat's bow and looked around. An open laptop was on the bunk, emitting a low blue light which illuminated the space. On reflex he reached out to grab the laptop, but snatched his hand back, remembering the words from his client: *Touch nothing. Take nothing. Just get the gun. Deviate from these instructions and not getting paid will be the least of your worries.*

The man slid his hands under the mattress on the bunk, but no luck there.

He thought for a moment, then exited the state room, careful not to disturb anything, and stood once more in the galley.

He looked at the galley table and realized that it doubled as a chart table. He reached underneath and eased out a long drawer. There was a tiny lock in the centre, and he pulled out the keychain and found the small bronze key. The drawer opened, and he grinned. A .22 calibre rifle and a box of bullets.

He grabbed the gun but left the box.

Didn't want to drop them all over the place, and his client hadn't said anything about bullets.

Estimating that he'd been in the boat over five minutes, he realized he needed to leave. He re-locked the drawer, pushed it back under the table with the charts and looked around one last time to make sure he hadn't left any cupboard doors open or cushions out of place.

Once out on the deck, the man put the gun down beside him and then stretched up again to replace the keys in the cubbyhole where he found them.

Then he was out of the boat carrying the rifle in one hand, scurrying up the dock as quiet as a rat, finally merging into the shadows.

CHAPTER TWO

Harry Brown brewed some coffee in the galley just as the pale sun edged out of the ocean, throwing its first rays across the glassy surface of the morning tide. The percolator spluttered steaming hot water through freshly ground beans, the same as it had done for the last thirty years, even when the boat was bucking and thrashing. The smell of fresh coffee and the morning ocean always revived Harry, even those mornings when he had seen the sun come up and go down several times without a hint of sleep in between.

Tied to the Coffin Cove Government Dock, Harry normally drank his first cup of the day sitting in a faded canvas chair placed on the stern of his pride and joy — a sixty-foot aluminium purse-seiner, the *Pipe Dream*. Not today, though. As Harry waited for his coffee, dark clouds obscured the late winter sun, and the first fat drops of rain splashed down the windows.

Harry sighed. He was used to bone-chilling wind and relentless rain, but today marked thirty-five straight days of rain, and even he was getting cabin fever.

Harry took up a lot of space in the tiny galley. Over six feet and nearing 300 pounds of solid muscle earned working on fish boats for his entire adult life, he looked as though he would be clumsy in such a small area. But he was used to confined spaces and knew that the secret to avoiding chaos was efficiency and organization. Everything in the galley had a use, and everything had its place.

He ran his fingers through his shock of greying curls and examined his beard in a cracked mirror above the tiny sink. It was also showing signs of salt and pepper. Even this early in the year, Harry had a weathered tan. He had inherited his father's dark skin.

Harry felt most comfortable on a boat. His happiest memories were with his father, Edward, on their tiny wooden trawler, leaving the dock before the sun rose, the smell of coffee on the old oil stove, and a day of jigging cod and pulling prawn traps. That was before the booze ravaged Ed's body and mind and left a spiteful whining husk in place of the laughing hulk of a man, with long dark hair and warm brown eyes that charmed many a barmaid over the years. Harry preferred to remember Ed that way. The smell of the coffee always took him back to that happy place.

Fishing was in Harry's blood, even though his father liked to remind him they weren't a fishing family.

"You'll never make it. Those people will step all over you. It's a pipe dream, son, go logging."

Harry had left school and gone to work on a fish boat when he was fifteen. The first summer he practically worked for nothing. His skipper, Lloyd, took him on only because a deckhand had quit, and he needed another body. He screamed orders at Harry all day long, had him running here and there, cleaning, sorting, sweeping, mending nets and cleaning out the one toilet that seemed, miraculously, to get plugged with shit every day.

But Harry wanted to learn, and when all the other deckies were snoring on their bunks, he snuck up to the wheelhouse and sat with Lloyd, learning how to read the charts and the tides. He soaked up knowledge. And saved every penny he could.

Three years later, he made a down payment on his own boat, and Lloyd co-signed for the loan. Harry remembered picking up Ed and taking him down to the dock to show him the tiny vessel, piled up with second-hand prawn traps, and rope and equipment that Lloyd let him take from his net sheds.

"See, Dad? I told you I could do it!"

"You fucking idiot," Ed sneered at him. "You'll be selling that before the season's out, and you'll be broke." He turned and walked away.

Eighteen-year-old Harry had wiped away the last tears he would ever cry over his father and gone fishing. He did sell the boat. He traded up for the *Pipe Dream* a few years later.

Harry had stopped being angry at his father as he watched good men, great fishermen, beaten down by booze, and sometimes drugs, over the years. He forgave Ed finally, and dropped off a few fresh prawns and salmon now and then to the rundown trailer that Ed moved into when Greta, Harry's mother, had finally had enough of the drinking and left, taking Harry's baby sister with her.

Harry sat at the galley table with his coffee and let his mind wander back to the golden years of fishing, indulging himself with memories of the glory days.

And it had been like a gold rush back then. Fresh seafood from the pristine Canadian waters suddenly became a prized commodity in Japan. Buyers arrived in their chartered jets, with their slick suits, immaculate shoes and briefcases full of cash, in return for the finest sashimi-grade seafood in the world.

With cash came trouble.

Harry recalled sitting at his galley table doling out hundred-dollar bills to his crew with a loaded shotgun resting by his side. Mugging was a common occurrence in Coffin Cove. Drunk deckhands with their pockets full of cash in between openings were easy pickings for the drifters and grifters who always seemed to blow in wherever they thought there was easy money to be had.

Coffin Cove was a lot less sleepy then, Harry remembered. The rain had let up enough for Harry to take his second cup of coffee out to the deck, and from there he watched the trickle of trucks congregate in the Pulp Mill parking lot for the shift change. In the eighties, the Pulp Mill employed 2,000 men, and there were a hundred purse-seiners and gill-netters jostling for position at the docks. The fish plant was heaving with tons of product being processed and flash-frozen every day, and anyone who had any kind of trade experience was sought after and paid handsomely.

Young men graduated (or not) from the now boarded-up high school and either walked into a job at the mill, or down to the docks.

Harry looked around.

Twenty, maybe thirty boats? Sporties in among the commercial guys. The fish plant was boarded up, the warehouses derelict. These days, the boats unloaded further up the coast or in Vancouver. The small fish markets were gone. Instead of multiple buyers vying for their product, the fishermen had to take the price on offer — which often barely covered fuel and expenses. Quotas and licenses had been bought up by major corporations and they could screw down the prices because they owned the quotas, the processing plants, even the reefer trucks that collected the fish. The industry had changed beyond Harry's recognition. He missed being on the water but was glad he wasn't in the thick of it anymore. The boats were high speed, fitted with all the electronics and radar equipment they felt they needed to find the fish, and to pay for all that and make a slim profit, there was no room for the camaraderie of the old days. When Harry had first started fishing, it was the unspoken etiquette to hand over spare parts if a boat had broken down or needed a tow. Now, a boat drifting, unable to set a net, was a competitive advantage to the next man.

Harry sighed. He still went to all the meetings and felt sorry for the young guys as they argued against dwindling quotas, an increasing stranglehold on the industry by unscrupulous buyers and an uninterested government. Their complaints were met with more regulations and paperwork.

10

No point in looking back, Harry thought.

Fishing had served him (and his ex-wife) well. The *Pipe Dream* was paid for, as was a little house on top of the cliff with a spectacular view of the ocean — currently rented out to his sister Hephzibah. His daughter was a teacher, and Harry owed money to no one. He lived unofficially on the *Pipe Dream* (against the rules, but tolerated because his constant presence deterred thieves), he made a little cash by hiring himself out as a boat mechanic once in a while, or filling in for an absent deckhand, and he sportfished a few prawns and salmon from his little skiff when he felt like some fresh seafood.

Once in a while he frequented the Fat Chicken, the only pub left in town. It used to be called the Timberman's Pub until it burned down after a fight broke out between fishermen and loggers (all because of a squabble over a bout of arm-wrestling). The only item intact when they sorted through the smoking debris was a porcelain chicken without a chip or a scratch on it.

Harry had been there last night and had left early. Usually he chatted with the owner, Walter, an old school buddy, and spent time making a fuss of Bruno, the pub dog that waited for Harry every night by the stool at the bar where he always sat. Bruno had met Harry as usual with tail-wagging, but Walter was distracted by a raucous group of five or six students (Harry guessed) with weird-coloured hair, ugly tattoos and piercings with attitudes to match.

A grubby-looking kid with dreadlocks banging on some kind of hand drum had interrupted his quiet beer and burger, singing a protest song about the environment. The kid, with his sneering, cocky attitude, reminded Harry of the last clash with the greenies — especially when Walter tried to quieten him down.

"Fuck off," the kid had said, standing up and coming within two inches of Walter's face.

Harry had braced, watching from his seat at the bar, ready to step in, and Bruno was on his feet, attentive and growling.

"There's no law against singing, is there?"

Harry noticed that the kid was wearing army fatigues. A few months in the actual military might do this little pecker-head some good, he thought.

"Nope, no law, just a request for you to respect the other customers in my pub," Walter replied.

Harry knew that Walter could de-escalate a situation when he needed to, he'd had plenty of practice breaking up fights, and knew it was easier to just not let them start. He sat and watched.

The kid made as if to argue, but changed his mind, shrugged and sat down.

Walter rolled his eyes at Harry. "That's the third night these little assholes have tried to cause trouble."

"Who are they?" Harry asked. "Not seen them around before."

"Activists, apparently," Walter answered, and before he could elaborate, someone else had ordered a drink, and Harry slipped out, leaving payment on the bar.

As Harry mulled over the dregs of his coffee, he snorted to himself.

Greenies.

That's one thing that hadn't changed. Hyped-up city kids with nothing better to do than meddle in what they didn't understand. He felt his anger rise as he remembered the mid-eighties, when Greenpeace launched their *Ocean Crusader*, protesting against fishing practices in the British Columbian waters. A part of Harry understood their point — the demand for seafood was so hot, and the rewards so high, that some fishermen were breaking the rules. For a while, it had been everyone for themselves, and fish stocks were suffering. But the real fishermen policed themselves. The true fishermen knew that their industry would only survive if they looked after their own product, with future generations in mind. No, it was the tactics they used.

Harry's pulse quickened as he thought about that time when the *Pipe Dream* and the *Ocean Crusader* had had a near collision. The *Crusader*, a much faster vessel, was steaming towards the *Pipe Dream*. Harry had just set his net and did not believe for a second that the *Crusader* would deliberately ram his boat, so he held his position and kept on fishing. The skipper on the *Crusader* had other ideas, and it was only a last-minute manoeuvre, when Harry realized that the *Crusader* wasn't slowing or turning, that saved the *Pipe Dream*. Harry lost his net and the fish, but what really incensed him was the skipper laughing as the boats passed each other so closely that paint was nearly scraped off the hulls. Harry remembered the red-hot rage that consumed him. His deckhands talked him down, worried that he would really get into trouble when he grabbed his shotgun and aimed it at the *Crusader*'s skipper.

That wiped the grin off his face, Harry thought. But in the end, it was the *Crusader*'s crew and the greenies who had the last laugh. Harry narrowly avoided being charged, and the protestors hogged the media, using the incident as another example of the Cowboy Fishermen who were out of control.

Harry snapped out of his reverie when he heard a sound, like a scream, he thought, muffled by the morning breeze.

He stood up, looking towards the beach.

Light was now illuminating the east-facing cliff, as the drizzle gave way to watery blue sky, and Harry could see a figure running towards the steps up to the boardwalk. He reached into the galley, grabbed his binoculars and trained them first on the figure running and then back on the beach.

He tossed the rest of his coffee overboard.

Time for breakfast, he thought, as he stepped off the boat, and walked up the dock towards Hephzibah's tiny café.

CHAPTER THREE

For a couple of moments, Andi Silvers thought she might have got away with it.

She lay still and, without moving her head, she just opened her eyes.

Huh. Gritty and dry, but no headache . . . yet.

Andi tested each limb nervously, just stretching out, feeling the change on her skin from the clammy indentation of her sleeping position, to cooler dry sheets. Too much, too soon, she thought, as a familiar queasiness in the pit of her stomach gathered strength into a wave of full-blown nausea. She took a deep breath and pulled herself to a sitting position, and then carefully and slowly swung her legs over the side of the bed. Andi clenched both hands into fists and willed the light-headed, detached sensation to pass. After a moment, she surrendered and staggered to the bathroom. As she gagged into the toilet, the throbbing started behind her eyeballs.

There it is.

Hung-over.

Again.

She sunk to her knees and then lay down, keeping still on the bathroom floor, her burning cheek against the cool porcelain tiles.

Just a few minutes.

She knew only stillness and time would bring relief at this point.

How much did I drink last night?

She counted them off in her mind — one glass of wine when she got in from work, then two glasses of wine downstairs at the pub, or was it three?

She remembered someone telling her an uproariously funny story about tequila — did she have a couple of shots too? She couldn't remember, but it would explain the vomiting — she rarely got this bad just on wine.

Water. That's what she needed now.

Wincing, she heaved herself off the floor. And then slowly, so the room wouldn't spin too badly, she pulled herself to her feet, hanging on to the washbasin to steady herself.

OK. Not too bad.

She shuffled out of the bathroom to the kitchen corner of her studio apartment and looked for something other than slightly rust-coloured tap water to quench her desert thirst.

Shit. No fizzy water. Nothing in her tiny fridge, except the bottle of wine from yesterday.

Empty. Shit. I must have finished that last night. She mentally added that to her drinking inventory.

She poured some water into a grimy glass, considered and rejected food almost in the same thought.

Andi sat on the edge of her bed and sipped the warm tap water, and attempted to piece together the previous night.

Why did I stay so long at the bar? She had promised herself she wouldn't do that again.

She sighed and looked round her little one-room apartment. Clothes crumpled on the floor. Several greasy pizza containers. An open box of junk balanced on the only chair in the room.

She sniffed.

Funny smell. Grime, booze and sweat.

She'd clean up today. This room was an unwelcome reminder of her childhood. She shut her eyes to get rid of the vision of her passed-out parents, slumped on the couch after another night of partying. She'd fought so hard to get out of that life. What the hell was she doing to herself now?

She turned slightly away from the packing boxes piled against a wall. She didn't want to look at them. Unpacking them, she felt, was surrendering. An acceptance that this move was permanent.

"Permanent," she said aloud, and let the word hang ominously in the stale air. She didn't know what to think about that yet. She didn't want to think about her future at all. As if thinking about what might happen tomorrow or making plans that didn't include *him* would jinx everything. Make it all real. *Permanent.*

Andi's phone trilled, the sound echoing around the room, jarring her whole body. She rummaged through the bedclothes, moving quicker than she wanted to, attempting to grab the phone before it went to voicemail. Seeing the number displayed, she sighed and returned to sit on the bed, the sudden movement causing the blood to pound behind her eyes once more.

Work. Not Gavin.

She turned the phone over and over in her hand. It made a soft dinging sound to tell her that the caller had left a message.

She wondered what she would say to Gavin if he called.

Andi admitted to herself that it was likely a situation that she wouldn't need to deal with. The second-to-last time she spoke to Gavin it was face to face, a showdown that made her flush with embarrassment just at the memory.

* * *

Not that the memory was entirely clear. They had celebrated that evening. Gavin had brought over two bottles of wine, and she had downed most of a bottle, both exhilarated and exhausted at the end of a six-month-long assignment.

Andi remembered how he held her in his arms as they slow-danced in her small apartment.

16

"You make me feel like I'm eighteen again, and everything is possible," Gavin whispered.

And then the same old argument.

"I have to go," he said flatly.

"When is this going to end?" Andi demanded. "When are you going to tell her?"

And as usual, he sighed and asked, "Why do you have to be like this?" Then he left.

An hour (and the other bottle of wine) later, Andi's phone rang.

"Gavin?" Her heart jumped with hope.

"Hi honey, how was your day? I'll get some dinner warmed up for you."

An inaudible reply.

"Geez, they're working you hard on this assignment, aren't they?"

The muffled sounds of kissing.

A warm comfortable exchange between married people. *Happily married people.*

Looking back, Andi couldn't piece together exactly what happened next — she was too drunk — but she knew that after that pocket-dialled call, she had got into her car and driven across town to the quiet, neat suburb where Gavin lived with his wife of twelve years and their two children.

Blinking back tears of shame, Andi recalled clearly how she'd marched up the crazy-paving pathway through an immaculately manicured front garden, ignoring the buzzer and the cute brass doorknocker shaped like a dog's head, and announcing her presence by pounding her fists on the door.

"What the fu—?" Gavin had bellowed, his facial expression turning from fury to shock as he saw Andi standing on his doorstep.

"You fucker!" Andi screamed at him. "You lied to me!"

"Gavin?" A tall blonde woman wearing pyjamas and fluffy slippers appeared at Gavin's shoulder before he could say anything. "Who is this? What's going on?"

"Yes, *Gavin*," Andi sneered. "Who am I? Don't you think she should know?"

Gavin stood silent for a second, his eyes filled with disgust.

To Andi's shock, Gavin's wife had stepped forward. "I think this lady has come to the wrong house, don't you, darling?" And then in a harder tone to Andi, "I think you have my husband confused with someone else."

"Daddy? What's going on? Who's that lady?"

To Andi's dismay, a small child with Gavin's dark eyes and his wife's blonde hair had squeezed past Gavin's legs.

"No one, darling. This lady came to the wrong house. Take her back to bed, Gavin." Wordlessly, Gavin swept up his daughter and retreated into the house.

"This lady is nobody," Gavin's wife repeated calmly, as she eyed Andi up and down before closing the door firmly.

Andi was in the office early the next day, red-eyed and unshowered.

"*I'm sorry*," she had texted. "*I'm so sorry.*"

No reply.

Eventually, Gavin appeared at the office door, clean-shaven, neatly dressed as ever, slight shadows under his eyes the only sign of any stress.

"Get into the senior editor's office now," were the very last words he uttered to Andi, before turning his back and walking away from her.

Andi hadn't had time to tend her broken heart. The next two hours were spent trying — and failing — to save her job.

She had screwed up. She had failed to corroborate a tip-off from a source. She had written an article, sure that everything was fine (and assuring Gavin that the source was solid). It wasn't fine. The tip had been bogus, a prominent businessman had threatened to sue. It was a horrible mess. The newspaper would have to apologize publicly.

Andi was fired. She still felt the sting of humiliation. They issued Gavin a warning, she discovered later. She had tried to contact him, calling, texting, and even emailing. One curt text came back that filled her with a little hope:

"*We'll talk later.*"

Three months later and they still hadn't spoken.

In a month, Andi's money ran out. She hadn't found another job. She was toxic now. She had been a rising star, a tenacious reporter and talented writer. But nobody would touch her résumé or even return her calls.

In desperation, she answered a small ad for a reporter/assistant editor/administrator for a place she had never heard of on Vancouver Island. To her surprise, the *Coffin Cove Gazette*, an independent publication, offered her an interview immediately.

She accepted, hoping that the owner would not probe too far beyond the carefully presented portfolio she sent ahead of her appointment.

A two-hour ferry journey and Andi was on the island, following the directions that Jim Peters, the owner and editor of the *Gazette*, had sent her.

After half an hour driving from the ferry terminal, she assumed she must have read the directions incorrectly. She was driving north, and after turning off the main island highway, she found herself driving along a small winding road along a cliff edge. She pulled over and checked the directions again. Frowning, she pulled out her cell phone. No service.

Shit.

On impulse, she got out of the car. The salty breeze on her face and the expansive view of the ocean both calmed her and reminded her of her aloneness. Standing on top of the cliff, she acknowledged — painfully — that Gavin had been more than an office fling. She had become obsessed with him. Her whole life had revolved around him. She had spent her spare time waiting for him to call or text. She lived for the stolen afternoons when they would sneak out of the office "on assignment". He had never lied about his marriage. But he had allowed her to believe that eventually the affair would be much more.

"And now I'm just a cliché."

Standing on the cliff, plunging into the unknown, Andi wiped angry tears away. *Stupid, stupid, stupid* — for allowing herself to think it could be anything more. The cool way she had been dispatched out of Gavin's life by his wife told her that this probably wasn't the first time. She hadn't been special. A sudden surge of fury motivated her to get back in the car.

Jim Peters, her new boss, had given her a chance.

When she finally arrived at the *Coffin Cove Gazette* that day, there was no efficient receptionist to announce her arrival. Just a shabby office with an ancient photocopier in one corner and an oversized desk in the other. A man with glasses perched on his balding head was typing furiously and made no sign to acknowledge Andi's presence.

Not sure what to do, Andi nervously cleared her throat and opened her mouth to announce herself.

"One minute." The man squinted at his screen, and then typed again for a few seconds.

"There. OK. Andi, is it?" He gestured to a seat in front of his desk.

"Hi, yes, sorry, I'm a few minutes late . . ." Andi sat in the sagging chair opposite the man she assumed was Jim Peters.

"Yes, yes, not a problem, we are hard to find. So, tell me about yourself and your work." The man leaned back and folded his arms across his chest. Andi noticed that his hands were bony and wrinkled, an elderly man's hands. But as he interrupted her, and questioned and assessed her with intense blue eyes, Andi realized that whatever his age, this man's intellect and curiosity made him a match for any journalist she had ever worked with before. And she realized something else. She really wanted this job.

After an hour of probing questions, Jim Peters got up from behind the desk and perched in front of Andi.

"I know what happened. There's no excuse for what you did. I won't tolerate any corner-cutting. This is a small community. We report on the things that matter to the people who live here, and we are only concerned with the facts and truth, got it?"

Andi nodded.

"OK, then. You can start tomorrow, if that works."

Andi remembered the relief she felt. A completely clean slate. A chance to start again.

Now, hung-over in her new apartment, she dialled her voicemail and listened to the message.

CHAPTER FOUR

Andi pounded her steering wheel in annoyance.

"Not one fucking place to park."

The normally deserted parking lot at the Government Docks was full.

Andi crawled slowly around, twice, as people milled in front of her, not in a hurry to get out of the way.

Andi didn't know there were this many people in town. She gave up the search and ended up driving almost all the way back to the Fat Chicken. Jim had made one phone call after her interview, and after her hasty acceptance of the job offer, she also had a new apartment. It was above the only pub in town, but at least it came with its own parking space. Since she'd moved in, Andi had spent a good deal of time in the bar. Too much time, she thought, as she struggled to ignore the throbbing behind her tired eyes.

Coffin Cove was built on a hill overlooking the ocean. Narrow roads wound up to the pinnacle, where back in the glory days of coal and logging, the owners and managers of the local mines and sawmills had built the fanciest homes with the best views of the bay.

Further down, the houses got smaller and more crammed together, and just before the boardwalk and the marina, there was one strip of stores, a bank, a post office and the only café in town, Hephzibah's. Andi wondered again why Coffin Cove had not flourished like other coastal communities on Vancouver Island. Other cities and towns had embraced tourism, built malls, encouraged retirees to settle in clusters of cookie-cutter ranches, and had built up service economies and leisure industries around the aging baby boomer population. Coffin Cove seemed stuck in the past, in a futile waiting pattern — waiting for the fishing industry to return or for a miraculous revitalization of logging. In the meantime, some people tried to launch new businesses, optimistically creating window displays and hanging out balloons, until the *Under New Management — Come On In!* signs faded. Andi had noticed some stores having closing-down sales when she had arrived in Coffin Cove a month ago, and they were showing no indications of finishing.

She parked her car and strode briskly down to the dock, feeling better for the walk in the persistent drizzle.

She had listened to the voicemail from Jim and nearly hadn't bothered with a shower. But as it was, she had let the hot water cascade over her, washing away the stale booze and cigarette smell. She'd dried her hair, put on some makeup and rummaged around in the dilapidated kitchen cupboards for breakfast food that wasn't chips or chocolate. She settled on a fried egg sandwich. The grease was already doing its job on her acid stomach, and a large black coffee combined with the damp salt air was keeping her headache at a manageable level.

Andi had her camera slung over her shoulder and her phone in her pocket — all the equipment she needed as a reporter. She took her own photos and used the voice recording app on her phone for interviews. Until two months ago, her writing skills plus her instinct for a good (or at least "sellable") story made her a successful journalist. But her real asset was her ability to blend in with the crowd. Her small, unobtrusive figure was barely noticeable at crime scenes, courthouses and even in the homes of people in the throes of scandals or tragedy. People let their guard down with Andi — an unthreatening, diminutive woman who knew how to listen sympathetically, murmuring encouragement as the real story came spilling out. *She was on their side. She would never sell them out.*

Down at the dock, Andi scanned the crowd looking for Jim. He had only left a short, terse message for Andi to meet him at the marina. He had said nothing else, but Andi got the impression something significant was going on. She spotted him standing by the boat ramp talking to . . . *Shit, a TV crew.*

Jim waved at her to meet him by the boat ramp.

"What's g—" Andi started to ask, but took a step back in horror as she got near.

"Holy shit," she gasped, as her fried egg sandwich thrashed around in her already sensitive stomach. It wasn't what she could see that caused her reaction. Andi couldn't even tell what the swollen mottled mounds were, slumped on the concrete slope. No, it was the putrid stench of decomposition coming from these . . . dead animals? Two officials in matching yellow rain gear were taking pictures and examining the mounds. Someone had cordoned off the entrance to the boat ramp with tape so the gathering crowd couldn't get any nearer. Not that anyone would want to, surely. The odour was thick — a mixture of dead fish and rotten eggs. It wafted like an invisible curtain in the slight breeze off the ocean and invaded Andi's nostrils and clung to her hair. She clamped her mouth shut and walked abruptly away from Jim, desperate not to vomit in front of him.

Jim followed her. He took her arm and steered her to the far end of the parking lot.

"It's better here," he said. "Is it the tequila or the stink?"

Andi looked at him. She couldn't remember him being in the pub last night.

"Everybody knows everybody's business in this small town," Jim answered her unspoken question.

Was that a hint of amusement on his face? She struggled to control her nausea.

"That's a body." She tried to focus on the reason she was here.

"Well, technically there are two bodies," Jim stated. "Two sea lions. No human bodies," he added. "Sorry about that."

Slightly irritated at Jim's tone, and because he had correctly noted her disappointment, she said, "So what's the story here? And why the camera crew?"

"It's a federal crime to kill sea lions. And these aren't the first to appear on the beach or the boat ramp. They were shot," Jim added.

"Why?" Andi was mystified and shocked. "Why would anyone want to hurt them?"

"Sea lions have multiplied in the last few years. They eat salmon. Lots and lots of salmon. The fishermen believe they'll wipe out the commercial fishery . . . eventually. So to fishermen, they are a pest. Plus, they're filthy and they're wrecking the breakwater."

"Can't they be culled?" Andi asked, her flip-flopping stomach forgotten for a moment.

"No, says the DFO . . . Department of Fisheries and Oceans," Jim corrected himself for Andi's benefit. "Those two are DFO officers." He gestured at the two men probing the dead sea lions, apparently unaffected by the smell.

"They say the science doesn't support it. But the fishermen say they're being influenced by *those guys*."

Jim gestured at a group of onlookers who had edged towards the boat ramp, flashing camera phones and jostling to get a better view of the bloated corpses.

Andi noticed that most were dressed all in black and wore bandanas across their mouths. First, she thought they were merely trying to avoid the stench. But there was tension in the air as the group, in one purposeful move, pushed forward and swarmed around the entrance of the ramp, blocking the exit of the officials who were still examining the dead sea lions. The fishermen and other local workers, in their own uniform of grey woollen Stanfields and overalls, had backed away.

It felt like a standoff, Andi thought. The sudden mood change from curiosity to hostility, the division of the crowd into two factions — she had seen and felt this before. A gaggle of seemingly unconnected people, tension sparked by a small random act, a flash of anger that erupts and engulfs everyone, until a crowd becomes a mob.

"Protesters," she said to Jim. "Which organization?"

"The Ocean Protection Society," Jim replied. "Commonly known as Black OPS. This has been building all week. The Coast Guard and DFO have been getting calls since herring season opened, about fishermen who aren't wearing lifejackets or don't have safety equipment on board — minor infractions, but they all have to be investigated, so some fishermen are tied to dock instead of fishing. They're not happy about it. And this morning, there was an anonymous tip-off that a fisherman was shooting at sea lions."

Andi already had the lens cap off her camera and was focusing in on the protestors. They all wore black from head to foot. Commando-style jackets, baseball caps pulled as far down as they would go, and the bandanas serving as face masks made it hard to distinguish gender, let alone identity. All save one figure who stood slightly apart. A slightly built man, with a military-style buzz cut and the posture to match, took a slow look around the parking lot, as if surveying an audience.

Slowly and deliberately he folded his arms and shouted something that Andi couldn't quite hear. Like an army of foot soldiers obeying a sergeant, the Black OPS group parted and let the DFO officials leave the boat ramp. Then, with the arrogance and self-assuredness of a movie star on a red carpet, he gestured at the local TV crew.

"He's the story," Jim continued, as a TV reporter and cameraman rushed forward and held a microphone under the man's nose.

"Who is he?" Andi asked. "Why are the DFO listening to him more than the fishermen?" She swung her camera over her shoulder, grabbed her phone, and started to move, now understanding that there was far more to this story than two dead sea lions.

"Shouldn't we be getting an interview?" She looked over her shoulder and saw that Jim hadn't moved. He was still standing in the rain, quietly observing the man giving an animated interview surrounded by his black-garbed disciples.

The locals had dispersed, drifting back to their boats.

"No, it's OK," he said. "You won't get any more than a one-sided rant out of him. And he'll never talk to a reporter from the *Gazette*, anyway."

Andi persisted. "We're supposed to be reporting the news, right? His 'rant' is news, even if we — or you — don't agree with it."

Jim stared at Andi. To her annoyance, he spoke slowly, as if to a small child. "You look like you could do with a coffee. Let's go to Hephzibah's and I'll tell you why this is the biggest story for the *Gazette* in twenty years. Looks like you arrived in Coffin Cove at exactly the right time."

CHAPTER FIVE

"Morning Glory," Hephzibah declared, as she put a plate with two muffins in front of Jim and Andi. "Coffee?"

Andi nodded. Her fried egg sandwich was a distant memory and her head was throbbing again. As she waited for her coffee, she checked her phone again. Nothing from Gavin, but she saw Jim had left three messages for her that morning. How embarrassing. She'd nearly missed all the action at the dock. She had to do better if she was going to hang on to this job.

The late afternoon sun had lost all warmth. It had started to rain. Andi and Jim had loitered at the dock until the crowd slowly dispersed. Fishermen faded back to their boats, some of them nodding to Jim but not wanting to speak. At least, not on the record. Andi guessed that the fishermen did not want to be cornered by the official examining the dead sea lions. The protestors had also melted away, now that they had achieved their aim — attention from the media. Andi had covered protests before and knew how it worked.

Apart from Jim and Andi, Hephzibah's café was empty. The only noise came from Hephzibah herself, chinking cups and saucers as she emptied her ancient dishwasher. Clouds of steam from the hot water misted up the windows that looked over the bay.

Hephzibah enjoyed almost exclusive control over the coffee trade in Coffin Cove. The big chain stores, if they had even heard of Coffin Cove, had not bothered to expand their corporate tentacles into the little town, sensing perhaps that it would be hard to coax customers away from Hephzibah's ramshackle café. She was not a rich woman, despite her lack of competition. Coffee was cheap — free for many inhabitants, if they were financially pressured, or even if they were having a bad day. Other customers were often forced to wait while Hephzibah doled out free hugs and motherly advice.

Andi had found Hephzibah on the day she arrived in Coffin Cove with her suitcase and all her belongings stuffed into her car. Jim had arranged her tiny apartment above the Fat Chicken, and after dumping all her stuff, she went in search of a decent cup of coffee. She found a surprisingly good brew and barely missed the array of options and additions on offer at the sleek branded coffee emporiums she frequented in the city. Over the next weeks, Andi found that a tiny table squeezed in by the café window was where she liked to write. Jim had given her a desk at the *Gazette* office, but the dingy surroundings reminded her too much of her apartment. Depressing. So Andi escaped with her laptop to the café, avoiding Jim's curt comments about her hung-over appearance, and attempted to throw herself into the few "starter assignments" he'd given her. Every day she promised herself she would drink less. She planned to start a blog, or that novel she had always said she would write. But most days she found herself nursing a throbbing headache and hastily writing enough to avoid more disapproving looks from her boss. Working had always kept Andi's mind occupied, but still she found her thoughts wandering back to Gavin. At least the chatter and hum of the café kept her loneliness at bay. Not only that: Andi was drawn to the owner of the café, a tall angular woman who seemed comfortable in her own skin. Hephzibah was single and about the same age as Andi, but she had the confident aura of an older woman who had her life in order. Andi envied that. Hephzibah appeared to know everyone and everything that was going on in Coffin Cove. None of her gossip was malicious, and Andi recognized a golden source of information when she saw one.

Andi and Jim settled into the comfy armchairs by the woodstove at the back of the café. The days were getting warmer, hinting at spring, but Hephzibah lit the stove anyway as marine air often rolled in from the Pacific Ocean, enveloping the dips and crevices and valleys along the coast, leaving continuous moisture hanging in the air.

"Sorry again for missing your calls." Andi coughed awkwardly. "I, uh, must have left my phone off."

Jim shrugged. In the short time that she had known Jim, Andi had discovered he seldom wasted his breath on small talk. She changed tack. "So what's the deal? Who's the main guy and what's the story?"

"Pierre Mason," Jim answered. "Originally from Quebec, likes to be known as an eco-terrorist," he snorted. "Fired, it's believed, from Greenpeace back in the early nineties. They were apparently tired of getting lawsuits following Mason's dangerous stunts, which almost always involved damaging property." Jim hesitated. "But not before he raised a significant amount of cash from his own brand of publicity."

"Sometimes those kind of shock tactics are effective," Andi said. "To get media coverage for their cause."

Jim shrugged. "I suppose. But Pierre Mason is known to be violent. Well . . ." He took a gulp of his coffee and seemed to weigh up his words. "He's not *directly* violent. But he's not above inciting the odd riot, as you saw today. He's charismatic, and impressionable kids hang off his every word."

Andi nodded. She'd seen how his Black OPS had swarmed on his command.

"After Greenpeace," Jim carried on, "Mason freelanced for a bit. Kind of like an environmental mercenary — he'd organize protests, stunts, pickets, that sort of thing, paid for by whatever organization needed his expertise. That's how he ended up in Coffin Cove."

"To protest against the fishing industry?"

"No," Jim said, "the War in the Woods."

Andi shook her head.

"Back in the nineties, environmentalists blockaded forestry operations, protesting clear-cutting — that's felling every tree in one area at a time," he added.

Andi nodded, not wanting to give away her ignorance.

"Also, local bands — local First Nations," Jim corrected himself, "they got caught up in the protest because their traditional territories were being logged, and they weren't getting compensated. Also, the clear-cutting was affecting the water supply. When the water contamination spread into the river and then the main reservoir that supplies the town, the city council was inundated with complaints." Jim looked at Andi. "You have to bear in mind that back then, the entire local economy was built on the resources industry. There wasn't one family in town who didn't have some income coming directly from fishing or logging. And every small business depended on those families spending that money. So it was unprecedented when one of the biggest logging companies, McIntosh & Co, agreed to change their logging practices and clean up the pollution."

Jim stopped to take a gulp of his coffee.

"What about the First Nation claims?" Andi asked.

"I'm coming to that. Joe McIntosh was forward-thinking. He could see that the future of logging was in decline. The environmental lobby had a louder voice, and indigenous land claims were being taken seriously. Joe figured that his company and the industry in general would have a longer lifespan if they adapted."

"Sounds like a smart guy," Andi commented. "So why the war?"

"It started much like today," Jim said. "A few protestors showed up, stirred up a bit of trouble, nothing significant to start with. Joe headed up a committee and involved the band elders, local environmentalists, the union, and they hashed out a plan. Everyone was happy, or so Joe thought. Then one day, one of his crews came in to work and found that someone had sabotaged their machinery — and worse than that, they spiked trees."

"What's that?" Andi asked.

"The protestors had driven spikes or long nails into the trees. The logger can't see the spike until his chainsaw hits it, and then the saw explodes. Imagine thousands of razor-sharp pieces of steel flying up in your face."

"Holy shit," Andi said, horrified.

"Yes," Jim said grimly. "If the logger misses it, and the tree ends up in a sawmill — then it can be even worse when the spike is hit by a high-speed blade on a conveyer belt. Some poor kid was torn apart just like that, down in a California sawmill. It split his jaw in half. A bit more than 'shock tactics', don't you think?"

"Was anyone hurt here?" Andi ignored Jim's sarcasm.

"No, Joe shut down operations immediately. A few days later, Coffin Cove was swarming with so-called eco-terrorists, led by our friend out there." Jim gestured towards the marina.

"So what happened?"

"Well," Jim paused, looking down into his coffee cup, seemingly lost in memories for a moment, "it was a difficult time. Mason recruited some young people in the town, who were only too happy to hang out at blockades . . . You might have noticed, there's not too much for teenagers to do in this town," Jim added wryly, "and Joe kept attempting to negotiate with anyone who would listen. But the environmentalists wanted the whole show shut down, and the band wanted to take over the entire operation. And this is the weird thing—" Jim shifted forward in his chair — "Mason always seemed to be one step ahead of Joe. Every time Joe set up a meeting, Mason knew about it."

"Someone on the inside," Andi said. "But why all the focus on Joe's operation? There had to have been other logging companies clear-cutting at the time?"

"Yes, but none as big as Joe's and still privately owned."

Andi drained her coffee. "So who was paying Mason?"

"A large American corporation, we think. But we were too late. Joe sold before we could find evidence."

"He sold?" Andi was surprised. "Why?"

"Here's the tragic part. And the reason it's such a big deal that Mason's back."

Jim ran his finger through his hair and looked tired for a moment.

"Joe's daughter, Sarah, went missing. Joe thought she was just acting up and hanging out at the blockades — you know what teenagers are like, anything for a bit of excitement. But she didn't come home, so he called the police. They searched for days. But they suspected she might have been taken by the eco-terrorists."

"What, you mean kidnapped?"

Jim nodded. "Yes, but there was no ransom demand. And then—" he paused and looked down — "her body washed up on the beach."

"Oh, I'm sorry." Andi could see Jim was getting emotional.

"Yes." He sat up and looked Andi in the eye. "It was definitely foul play. They tied her legs and arms."

"Oh no."

Andi and Jim sat silent for a moment. Andi had questions but waited respectfully until Jim spoke again.

"It devastated Joe. Sarah was his only child."

"There must have been an investigation?"

"Yes. It hit the town hard. Everyone knew Sarah, she was well liked, she lived with her mother most of the time — she and Joe split up when Sarah was little. She got on well with Joe . . ." Jim paused.

"But?" Andi prompted him.

"She didn't like his new wife much. But that's normal, I guess. The popular opinion was Sarah was abducted and something went wrong."

"Abducted by the protestors? That's pretty drastic," Andi thought out loud.

"Not for those bastards."

Andi was so lost in thought she hadn't noticed someone behind her.

"Harry." Jim gestured to a large man who had overheard Andi's musing. "Sit down. This is Andi, the *Gazette*'s new reporter."

Harry pulled up a chair. Andi could see he was a fisherman. He was wearing overalls and boots, the same as the crowd on the dock earlier. Even sitting, Harry towered over them. He looked familiar to Andi, but she couldn't place him.

"Those bastards thought it was OK to spike trees and put loggers' lives in danger, you reckon they'd think twice about taking a kid?" he asked. He was matter-of-fact, not ranting, but he looked directly at her and held her gaze, waiting for a response.

"Harry—" Hephzibah interrupted them with coffee refills — "leave the girl alone. She wasn't here, she doesn't know what it was like."

Andi realized why Harry seemed familiar. He and Hephzibah could have been twins — except that he was built powerfully and she was tall and graceful, like a dancer. And Harry was clearly older — in his fifties, Andi estimated.

"My big brother," Hephzibah confirmed. "He's quite direct," she added unnecessarily.

"So, what was it like?" Andi asked. "Was there evidence that the protestors — and Mason — were involved? And if so, what is he doing here now?"

"He's getting paid." Jim answered the last part of Andi's question first. "And no, there was no direct evidence. We couldn't link him to the American company that bought out McIntosh. We found out he was recruiting and paying protestors. Every Wednesday, they would all disappear. Turns out that Mason was bussing them back to Victoria, so they could pick up their welfare cheque. The police questioned him but couldn't find any link to Sarah. Then they received a tip-off that Sarah and Mason were seen together just before she vanished. There was still no evidence that he had anything to do with her disappearance or murder, but there were no other leads. Then the rumour mill took over. Maybe Mason seduced Sarah and it all went wrong — that kind of thing. It was a bad time."

"And he's back in Coffin Cove," Andi said. "Doesn't seem like something a guilty man would do, right?"

"He's an arrogant prick," Harry grunted. "Doesn't mean anything."

"So why would he get involved in a sea lion shooting?" Andi asked, feeling confused.

"It's not just the sea lions. His Black OPS have been phoning in minor safety issues and infractions, meaning that some fishermen are tied to the dock for a day or so, rather than fishing."

"OK, I get that," Andi said. "But *who* is he working for, and *why* do they want to disrupt your fishing?" She was getting impatient.

"Don't know," said Harry. "Could be the Americans. They're always whining."

"Fish farms?" Jim suggested.

"Could be them too." Harry shrugged.

"Fish farms?" Andi asked.

"Great big pens in the ocean where they breed mutant fish and sell them to people who don't know better," Harry answered sarcastically.

"I know what fish farms are, thanks," Andi replied, thinking it was a bit rich of Harry to be accusing anyone else of being an arrogant prick. "I would have thought eco-terrorists would be more concerned about fish farms than a couple of sea lions being shot."

Harry shrugged again. "Well, you guys are the investigators," he said, standing up. "I'm going to see Joe tomorrow morning. It's best he knows about Mason being back in town from a friend, not town gossip."

"Joe still lives in town?" Andi asked, surprised again.

"Where would he go?" Harry responded. "All his friends and family are here."

"Good idea." Jim got up too. "Let me know how he is." He turned to Andi. "Let's talk about this in the office tomorrow, it's getting late."

The three of them said their goodbyes to Hephzibah, who was waiting to close up, and they stood for a minute in the dusk outside the café.

Harry looked at Andi. "You're staying at the Fat Chicken?" For a moment, Andi thought he was offering to walk her home.

"Yes, but—"

"Thought so. Saw you in the bar last night." Harry walked away, leaving his disapproval hanging in the air.

"Told you," Jim said to Andi. "Everyone knows everyone else's business around here."

Didn't help Sarah, did it? Andi nearly said. But she thought better of it and kept her mouth shut.

CHAPTER SIX

Joe carefully moved his ashtray, a packet of smokes and stained coffee cup so they lined up on the rusty metal fold-up table, next to his chair on his deck. He sat in his faded armchair, facing the view of Coffin Cove from high on this vantage point, as he did every day.

Anyone observing him — and there were few people who came near him these days — would see a near-motionless man, gazing into the distance, only moving to sip coffee or rye, light a cigarette, smoke it and stub it out. He smoked a pack a day, drank half a bottle of whiskey, ate a sandwich or two (only to stop Tara, his wife, from nagging him) and maintained the same robotic schedule every day. Up early (he only slept a couple of hours every night), straight to his chair in the same spot, wait out the daylight hours and then back to bed.

It was an existence. Joe knew that Tara stayed out of a sense of duty. Maybe pity? He wished she wouldn't. It was an extra layer of guilt that he didn't need.

Although he was physically deteriorating — his goal was to hasten his death — his mind would not stop. He could not turn off the constant stream of consciousness, a daily playback of moments and scenes from his life.

He was going mad, but the madness was safe.

One night he was shaken awake by Tara and found that he was sitting on the side of his bed.

"You were driving the tractor in your sleep!" she told him in amazement. "Operating the bucket and steering and everything."

He nodded miserably, sad that she had woken him. In his half-sleeping dream state, he was back forty years ago when he first purchased this property. Before . . . everything else.

Prime real estate, he told everyone proudly back then, when he paid cash for these three acres on top of a hill.

It took two years to pound in a driveway through all the rock and drill two wells before blasting and excavating to pour a foundation. Joseph did much of the work himself, operating the heavy machinery far into the night, pouring cement, framing, nailing, roofing, building his vision with his own hands. Nobody but Joseph had seen the potential in this rocky outcrop on top of the cliff. He was used to being underestimated. Nobody had seen the potential in Joseph either. A logger's son who wanted more than a life living paycheque to paycheque and getting drunk Friday through to Monday in the Timberlands Pub.

So he paid attention. He worked longer hours, turning up earlier than anyone in the morning, clear-headed and ready for work. At first, the old-timers treated him like any other greenhorn. His first day, they teamed him up with a wiry old goat of a logger. Unwashed and reeking of stale booze, he grabbed armfuls of equipment, taking an eighty-pound haulback block for gathering up the logging cables himself, and handing Joe the axe, cable strap and "Molly Hogan", a small piece of cable used for joining logging lines. The old guy eyed him, a cigarette hanging out one side of his mouth.

"Up there," he gestured to a vertical climb up the side of the mountain. Joe considered himself in good shape. He followed the old guy for about five minutes before he was gasping for breath. The old man stopped and grabbed the strap from Joe and added it to his load. Ten minutes later and Joe's lungs were burning as he struggled to keep up. The old guy hummed tunelessly as he scrambled over logs, looking back occasionally to check on Joseph. Just once he waited for Joe to reach him. Bent over double and wheezing, Joe stopped for a moment, only to find that he was choking on a pungent whiskey fart that the old man had timed perfectly. By the time they reached the top, Joe was carrying nothing except the Molly Hogan.

It took him six weeks to match the old logger stride for stride. After that he was part of the crew. He never missed a day, was never late and never had a hangover. He took every training course and learned everything he could about all the equipment.

Six years later he had enough money to apply for a timber claim. He didn't take a paycheque for a year. Three more years and McIntosh Logging was a going concern.

Joe let his memories wander back over the years, recalling each detail, fitting the pieces of his life together, as if watching a documentary in his mind.

There he was, sweating in the excavator, wiping dust out of his eyes.

There he was, on his deck for the first time, laughing in delight at the view of the ocean.

There he was, with Sue, cuddling in bed, watching the sunrise on their first morning as a married couple.

There he was, holding Sarah for the first time, gazing in wonder at the tiny, bloody, screaming infant.

There he was, chasing Sarah around the lawn, hearing her squeal. *Daddy, Daddy!*

There he was, with Sarah, grabbing her shoulder, angry at being disobeyed.

He rarely allowed the movie in his head to play any longer. He knew what happened next. He willed himself to hold his thoughts at the edge of the abyss, knowing that the following scenes of chaos and confusion would drag him down into a pit where he flailed in the darkness, out of control in grief and despair . . . If only he had forced her to stay home.

Instead, he sat here every day, clinging on to self-control, barely noticing Tara taking away his coffee mug and replacing it with his glass and bottle of rye, sometimes eating the sandwich she left, sometimes not. Just waiting. Waiting for his last breath, hoping that as the alcohol numbed his thoughts, he would black out for the last time and his movie would finally have an ending.

People didn't visit anymore. He was OK with that, because he couldn't raise the energy to speak. He couldn't think of what to say. He didn't care about their lives, didn't care about the town gossip, didn't care about anything, and had stopped listening even to Tara. In the early days, she had urged him to go back to work, to involve himself in the community. He didn't refuse. He just got up every morning and sat here as the daylight hours ticked by, finally stumbling to bed, another day of existence under his belt.

This morning, as Joe lit this third cigarette, he heard a truck groan and creak along his gravel drive, which was pockmarked with crevices and ditches filled with rivulets of muddy water from the continual rain.

He waited without interest until the truck appeared in the driveway and came to a stop.

* * *

Harry noted the decay and disrepair the McIntosh home had fallen into since his last visit. Which, he realized, was over a year ago. In the early days after Sarah's death, Harry brought his father, Ed, to sit with his grieving friend. But Ed had struggled to connect with Joe and asked Harry not to bring him anymore.

"What should I say to him?" Ed asked. "What should I talk about? My son and daughter? Who are still alive while his kid is dead?" He shook his head. "I'm making it worse."

Harry had to agree. Ed might be a selfish sonofabitch, Harry thought, but he had a point.

Gradually, everyone drifted away from Joe. The tragedy faded from the collective minds of the community, to be jolted back to the forefront only when Joe made a rare appearance in town or the *Gazette* ran an anniversary piece about Sarah, asking again for any new information that might solve her murder.

Harry didn't want to be here.

He sat for a moment, drumming his fingers on the steering wheel, figuring out what to say to Joe. He silently cursed Mason for coming back.

Why was he back here? He had to be fucking with them.

Harry remembered when Sarah went missing. He was out fishing when Ed had contacted him via the satellite phone. Harry didn't hesitate. He pulled his net in and headed back to the dock. He was just married, at the time, and his wife was expecting their daughter. Harry was already experiencing the parental fear of the unknown, and one of his biggest what-ifs was playing out for Joe.

Harry and most of the adult population of Coffin Cove had formed search parties. Even the protesters left their camps and helped. Police dogs on the ground and forestry helicopters in the air, but Sarah had vanished.

Worry turned into fear and then suspicion. What had happened? Who had done this? Who had taken her?

Everyone knew each other in Coffin Cove. It couldn't be anyone local. Whispers about the protesters and Mason got louder. Someone told the police that Sarah had a crush on Pierre Mason, that he and she were seen together, maybe even kissing. Speculation turned to rumour and gathered momentum.

Until that day on the beach, and Sarah wasn't missing anymore.

Harry got out of the truck, climbed the rotting wooden steps and stood over Joe.

"How are you, Joe?" Harry asked. The words seeming ridiculous, as he could see that Joe had shrunk into himself, his plaid shirt hanging over a skeletal frame. Joe's shrivelled, nicotine-stained fingers jerked up, and Harry thought for a second that Joe was ordering him off the deck.

Joe nodded in the same direction as his fingers and Harry realized that he was gesturing at a chair for Harry to sit in.

The two men sat in silence, broken only by Joe's wheezing breath.

"Joe, I have something to tell you," Harry began at last, and told him about Pierre Mason.

Joe tried to speak. His voice, low and rusty after years of silence, came out as a whisper. Harry bent his head to hear the words.

"I failed her," Joe said.

Harry touched Joe's shoulder, and that simple gesture shattered Joe's self-control. He bent his head to weep, and Harry backed away and left the broken man alone. Moments later, Harry was back in his truck, lurching back down the pitted driveway, cursing Pierre Mason.

CHAPTER SEVEN

"It's in here somewhere, I'm positive."

Andi waited impatiently, curbing her urge to push past Jim and start dragging boxes off the shelves of the archive cupboard. Instead, she tried to ignore the stench of rodents, and hoped that the files were still readable.

"Have you ever thought of creating digital records?" she asked, as Jim emerged, triumphantly carrying two heavy-looking boxes.

"No, never," he answered, setting down his load and disappearing back into the cupboard for a third.

"These are all the files and transcripts from my original investigation. Er, this one, I think, is the first . . ." Jim opened the lid of one of the boxes. "Yes, all dated and in order. The articles are in fact saved on microfiche," he said, ignoring Andi's smirk. "If you've never used microfiche, I'll be glad to help. I'm sure it's no more complicated than Google," he added.

Andi laughed. She was getting used to Jim's dry sense of humour.

"Thank you, but I'm fully trained."

Andi peered into the boxes. Each one was full of neat manila files, marked with names and dates.

"Lots of files," Andi said. "Lots of work."

"It was," Jim agreed. "But sadly, no conclusion. I handed all my files and notes to the police, but they hit a brick wall too. The case file is still open as far as I am aware, and I think Sarah's mother meets one of the original investigators on every anniversary of Sarah's death, but there hasn't been any new information since the first investigation."

"What about forensics? DNA?" Andi had reported on several cold cases where new scientific methods had resulted in breakthroughs and eventual convictions.

"No DNA. Sarah had been in the water for hours, there was no trace of DNA or helpful forensics by the time they found her on the beach. Her legs and hands were tied with hemp rope, which in those days was used by just about every fisherman on the coast — and anyone could have found some lying about on the docks, and the knots were common."

"So what linked her to Mason?" Andi asked. "Harry seemed totally convinced that Mason killed her."

"As did everyone in Coffin Cove," Jim sighed. "I tried to be objective, but most people close to Sarah thought she was having some kind of affair with Mason, who they said had a—" Jim fumbled for a word — "predilection for younger girls."

"But why kill her?" Andi said, almost to herself. "Unless she changed her mind about their affair? Or found out something about Mason he didn't want known?"

"There was a theory." Jim sat down behind his desk, and absent-mindedly began twirling a pencil in his fingers. "There was a theory that Sarah and Mason had staged her kidnapping to scare her father. Sarah and Joe had some serious arguments about the clear-cutting and what his business was doing to the environment. If she was mad at her dad and under Mason's spell . . . well, it could have all gone wrong . . ." Jim left his words hanging.

"Well . . ." Andi chose her words carefully. "If Joe and Sarah argued, is it possible . . . ?"

"That Joe did it?" Jim voiced her question. He shook his head. "No, the evening she went missing, she and Joe argued, but other people said they saw her after that. And I know Joe, he does have a temper, but he adored Sarah. Her death devastated him. He sold the business and spends his days just sitting and drinking. Waiting to die."

Andi pulled out the first file and flipped it open. A photograph of a smiling girl with blonde hair spilling over her shoulders was stapled to the inside of the cover. Andi studied it. No makeup, no earrings — just one silver cross on a chain, she noticed. And although it was just a headshot, Andi could see that Sarah was wearing some kind of dress or top with a lace collar. Very . . . wholesome? And yet, there was something — something about her smile — that had just the hint of mockery about it.

"Was this taken near to the time she died?" Andi asked. "She looks quite young, and a bit . . . old-fashioned? Unworldly?"

"Sarah's grandparents — her maternal grandparents — were very religious," Jim answered. "Sarah was a regular churchgoer until her parents split, and then, I believe, she began to rebel. Sue, her mother, moved back in with her parents when she and Joe split up. They never liked Joe, and I got the impression that they encouraged Sarah to stay away from her father and his new 'harlot'," Jim continued. "It must have been confusing for Sarah.

"If she was vulnerable, it would have been easy for a predator to befriend her," Andi said. "If Mason was — or is — a predator," she added.

"Whatever he was back then, they cleared him of any involvement in Sarah's death. And now he's back in Coffin Cove, and that's not the action of a guilty man, I suppose." Jim rubbed his hand over his eyes. "He's either innocent or stupid."

"Or arrogant? Or somebody made him an offer he couldn't refuse?" Andi added, recalling Harry's words.

"Yes. It could just be that Mason's been employed to cause a diversion, like last time."

Jim peered at Andi from behind the boxes of files. "Our job now is to report the story at hand. Who's killing the sea lions? Why are the Black OPS and Mason here? What's the impact on our fragile economy? These are the questions our readers want answered, Andi. The community mourned Sarah's death and it really did scare people. But as time has gone on, her death to most people is more like a legend than reality." Jim got up and walked around the desk. He took the file from Andi and replaced it in the box. "Look, you can review these files and see what you find, but I got a lot of heat from Mason's lawyer last time around, so *do not* start running around town and asking questions and stirring up shit. Remember, it's a small community and—"

"Everyone knows everyone else's business," Andi finished for him. "Yes, I get that. But don't you think we should at least visit Sarah's parents to get their reaction to Mason's return?"

"Look, Andi," Jim put up a hand, "I get that this is intriguing for you. Believe me, it's not just work that's in those boxes. It's my heart and soul. I wanted to solve this for Joe and Sue, just so they could get some peace." His voice cracked a little. "Nothing I could do would bring Sarah back. But knowing what happened might have helped a little."

Andi was silent a moment. She didn't know why, but this story had awakened her imagination. Instead of sitting in the bar the previous night, she'd gone straight up to her apartment and made notes about possible angles of investigation. "Let me just do a little digging," she pleaded. "Let me read the files. Who knows, a fresh set of eyes might turn up a new angle. And I do still have a few sources who will talk to me. I might find out who Mason is working for this time. I'll be working on both stories at once . . ." She let Jim mull it over for a moment.

"OK. But you do it in your own time, after you've finished the assignments you have at the moment. And by the way, you might have noticed—" he waved his hand, gesturing for Andi to look around the office — "I'm not flush with cash. I can't afford a lawsuit. So let's not forget that the most pressing story we have concerns dead sea lions."

CHAPTER EIGHT

Half an hour later they were both in Jim's truck on the way to Sue McIntosh's home. Although Jim was outwardly reluctant to stir up all this shit again, Andi sensed that pulling out all the old files had awakened his investigative impulses. He was a journalist. He hated to leave a story with no ending. So it was easy for Andi to persuade him to take her out to meet Sarah's mother, under the guise of letting her know that Mason was back in town.

"Doesn't seem right for her to just hear town gossip," Andi said. "We should at least tell her officially. So it isn't so much of a shock."

Jim didn't seem convinced that Andi's enthusiasm for a meeting with Sue was motivated by sympathy for the bereaved mother.

"We'll visit. And then we'll concentrate on getting the real assignments finished, right?"

Andi agreed, but already she was feeling a slight thrill of anticipation. It was a familiar feeling that started in the pit of her stomach. A literal gut reaction that Andi had learned to heed and ignored to her detriment.

Jim refused to let Andi drive. He saw the old papers and coffee cups strewn over the seats of Andi's beaten-up Toyota and said, "That's disgusting. We'll take my truck."

Now, Andi was sitting in the passenger seat without any coffee, as Jim had refused to stop at Hephzibah's. He seemed overly concerned about spillage and Andi resisted the temptation to point out the contrast between the spotless interior of Jim's truck and the grime and general disorganization of the *Gazette*'s office.

Instead, she questioned Jim about Sue, Sarah and Joe.

"She kept her married name," Jim explained. "Although she and Joe divorced legally, Sue didn't believe that they were divorced in God's eyes, so she is still a McIntosh."

"What about Joe's new wife?" Andi asked. "How does Sue rationalize that?"

Jim sighed. "She basically believes that Tara is the devil."

"Seriously?" Andi was incredulous. "No wonder Sarah was confused."

"After the divorce, Sue would not take any financial settlement. She just moved back in with her parents. She was always a regular churchgoer, but she got . . . I suppose you would describe it as more fanatical. Sue's father was a 'hellfire and brimstone' kind of religious zealot, and eventually none of the local churches were enough for him. And so . . . well, you'll see when we get there."

"When did Joe and Sue divorce?" Andi asked. "A long time before Sarah's death?

"Oh yes. Years. Sarah was about eight or nine, I think. Until then, Joe hadn't really paid a lot of attention to Sarah. Or to Sue, really. He was focused 100 per cent on his business."

"So what changed?" Andi pressed him to continue.

"Well, Sue had put Sarah in her father's church school."

"Wait," Andi interrupted, "her father's a teacher?"

"Not really," Jim answered. "He's more of a pastor who also runs a school."

"So is it an official school or what?" Andi was having a hard time getting her head around the concept. "Is it part of the school district? Don't they have rules about that?"

"They do now," Jim answered. "But back then, Fred, Sue's father, ran an offshoot of the Pentecostal Church, and he had a private school. It was thriving for a while. So that's where Sarah went, for a couple of years, anyway. It was more a gesture from Sue — an attempt to reconcile, I think. They hated Joe, they thought he was godless. I'm not certain, but I think Sue got pregnant on purpose to get away from her father. Joe and Sue weren't even dating, really, and suddenly they got married. Probably doomed from the start."

"And then they split up because . . . ?"

"Oh, Joe found out that Sarah couldn't read. She could recite Bible passages, but apart from that, she was eight years old and couldn't read or even write her own name. Joe pulled her out of the church school and put her in the Coffin Cove elementary with all the other kids. Fred was furious, and Sue left Joe in protest. Although Joe having an affair with Tara probably had more to do with it. They divorced, and Sue fought for sole custody of Sarah. Joe fought back, and for several years it was nasty."

"You don't think the whole situation had anything to do with Sarah's death?"

"Oh no. Sarah was fifteen, going on sixteen, and she had been making her own choices about seeing her father for a while. She even got on quite well with Tara." Jim hesitated for a moment. "Fred is an odd duck. There were rumours that he beat up his wife. Ruth — that's Sue's mother — often had a black eye, and no believable reasons for them. But I don't think he ever laid a hand on Sue, and he was pretty broken up after Sarah's death."

"How do you even start a church?" Andi mused. "Aren't there rules about that either?"

Jim laughed. "It's like the Wild Wild West to you, isn't it?"

"Yes!"

"It was a bit wild out here," Jim conceded. "It wasn't that many years ago Coffin Cove was just a logging camp and fishing dock. The town grew around that, and people made their own rules."

"And their own churches and schools?"

"Yes. But thirty years ago, there were eleven pubs in Coffin Cove. So it didn't hurt to have a few God-fearing men," said Jim, a bit defensively. "Anyway, when Joe pulled Sarah out of the church school, Fred never forgave him. Because after that, other parents started questioning his teachings and taking their kids out, and finally the school folded."

As they chatted back and forth, Jim had driven out of Coffin Cove on the single winding, narrow road that climbed up away from the ocean and eventually joined the island highway. They passed over a narrow bridge that crossed a fast-flowing river, and before they reached the intersection with the main highway, Jim took a sharp right turn onto a gravel road. Trees obscured the entrance and Andi couldn't see any signs. They seemed to immediately reverse their direction and head back towards Coffin Cove. The track descended at a steep angle and Andi was relieved they were in a truck, because the vehicle bounced through potholes and lost traction occasionally. Jim's expert steering kept the truck on the road, although it seemed to Andi, as she braced her arm against the dashboard, they were only narrowly avoiding crashing into the undergrowth. Finally, the track flattened out, and they were driving parallel to the same swift-moving river they crossed earlier. Andi understood now why Jim didn't want her to get coffee for the journey.

"A few more weeks of rain, and this road will be impassable," Jim said.

"Is this the only way to Sue's house?" Andi asked.

Jim nodded. "Yes. We call this area the Valley. Quite a few people used to live out here, but after all the clear-cutting, the valley flooded every spring. Most people left. They're cut off for weeks at a time," he said. "But nobody could persuade the old man to leave, not even when their house was four feet underwater. He said it was God's will if he lived or drowned, and he was staying exactly where he was. Now, it's just Sue and Fred. Sue tried to get him to move into town when Ruth died, but he wasn't having it."

Andi sat silently, processing this information and watching the scenery. The trees had thinned out and she could see now that they were surrounded by mountains. Andi tried to get her bearings and figure out where Coffin Cove was, but they had made so many turns that she was lost.

"We're going north," Jim said. "OK, try this," he added, noticing Andi's blank expression. "The town is over that mountain to the right. Over the left-hand mountain is the main island highway. And this here—" he braked and slowed the truck so Andi could look around — "is what's left of the valley community."

At first Andi didn't see anything. Just spindly trees and mounds of bushes covered with swamp grass. But as she looked closely, she saw rusty contortions of metal, almost devoured by Mother Nature. Piles of rotting wood, some with the faded outlines of painted words, threw eerie jagged shadows as weak sunlight filtered through the grey clouds. On the banks of the river she could see the crumbling remains of concrete structures and what looked like large plastic tanks and abandoned huts behind a chain-link fence.

"What's that?" she asked.

"The old hatchery," Jim replied. "I'll show you."

He parked the truck and they both got out. Andi shivered. It was raining heavily, and she could hear the river gushing behind the buildings.

Jim pushed open a rusty gate and kicked aside a rotting sign.

"The Valley Hatchery," Andi read out loud, and looked at Jim questioningly, not knowing why they had stopped.

"They built the hatchery to help conserve the wild salmon stocks," Jim explained. "Salmon return to the rivers to spawn. But their eggs and juvenile salmon are vulnerable to all kinds of predators. So the idea of the hatchery is to have a safe place for the eggs to hatch and the salmon to grow before they swim out to the ocean. These over here—" he pointed at the crumbling plastic tanks — "are the holding tanks for the eggs to incubate. They're transferred into spawning channels

51

— offshoots from the river — before they're released." He smiled. "It's a bit more complicated than that, but the basic idea is to give Mother Nature a helping hand."

"And does it work?" Andi asked.

"More or less," Jim said. "It's not perfect, but stocks, at least, weren't dropping while the hatchery was open."

"Why did it close?"

"The flooding," Jim said. "Every year in spring, the river floods. The clear-cutting meant that soil and gravel washed into the river and blocked up the spawning channels. The hatchery ran mainly on the efforts of volunteers and they just didn't have the budget to keep it open — another reason the fishermen are pissed off. The government pours thousands of taxpayers' dollars into enforcing the rules but gives no investment to enhance the fisheries. It's wrong."

"I see. But maybe the environmentalists have a point?" Andi still wasn't sure why they had toured the hatchery.

Jim ignored her. "Sarah spent a lot of time here. She volunteered. See that hut over there?" He pointed to a large battered Portakabin. "She helped organize fundraisers and open days for the public. She even had her own desk."

"It must have upset her when the hatchery closed."

"Devastated, according to Sue. Sarah blamed Joe for the clear-cutting. They argued about it a lot."

"It's a plausible explanation for her getting involved with Mason, then?"

Jim nodded. "Joe said that Sarah was punishing him. The thing is, Joe and Tara encouraged Sarah to go to college and study marine biology or something in that line. She had the grades. But she was adamant that she wouldn't take their money because it came from logging."

"What a mess," Andi said.

"Yes. And I'm sure that Sue and Fred made it harder. They hated the forestry industry too. So they would have pulled Sarah in two directions."

"But they wouldn't have approved of Mason, surely?" Andi asked.

"Absolutely not. Sue, I'm sure, isn't convinced that Mason wasn't involved."

"Did they do any kind of investigating themselves? Or offer a reward?" Andi had previously worked on stories where parents had offered large sums of money for information.

"They did, briefly. But the police advised against it after a while. Said they didn't have the resources to chase after every lead that the crazies phoned in."

Andi nodded.

They both got back into Jim's truck. His face was set into a grim expression, preoccupied with the past, Andi thought, so she asked no more questions. They travelled in silence until Jim pointed ahead at a collection of dilapidated buildings. At first Andi thought they were more crumbled remains, but as they got nearer, she could see a thin wisp of smoke coming from a tin chimney on one of the structures.

Jim brought the truck to a stop in front of three buildings. An old rusty truck was parked out front. The first building was larger and in better shape than the other two. A porch wrapped around three sides, but Andi couldn't see windows or any other sign of human occupants. Andi wasn't sure if it was a house or a barn. Steps at the side led up to the only entrance that Andi could see.

She got out of the truck and walked towards the building. When she got nearer, she saw a crude metal sign hanging above the wooden door.

"This is the church?" she asked Jim.

"Yes. And the old schoolhouse. Fred's house is out back."

It reminded Andi of post-apocalyptic movies, where people abandoned their homes in the nick of time to escape disaster. Rusting tools were strewn over the yard, as if the person using them had been called away in a hurry and had just dropped them where they stood.

Between the church and the house someone had planted tulips and daffodils in cracked flowerpots and arranged them under an old tyre that was suspended by rope from the branches of a moss-covered maple tree — a child's swing. It was the first sign of human life she'd seen.

The tyre moved slightly in a gust of wind and Andi shivered. Above the gush of the river, Andi could hear intermittent thuds, like someone chopping wood, and a low-level rumble coming from the same direction.

"Generator," Jim explained. "No other power out here."

Somebody had been doing a lot of digging. Wide shallow channels had been dug — by hand, Andi guessed, because she didn't see any heavy machinery — and it looked a bit like someone was trying to create a moat around the property. Mud was piled up on either side of the channels.

"Trying to divert floodwater," Jim explained.

The river was louder here than back at the hatchery and it didn't seem to Andi that these efforts would be successful.

They walked towards the thudding sounds.

The thud turned to more of a thwack as they walked around the church towards the back of the unkempt house. Paint peeled off old windowsills, and yellowing drapes hung limply in the dirty windows of the ugly stuccoed house. Once upon a time, it might have been painted pink, but now the stucco was grey and cracked, revealing damp rotting plywood underneath. A film of mildew was growing like a green skirt around the base of the house. Andi guessed that this was flood damage that had never been fixed. A cold wind whipped around the yard, but even in sunshine, Andi thought, this place would sag under an air of despondency and gloom.

The mystery of the thwacking sounds was solved when they got to the backyard. Under a makeshift shelter, erected with unfinished wooden posts and covered with a corrugated tin roof, a woman was rhythmically hacking at the biggest piece of raw meat that Andi had ever seen. The blade came down and sliced through flesh and sinew, making the thwacking sound as it connected with bone.

A deer's head lay in the grass, wide unseeing eyes staring at Andi directly from a pool of mud and blood. Andi wasn't squeamish, but the sight of the dismembered animal was unnerving. It occurred to her that dead animals were becoming a theme lately.

The woman was tall, with long grey hair pulled back in a ponytail. She was unsmiling, focused on her task, and her shoulders were pulled back in a combative stance. The only sign of exertion was the slight glisten of moisture on her forehead. She stopped, mid-swing, and stared.

"Sue, it's me, Jim Peters. How are you doing?"

She visibly relaxed.

"Jim. What are you doing out here? And who is this?" She stepped around the table and wiped her hands on a bloody rag. Still not smiling, but at least not hostile, Andi decided.

"I'm Andi, Jim's new assistant."

Sue ignored Andi's outstretched hand and turned to Jim.

"You must be doin' OK if you can afford an assistant, Jim."

"Not bad, Sue. And you? How's Fred?"

"He's inside." She turned abruptly away.

Andi called after her, "We have some news about your daughter."

Sue turned around, her expression blank. Andi could feel Jim's stare and it occurred to her that it wasn't a good idea to upset this woman, who was obviously skilled at handling a meat cleaver. But all Sue said was, "Tell Daddy. He deals with all that," and she walked back to her butcher's table and resumed her grisly task.

Andi followed Jim into the house. As he forcefully pushed open a wooden door, swollen with damp, they were both welcomed by an overpowering odour of mould. They were in a tiny hallway. On the wall facing them was a small carved plaque that read:

This is the day that the Lord has made; Let us rejoice and be glad in it. Psalm 118:24.

It seemed a strangely uplifting message in a place that hadn't seen any rejoicing for a long while, Andi decided.

Andi could just see a mustard-coloured stove in a tiny room to the left that must be the kitchen. To the right was an archway to what once might have been a living room, but now looked like an abandoned storage locker. There were books, magazines and cardboard boxes piled so high that the bottom ones were crushed and spilling out papers. The smell of mildew and damp competed with mouse urine, and Andi could see shredded paper and droppings scattered on the floor around piles of garbage. Heavy red velvet curtains hung miserably at one large window, partially blocking out the daylight. Rotting hems were held together with rusty safety pins and the curtains did nothing to stop a fierce draft from rushing through the cracked windowpanes.

"Who's there?" A man's voice came from somewhere in the depths of the room.

"Fred? It's me, Jim Peters."

Andi heard some shuffling. From the maze of boxes, a thin elderly man with a lion's mane of white hair appeared. He looked . . . biblical, Andi thought. How she imagined God would look — except in her mind, she expected God to have a kind, benevolent demeanour. This man had angry blue eyes and lips that curled back in a snarl. Andi remembered what Jim had told her about Fred's late wife, Ruth, and the unexplained black eyes.

This man gripped a cane in his hand, and Andi got the feeling that it could just as easily be a weapon as a walking aid.

"What brings you out here?" Fred demanded. His voice was strong and clear. If it hadn't been for the cane and the white hair, he could have passed for a much younger man than the eighty years plus that Andi had estimated.

"I have some news for you, Fred," Jim said. "This is Andi, my new assistant."

"Oh yes? What's the news?" Fred took no notice of Andi.

Jim answered calmly, "Pierre Mason is back in town. I thought you should know."

Fred stared at him for a moment, the same unblinking look they had got from Sue. Andi wasn't sure if he understood. She cleared her throat, which had become clogged in the heavy air, wanting to explain.

Jim touched her elbow.

Finally, Fred said, "Don't know what that's got to do with us. It's in God's hands now. Anything else?"

"No, that was it. Do you need anything out here? We don't see Sue in town much these days."

Fred answered sharply, "We got all we need. The girl shoots a deer when we need it." He stopped and thought for a moment. "You got any diesel?"

"I've got a jerrycan in the pick-up."

"The girl will pay. And don't you mind that deer." Fred pointed his cane at Jim. "We follow God's rules out here."

"Didn't see a thing, Fred."

The old man nodded, turned and shuffled back into the gloom and cardboard mountains.

Jim shrugged at Andi as if to say, *See? Told you so.*

They left the house. Andi was glad to be back in the fresh air.

Sue didn't look up when Jim placed the jerrycan of diesel beside her. She carried on slicing and tugging at the carcass, dropping chunks of flesh onto a growing bloody pile beside her.

"You here about Mason?" she asked suddenly.

"Yes," Jim answered. "You knew he was back?"

"Yep." Sue didn't make eye contact.

"How did you know?" Andi couldn't help asking.

Sue lowered the cleaver.

"People are always in a rush to tell you bad news," she said quietly. And then to Jim, "I don't have any cash here. I'll pay you for the diesel next week, when I'm in town."

Andi felt ashamed as they drove away. They had achieved nothing, she thought, except add to the weight of grief that already threatened to bury the decaying homestead.

Then she remembered something that Fred had said.

"What was that all about?" she asked, as they drove back on the gravel road. "God's rules and all that?"

"It's not open season for hunting," Jim answered. "Sue poached that deer."

CHAPTER NINE

Jim reminded Andi about her "priorities". They went back to the office, and together they stacked the boxes of the investigation files on Sarah McIntosh into Andi's car. Jim agreed to let Andi take a look in her spare time but made her promise some things in return.

"Get me more on the Black OPS and the dead sea lions." He handed her a list of stores and businesses to "hit up for some advertising". Andi reluctantly agreed, knowing that keeping the *Gazette* afloat was part of her job — and vital if she wanted to be paid.

When Andi arrived home, she found a note on her door from Walter, her landlord, reminding her that rent was due in a week — a reminder of her current financial situation.

Instead of drowning her worries with wine, Andi spent a few productive hours cleaning up her apartment. She collected up pizza boxes and plastic sandwich containers and dumped them in the garbage cans at the back of the pub, promising herself a healthier diet from now on. She assessed the state of her living quarters with fresh eyes, noting the strewn clothes, unmade bed and the pile of dirty cups and plates in the tiny kitchen sink.

OK, pity party's over. She stripped the bed, tidied up her clothes and cleaned the bathroom and kitchen area. As she worked, her mind turned over the events of the day. It was like stepping back in time, visiting Fred and Sue in the valley. Not at all like the romantic portrayal of homesteading she'd seen in the movies. She couldn't imagine how a fifteen-year-old would have felt, being isolated from friends. No TV, no Wi-Fi, no pizza, not even regular hot water — literally none of the trappings of modern teenage life. No wonder Sarah had rebelled. It made Andi's apartment seem luxurious in comparison.

She took down a bag of her laundry to the shared utility room at the back of the pub. She chatted with Cheryl, Walter's wife, as she filled the washing machine and promised that she would have her rent cheque in a few days. Feeling hungry, she slipped into the bar to order some food.

"Burger and wine?" Walter asked as Andi stood looking at the blackboard menu hanging over the fireplace.

It was quiet in the pub, too early for the evening regulars, so Andi jumped when a voice from the other end of the bar said, "Try the salmon."

She looked round and saw Harry.

"Ever eaten wild salmon?" he asked.

"I've had salmon before," Andi answered.

"From the grocery store, I bet. Old stinky farmed fish. Try the real thing," said Harry, almost challenging her.

She shrugged, and ordered the salmon, a salad and, remembering the promise to herself, a club soda rather than the wine.

"Did you supply the fish?" Andi asked Harry, heaving herself onto a bar stool.

"Nope," he said, "that would be illegal."

"Why?" Andi asked.

"Because I don't have a commercial license anymore," Harry replied.

"But you are still involved with the fishing industry, right?" Andi asked, thinking she might get some good information for her outstanding assignments.

Harry ignored her question, drained his glass, and set it on the bar.

"What do you want to know about fishing?" he asked.

"I'm a reporter. I report on all sides of the story."

"That's your job, is it? To write the truth?" A mocking note in his tone made Andi study his face for a second, wondering if he knew anything about her past.

"Yes. That's my job," she said evenly, deciding she was being paranoid. She was saved from further conversation as Walter arrived with her meal.

"Enjoy your salmon." Harry got up to go just as Walter set the plate in front of Andi.

"That looks amazing," Andi said. It really did.

"That's the best way to have salmon," Harry said as she took her first bite of the moist flakes of pink flesh.

"How?" Andi asked between mouthfuls.

"Poached."

Both Walter and Harry laughed.

Andi, confused, asked, "What's funny?"

"Doesn't matter," Harry said, still chuckling, and Andi realized that it was the first time in her few encounters with Harry that he had displayed any humour at all. It was short-lived.

"We're meeting tomorrow at Hephzibah's," Harry said abruptly. "Be there early if you want your story. You'll find out it's not the fucking sea lions that need saving, it's us. The fishermen are the only endangered species around here."

He turned and walked away before Andi could answer.

As Harry left the Fat Chicken, two young men dressed in army fatigues, but sporting ponytails and nose piercings so that nobody could mistake them for military men, pushed past him when he swung open the door.

"What the fuck?" Harry said, loud enough for Walter to pay attention.

The men ignored Harry as he let the door swing shut behind him, obviously irritated. They laughed, and Andi watched them slide into a booth. She guessed from Harry's reaction that they must be members of the so-called Black OPS protest group.

"Fuckin' fisherman."

That confirmed it. Andi couldn't see them from the bar but heard clearly enough. She wondered how she could shuffle along the bar so she could listen in to their conversation without being noticed.

Walter took their order for two beers, and the two started talking in low tones.

Andi kept her back to the booth and carried on eating, straining to hear. She caught a couple of references to "Pierre" and "Mason", and the word "march", but Walter put an end to her eavesdropping. "How was the fish?"

"Really good," Andi said, meaning it. "The salad too."

"Another soda?" Walter picked up her empty glass.

Andi shook her head. "No thanks. My laundry is probably finished by now, and I've got work to do."

"Jim got you hard at it, eh?" Walter asked. "I hear you were out at Fred and Sue's place today. You doing a story on Mason and Sarah?"

The low murmur from the booth stopped. Andi guessed that the two men had heard Walter mention Mason.

She answered loudly enough for them to hear. "Yes. It's a real mystery. I'd like to help those poor people find some answers about Sarah's death. So they can finally have some peace, at least."

"That's good," Walter nodded in approval and waved off Andi's attempt to pay for her meal.

"It's on the house. Your first poached salmon meal." He winked at her.

Andi, still mystified, lingered over her soda water.

The two men finished their beer and left the bar. Andi scrolled through her phone and began tapping in a few notes about the meeting with Sue and Fred McIntosh.

"May I buy you a drink?" A man sat on the stool beside Andi.

"Thanks, but I'm . . . oh." Andi looked up and saw Pierre Mason sitting beside her. He wasn't smiling.

"Then perhaps I could take up a few minutes of your time?" he asked, gesturing at the booth behind them recently vacated by his colleagues. Andi nodded, guessing that after the two men overheard her mentioning Mason in connection with Sarah McIntosh, they had immediately reported back to Mason.

She was right.

"Andi — may I call you Andi?" Mason began after they were seated, and having waved off Walter, who hovered for a moment, probably displeased that Mason was there.

Andi tensed. Mason must have looked her up. Maybe he'd read her articles. She'd covered environmental protests before, but she couldn't recall their paths crossing. She tried to keep her face expressionless, not wanting to let him know she was bothered. She nodded for Mason to continue.

"Andi, you probably know that I was falsely accused of being involved in the death of that poor girl," Mason started.

"You mean Sarah McIntosh?" Andi interrupted, wishing that she had her phone set to voice record.

"I mean Sarah McIntosh, yes," Mason confirmed. He had a slight French accent and a formal way of speaking that gave away his Quebec roots. He was neat — head shaved closely to disguise that he was going bald, his sweater unrumpled — and he sat upright. Again, Andi was reminded of someone in the military. He had an air of preciseness.

"The police cleared me at the time of any involvement whatsoever," Mason continued. "Unfortunately, Jim Peters and his father continued to publish unfounded accusations, tarnishing my reputation." He smiled unpleasantly and leaned forward. "I had to involve my lawyer back then, Andi, and I won't hesitate to do so again."

Andi didn't move, not wanting Mason to think she was intimidated.

"I'm only interested in uncovering the truth for the McIntosh family," she said.

"Ah, but that's the problem, isn't it, Andi?" Mason said quickly. "The reason you are here in this backwater is because of your . . . let's say . . . unfortunate relationship with the truth, isn't that so?"

Andi felt herself redden. Mason had done his homework, all right. She decided to let that go. "Mr Mason, you must have known that your arrival in Coffin Cove would attract attention from the locals, right? So why are you here? Surely not for a couple of dead sea lions?"

"I'm an environmental activist, Andi," Mason replied sternly. "It's what I do, what I've always done. Take action against poaching, overfishing, protect our wildlife, our oceans—"

"And you believe that the fishermen here are involved in illegal activities?" Andi asked. "They seem to think your Black OPS Group are unfairly harassing them."

"Ocean Protection Society," Mason corrected her. "And we reported safety infractions to the relevant authorities, Andi. How is that harassment?"

"Is someone paying you, Mr Mason?" Andi tried another approach.

Mason smiled and ignored the question.

"You're missing the bigger picture, Andi. And this surprises me, because I've read some of your previous work, and it seems you've always been able to maintain some perspective. Until now."

Andi tried again. "Did you have a relationship with Sarah, Mr Mason?" she asked. "Because you were seen with her just before she disappeared. You'd have been, what . . . thirty-ish? And she was fifteen, right? Is that what you've always done, Mr Mason? Take advantage of starry-eyed little girls?"

Mason looked as though he wanted to lean across and grab Andi round the throat.

"You don't know what you're talking about," he practically spat at Andi. "But I'm warning you—"

"Warning me? Or threatening me?" Andi could see that Mason was finally rattled by her questions.

"Everything OK, Andi?" Walter appeared beside the booth.

Andi nodded. "Yes, thanks, all good." Walter, not convinced, retreated behind the bar and set about polishing beer glasses, not taking his eyes off the booth.

Mason had regained his composure.

"You're not really bothered about a dead teenager from twenty years ago, are you, Andi? What you want is a good story. A way to redeem yourself — professionally speaking, of course."

Andi, with difficulty, kept eye contact.

"Maybe that makes two of us, Mr Mason."

Mason rested his hands on the table. He was silent, but clasped and unclasped his fingers.

Andi felt her heart beat a little quicker, sensing that he was on the brink of divulging some information.

But then the door to the pub swung open, and she heard Walter greet customers at the bar. The moment passed.

Mason smiled at her. "Time for me to leave, Andi. I'm sure we'll chat again."

Mason slid out of the booth and turned to leave. He hesitated for a moment.

"Just a reminder though, Andi. You'll be hearing from my lawyer if you print anything libellous about me." He strode towards to door.

"The truth is never libellous, Mr Mason," Andi called after him, but he didn't look back.

Andi looked down and saw her hands were shaking. The encounter had unnerved her.

"Walter, can I have a glass of wine, please?"

Walter obliged, and Andi sipped it, letting the alcohol dull her heightened senses.

She sat there processing the conversation in her mind. Was Mason really a victim? The locals despised him and his environmental causes — were they blinded by their prejudices?

Then, knowing that she needed to document the new information before she forgot any details, she drained her glass.

She hesitated before she left the bar, fighting a familiar impulse for a moment. Then she purchased a bottle of wine. Forgetting her laundry, she headed back to her apartment.

CHAPTER TEN

The man was feeling very pleased with himself. This had been a good week. In fact, he reasoned, this could be the start of a new career. He was a natural fixer, he thought. Solving problems for a price.

"A high price," he laughed to himself. "You get what you pay for." He acted out a new scene in his head, where people — important people — begged for his services, willing to pay him hundreds . . . no, thousands for his special talents! He savoured his imagined adulation for a moment and took a swig out of a bottle of vodka that he had paid for proudly with his wages.

He'd been disrespected, he thought. Nobody had ever taken him seriously. But all of that would change, he'd show them. He had skills that people needed, people would pay for . . .

He got agitated as another real memory intruded on his fantasies.

"Where'd you get the money?" Walter had asked him suspiciously at the Fat Chicken, where he went to buy his vodka.

The man had paid with a crisp fifty-dollar bill. Walter had held it up to the light and made the man wait.

"I earned it." The man had tried to sound outraged, but it had come out as a whine.

Walter hadn't believed him, the man could tell. That fucker. But Walter had sold him the vodka anyway, ushering him out, wanting the stench out of the pub.

"I'll fuckin' show 'em all," he shouted out loud, startling a seagull that was perched on the window of the man's home.

His living quarters were the old offices on the mezzanine floor of the disused fish plant. He'd been here for a year or so, he reckoned. It was dry, and being up high, the rats didn't bother him much. There were two entrances — one through the main door and the other upstairs, which was obscured from the view of any casual observer in the back corner of the warehouse. Piles of old packing boxes and fish totes blocked most people from poking around too much. From one office, there was a door to an old metal fire escape that led down to the rotting pier where the fish boats used to tie up and deliver their load. It was dangerous, missing a few rungs, and the man had to be especially careful if he had been drinking, but it was useful if the police came looking for him.

He was blamed unfairly for all the shit that went on, he thought, familiar waves of self-pity engulfing him, which could only be subdued by more vodka.

The man was dirty. He couldn't remember the last time he'd had a wash. In the summer, the showers and laundry were open for tourists, and he would occasionally sneak in, until he got caught stealing the change out of the detergent dispenser. He hadn't bothered since then. His matted hair was scraped back into a straggly ponytail, and a greasy base-ball cap hid a bald spot. He'd lost track of the years, but he figured he must be sixty.

Sometimes, he got free coffee from Hephzibah if he told her it was his birthday.

But most people avoided or didn't notice him.

He didn't mind.

Easier to do my work, he thought, and he took another shot of vodka. His work was stealing what he could from the boats and the dock. Most of his theft was wallets and cash left lying on galley tables. He was too well-known in Coffin Cove to sell stolen goods, but he couldn't help himself sometimes. Stealing was a compulsion. Laptops and electronic devices he mostly tossed in the ocean, but he managed to acquire some useful stuff too. He'd furnished his home with the proceeds of his petty theft. A new-ish sleeping bag lay in one corner, now stained with piss and vomit, and a barbeque that used to be attached to the stern of a yacht was in the other. He loved shiny objects and often added to his collection of "treasures" — jewellery and trinkets he would pull out and croon over, Fagin-like, when he was high or drunk. A pile of empty food containers and booze bottles were piled up against the wall, next to an old bucket that served as his toilet if he was too far gone to shit outside.

In his more lucid moments, he disgusted himself.

But today was a celebration. A new start. Soon those bastards would all be fuckin'—

The man stiffened as an unfamiliar noise stopped his train of thought. He automatically crouched down on the floor, even though he was hidden from view. He'd heard a truck. It was near, he figured, right outside the fish plant. He heard a door bang, and then the sound of another vehicle, then another door and then voices.

Police? He didn't think so. Those fuckers turned up with lights flashing. But he kept his crouched position and shuffled as near as he dared to the edge of the mezzanine, ready to make a run for it down the fire escape if he had to.

The main door creaked open and let in a streak of grey light. It was twilight outside, and all the man could see was the outline of two men. The door banged shut, the echo reverberating around the deserted warehouse. It was pitch black, and the man heard one voice exclaim in irritation. The door opened again, just a crack, to provide a little light.

The man couldn't see faces, but he could make out the shapes of two men. The taller one looked familiar.

Outside, disturbed seagulls were crying, and the man edged forward a little more without being heard.

Information was currency. The man had profited from secrets before, so he strained to hear what the visitors were saying.

It was too muffled. The echoes from the high metal ceiling distorted the sounds, and the man only caught a few words, but he could see that they were arguing. The smaller man was gesturing and doing most of the talking.

It had only been a few seconds, but the man was starting to cramp. Not hearing anything useful and thinking he was best out of sight in his hidey hole, he started to crawl backwards, when he heard one of the men laugh. It wasn't humorous, as though one of them had said something funny, it was a mocking laugh.

The door slammed again.

The man peered back over the edge. The door was shut tight, but the outline of the remaining visitor was still visible from cracks of light in the dilapidated roof.

The trill of a cell phone made the man jump, high up on the mezzanine, and he let out an involuntary gasp. Frightened that he may have given himself away, he waited and then nervously stuck his head out again.

He needn't have worried.

The remaining visitor was intent on looking at his cell phone. The blue light from the screen lit up the visitor's face, and the man immediately recognized him.

Congratulating himself, the man again started to slowly retreat, grinning in the darkness at this new morsel that he could maybe trade away.

He heard the creak of the door. He stopped. He was too far back now to have a full view, but he saw the blue glow of the cell phone wave back and forth. The visitor was startled.

"Wha—?" the man heard, and then a hard crack that echoed and bounced off the roof and wall, followed by a thud. The blue light tilted out of view and disappeared. The man heard the slithering sound of a dropped phone sliding into darkness.

He dared not move. He waited and waited, hearing only a few footsteps that stopped, and then started again, but going in the opposite direction. He heard the door creak and then silence.

The man waited again. No groaning or sounds of movement.

Carefully and quietly as possible, he went down the stairs onto the warehouse floor. His eyes were accustomed enough to the gloom to make out a heap on the floor. The metallic smell of blood mingled with shit told the man all he needed to know.

Not worried about noise now, but knowing that he had to hurry, he skirted around the dead body, not wanting to step in blood and leave footprints. He knelt and felt around the floor at the edge of the warehouse, in the last direction that he had seen the blue light.

It didn't take long. He soon found the phone, which didn't seem to be damaged, and shoved it in his back pocket. He quickly stumbled back up the stairs, adrenaline flowing, and stood for a second at the top, catching his breath. He badly wanted more vodka, but he knew that the last thing he needed was a blackout. He thought for a moment, and then gathered up the sleeping bag, the bottle of vodka, and his bag of treasures. He kicked around the empty bottles and garbage. For good measure, he tipped over the shit bucket and watched the putrid sludge seep over the floor.

Not many people would be examining the room too closely now, he figured.

He left, taking the back exit down the fire escape into the night, clutching his filthy possessions and shiny secrets close to his chest.

CHAPTER ELEVEN

Andi woke early. As she opened her eyes, the empty wine bottle came into focus first. Andi sighed. She had to stop doing this. She pulled herself out of bed, trying to remember the last time she'd got up feeling clear-headed and energetic.

She blinked in the early morning sun that brightened her apartment, and drank a large glass of water while she brewed coffee.

At least she'd got some work done last night. For the first time since she moved to Coffin Cove, she felt a sense of purpose. A story was within her grasp.

The previous evening, Andi had scribbled down some notes on her encounter with Pierre Mason. She then sat sipping her wine, trying to fit together the pieces of the story she'd discovered so far.

Nothing was making much sense. Andi knew what she had to do. When she was consumed by a complex investigation, Andi found it easier to figure out how all the different strands of details came together if she created a visual story wall. It clarified her thoughts and allowed her to see relationships and connections that might have otherwise been lost in the mass of information she collected.

It was a process that served her well, and she remembered with irritation that she had stopped doing this when she was with Gavin. He had teased her about it and called her Nancy Drew. Desperate to impress him, she'd laughed and agreed that it was ridiculous.

And look what happened, she thought. But she didn't want to wallow in the past. Instead, she put her wine glass down and rearranged the few pieces of furniture in the apartment so she had one clear wall. Then she worked through Jim's files and her own notes and created a spider's web on the wall using postcards, pins and string.

A few hours in, and she already had half the wall covered. Jim had been thorough. Andi found notes of interviews with people she hadn't heard of. He'd spoken to Sarah's friends and schoolteachers, there were multiple notes about Joe, Sue, Fred and his late wife, Ruth, plus photographs of a much younger Pierre Mason.

By the time she had finished the bottle of wine, she had been through all the files and it was after midnight.

This morning Andi's story wall prompted more questions than answers. This was usual. It was the beauty of the wall. Eventually, the story would tell itself, Andi theorized, as she drained her coffee cup. She felt better. She threw her notebook and phone in her purse and headed to Hephzibah's for her second shot of caffeine.

Hephzibah had arranged a few mismatched tables and chairs outside the café for customers to make the most of the morning sunshine. The sun made all the difference to the town, Andi thought. The sky was already a deep blue, and the ocean sparkled as far as she could see. This had to be the prettiest day yet in Coffin Cove, and Andi felt lighter. She felt free. No secrets to keep, no facade to keep up. She promised herself again that she would leave the wine alone for a while and really get to grips with this story.

She realized as she got nearer the café that not everyone was sharing the same positive vibe.

Harry sat at one of Hephzibah's outside tables, his hand gripping his coffee. A gaggle of fishermen surrounded him. Andi couldn't hear what they were saying until she got closer, but she could see by their folded arms and hostile demeanour that they were not very cheery at all. She caught snippets of the conversation as she slipped past them into the café.

"It's all right for you, Harry," one of them was saying, "but I can't be tied up for another day."

Hephzibah was pouring her coffee before Andi got to the service bar.

"What's going on with those guys?" Andi asked.

"Another day tied at the dock," Hephzibah answered. "Those protestors called in a bunch of so-called infractions to DFO and they can't go fishing until they get inspected."

"Oh, that's not good." Andi was beginning to understand what this all meant to the angry men outside.

"You'll understand more when you sit in at the meeting. Harry wanted you to be here."

"Really?" Andi thought back to the previous evening. "I'm not sure Harry has a high opinion of reporters."

"It's true, he hasn't had good experiences with the media. But he trusts Jim, and Jim employed you, so he thinks you must be OK."

Hephzibah smiled at Andi.

"Harry spends too much time on the ocean or with other fishermen. He doesn't have much practice talking to women these days."

"He's not married?" Andi looked outside where Harry was talking animatedly. Not bad looking, she thought.

"He was. Divorced, and one daughter. My niece is all grown-up now."

"Harry's a lot older than you?"

"Fifteen years. My mother left Ed, my dad, when I was a baby and I went with her. I never knew Harry until my mother died. Harry was married then, but he still took me in. We're very close now. He's a good man. Lots of fun when you get to know him."

"I see." Andi was curious. Harry wasn't like any other man she'd met before. But then, she'd never lived anywhere like Coffin Cove either.

"Look over there, the sharks have started circling already." Hephzibah nodded towards a blonde florid-faced man sat in an armchair at the back of the café. He was sipping tea from a cup and saucer that he perched on his knee.

He was dressed in the same fisherman's uniform as the men outside but didn't quite fit in, Andi thought. His hair was neatly combed, and as he bent to take another mouthful of tea, the sunlight glinted on a gold stud in his ear.

He was spotlessly clean. His canvas bib overalls were creased as though he had just unpacked them. He wore white runners and socks. His hands were soft and white, with manicured nails. Andi could see a large pinkie ring on one hand.

This was a guy, Andi thought, who wanted to look like a fisherman. But it wasn't working.

"Who is that?" Andi asked, lowering her voice, so the man wouldn't hear.

"I call him Slippery Steve," Hephzibah whispered back. "It's Steve something, I can't remember his real name. He works for Hades Fish Co."

"Why is he here?"

"To find out what's going on. These guys," Hephzibah nodded at Harry's group outside, "work for Hades. Well, more than that, really — Hades either owns or part-owns their boats and licences. If they don't deliver herring, a lot of them won't make their boat payments."

"I see. He does look . . ." Andi fumbled for a word.

"Slippery," Hephzibah finished for her. "Right?"

"Can't Hades help? I mean, with sorting out the infractions or talking to the DFO or something?" Andi asked.

"It's not as simple as that."

Before Hephzibah could explain further, a thin, grimy man slapped some change on the counter. He was clutching a roll of stained material, which Andi saw was a sleeping bag, and had an old canvas bag slung over one shoulder. Andi assumed he was homeless.

"Can I have a coffee, Hep?" He had a high-pitched voice, and as he spoke, flashed broken brown teeth. He was standing a few feet away from Andi, but a stench of faeces and urine wafted in her direction.

Hephzibah pulled a face. "Geez, Brian, when was the last time you washed?" She set down a cup of coffee in a paper to-go cup. "Take it outside." She waved at him to take his change.

Andi had seen Hephzibah be much kinder to homeless people, and it seemed unlike her to be so dismissive.

"Who was that?" she asked as the man grabbed his coffee without a thank you and slouched outside.

"Brian McIntosh," Hephzibah answered.

"McIntosh?" Andi opened her mouth to ask more questions, but Harry and the fishermen, grumbling about "that stinkin' rummy", filed inside to get refills from Hephzibah and take seats around Slippery Steve.

Harry acknowledged Andi with a nod.

Slippery Steve waved his hand at Harry. "Who is this?" he asked, looking at Andi.

"She's the girl from the *Gazette*," Harry answered, before Andi could introduce herself. "Mason's been getting all the media attention, I thought it was about time we got some."

"And the *Gazette* counts as media these days, does it?" The man smiled, but it wasn't pleasant.

The sound of a police siren diverted his attention, wailing near to the café. As if jolted by an electric force, the homeless man, Brian, leaped up and started to run. In his haste he overturned the table and dropped something out of his pocket.

The fishermen and Hephzibah laughed.

"Brian always has that reaction around police," Hephzibah explained to Andi, who didn't see the joke.

Andi went outside and set the table upright. She saw that Brian, in his haste to avoid the police, had dropped his phone. She held it up for Hephzibah to see.

"Almost certainly not his," Hephzibah called to her. "Take it to the—" Her suggestion was drowned out by another blast from the police siren.

"That's weird. There must be an accident." Hephzibah joined Andi outside and walked down the boardwalk.

"Hey, something's happening over at the fish plant," she called back to Andi.

Andi felt the stolen phone buzz in her hand. She looked at the screen, and one word announced a call: *HADES*.

Before Andi could think about that coincidence, she heard the trill of her own phone from deep in her purse.

She rummaged with one hand and shoved the other phone in her pocket, mentally making a note to take it to the detachment later.

She held her phone to her ear.

"Where are you?" Jim's voice demanded.

"At Hephzibah's," Andi said. "Harry asked me—"

"Get over to the old fish plant," Jim interrupted.

"What's going on?" Andi asked.

"There's a dead body," Jim said. "And this time, it's human."

CHAPTER TWELVE

In a small town, rumours spread like grass fires, and twice as fast, Andi discovered.

After Jim's phone call, she'd taken off running towards the fish plant. She could hear Hephzibah calling after her, but Andi knew there wasn't any time to explain.

Andi slowed to a walk when she saw a woman sitting on a chair outside the bait and tackle shop, across the road from the fish plant. Already a small group of people were gathered around her. As Andi got closer, she saw the woman was Peggy Wilson, owner of the only motel in Coffin Cove. Her dog was by her side and whining as Peggy alternated between covering her face with her hands and gesturing furiously towards the fish plant.

Andi looked from Peggy to the fish plant, knowing she didn't have much time before the police arrived.

Andi made a decision. She could hear what Peggy had to say in a few minutes. Right now, she wanted to see as much as possible for herself.

The police were already at the scene. The police cruiser was parked outside the fish plant, and the driver door had been left open. There was nobody in sight, so Andi walked to the fish plant door, pushed it wide open and stepped inside.

It took a few moments for Andi's eyes to adjust to the dim light. The smell of decay hit her nostrils. There was a dark mound on the floor, and Andi could see it was the dead body. There was a metallic odour, mixed with the stench of faeces. Andi saw stagnant pools of blood that had seeped out from under the corpse and were now congealing on the concrete floor. How long had the body been here?

Andi had seen dead people before. She'd been to the scenes of traffic accidents and gang shootings on the mainland. But usually, she only caught a glimpse before the first responders ushered her away.

Where are the police now? she thought, expecting someone to stop her at any minute. The place was eerily quiet.

Andi moved forward, her stomach churning. Her legs felt a little unsteady, and she willed herself to focus.

The body was male, Andi was certain. He was face down on the concrete, an arm thrown out to his side at an impossible angle. Andi tiptoed around him, making sure not to step in the blood. She crouched down to get a closer look. One side of his face was mottled with patches of purple lividity.

Andi gasped as she saw the other side of his face and head was reduced to clumps of shattered bone and bloody tissue.

Andi swallowed hard, trying not to gag, but she let out a small cry as she realized she knew the dead man. Although his face was destroyed, she recognized his jacket.

A gunshot wound? Andi looked around to see if there was a weapon lying near the body. Could he have done this to himself? She couldn't see a gun, but she felt her stomach heave again when she saw dark patches of blood splatter on the wall in front of the body.

Andi covered her mouth with her own jacket and steadied herself with two deep breaths.

"Be professional," she muttered to herself as she pulled out her phone and took two photos. She had just changed the mode to video recording when she heard footsteps.

"Hey, get away from there!"

Andi looked up to see a police constable standing over her. Even in the dim light, she could see his young face was white. He was holding his hand over his mouth. Andi was instantly sympathetic. It had taken enormous willpower for her not to vomit or run from the building.

"Who are you? What are you doing here?" The young constable bent forward, and put his hands on his knees. For a moment, Andi thought he might be sick again.

"I'm Andi. The door was open . . ."

"You have to leave," he said, his voice shaky.

Andi didn't argue. She could see the constable was distraught, and Andi knew he'd be in trouble. He'd left a dead body lying in an unsecured building and allowed a reporter to trample over a potential crime scene.

"I'm going right now." She had everything she needed anyway.

* * *

Jim got to the fish plant just as RCMP officers from the Nanaimo detachment were cordoning off the parking lot. So they'd already called out the big guns, Jim mused. It was more than the small Coffin Cove detachment could handle.

Three police cruisers were blocking the entrance. Jim could see one older officer with his hand on the shoulder of the constable from Coffin Cove. The young lad was bent over slightly.

He must have been first on scene, and judging by the way he looked, it must have been bad. Especially if this was his first dead body.

Jim looked around for Andi but couldn't see her. He frowned. This was a chance for Andi to shine. Was she hungover again?

A group of people had gathered around Peggy Wilson, who was sitting in a chair outside Bill Richard's bait store. Bill gestured for Jim to come over.

"I couldn't believe what I was seeing." Peggy's voice was agitated. "I thought Rocky was chasing a rat so I went in the fish plant to get him. And then . . . then I saw the body." Her voice dropped to a dramatic whisper. "I felt frozen, I couldn't move. And then I just screamed at Rocky to *come now*, and then I just ran here." She buried her head in her hands.

Jim knew this wasn't the first time Peggy had told her story. Anything she was saying now would be embellished as more people joined her audience. Too late for any accurate information from a key source for the story. How irritating.

"Jim!"

Andi touched his elbow and gestured for him to move away from the crowd. Jim followed her, hoping she had questioned Peggy before the crowd had gathered.

"It's Pierre Mason," Andi said.

"The dead body? Is that what Peggy's saying?"

"No, that's what I'm saying. And look for yourself."

Andi thrust her cell phone under Jim's nose.

"How the hell . . ." he began to say, horrified at the image he was seeing, but Andi interrupted him. "Never mind that. It's Mason, isn't it? Is that a gunshot wound?"

Jim looked closer and couldn't help flinching. It wasn't pleasant. Eventually he looked up.

"Yes, I think it is Mason. Hard to tell for sure, not with most of his face blown off."

"But the wound? Is it a gunshot wound?"

Jim ignored Andi's impatient tone and looked closely again.

Eventually he nodded. He'd seen the aftermath of a hunting accident once before.

"I'm sure as I can be from a photo. The coroner will confirm, of course. And the crime scene guys."

Andi was looking at him strangely. It took a minute before he realized what she was thinking.

"You didn't see a gun," he stated.

She shook her head.

"Pierre Mason was murdered."

CHAPTER THIRTEEN

Adrian Palmer slammed his cell phone onto his desk in irritation. Another fisherman whining about payment. How the hell did these calls get through to him anyway?

"Everything OK?" Brenda, his secretary, appeared at the door. She had a bored expression on her face and they both knew that she didn't care if he was OK or not. Brenda was the one non-negotiable that Nikos, Mr Palmer senior, had insisted on before signing Hades Fish Co. over to his son.

Adrian had hoped that Brenda would leave of her own accord, but dear old Dad had virtually guaranteed that she would be a fixture for the next twenty years. He'd even made her salary and yearly increases non-negotiable.

"I'm fine, thank you, Brenda." He smiled as winningly as possible. "Maybe just a fresh coffee?"

No way was he going to tell her about the call. He was certain that she spied on him and reported back to Nikos.

"No problem, dear."

He winced. She never called him "Mr Palmer". It was either "Adrian" or "dear", no matter how many times he corrected her.

"It's more professional if you call me Mr Palmer in front of visitors, or even the fishermen," he'd said just yesterday for the thousandth time.

"But if I do that," she had replied seriously, "they would think I was talking about your father, and I wouldn't want to disappoint anyone, eh, dear?"

It was infuriating. Brenda had been with Hades Fish Co. since his father started the business back in the seventies with one reefer truck. She helped him buy the fish at the docks and deliver to restaurants and stores all over the Lower Mainland. She had an impressive memory, never forgetting a fisherman's name, or his crew, or even his family. When Hades expanded into three refrigerated trucks and then a warehouse, and then the immaculate processing plant situated on prime riverfront real estate, it was Brenda who worked sixteen hours a day with Nikos Palmer.

Adrian often thought his father spent more time with Brenda than his family. He remembered his beautiful dark-haired mother, Iris, with a pang. She never complained.

"Your father works so hard so we can have all the nice things we want," she used to say fondly, whenever her hot-tempered son ranted about his father.

It was true, Adrian had to admit.

Hades provided him with a private school education, brand new clothes, the latest electronic gadgets and, according to Brenda's blunt assessment, "an enormous sense of entitlement".

Adrian recalled with a shudder the time when his father dispatched Brenda to bail him out of jail after a drunken party at a friend's house. Full of booze and bravado, he'd tried to kiss and grope a female RCMP officer. As she cuffed him, his friends were still whooping and cheering, but when he got to the jail cell, sobriety and panic set in.

Adrian was horrified when Brenda showed up the next morning. She acted as if bailing her employer's son out of jail was all part of the job, driving him in silence back to his house.

Just as he was about to get out of her car, mumbling a half-hearted "thanks", Brenda touched his elbow.

"You're breaking your parents' hearts," she said. "You really are an entitled piece of shit. I hope for your sake that you grow out of it. Soon."

It took a month for his father to say more than a few words to him, and for punishment, Adrian was assigned to the processing line of the fish plant for the entire summer.

He remembered the horror of those weeks. Dressed in the same overalls and hygiene bonnets, he'd been indistinguishable from every other worker in the plant. For twelve-hour shifts, his job was to scrape out the fish eggs or roe from the bellies of the salmon. The boats docked beside the plant, and heavy hoses sucked up tonnes of slippery shining salmon from the bowels of the vessels and deposited them on steel conveyor belts. The fish then efficiently trundled around the plant, as fast hands sorted, cut and scraped before they slid into large freezers. There was no time to chat (although Adrian didn't want to make friends), and apart from the official breaks, there was no time to slack off. If he missed a fish, the supervisor would scream at him, compounding his misery and humiliation. And despite the heavy-duty gloves that fit all the way up his elbows, fish blood and slime managed to seep in.

At the end of each shift, Adrian stood in the shower, turning the temperature to scalding hot and scrubbing his skin to get rid of the fishy stench. At the end of the summer, his father clapped him on the back.

"Well done, son. I'm proud of you."

For the life of him, Adrian still couldn't understand why a father would be proud of his son being covered in blood and filth every day.

Sat at his mahogany desk, and lost in his nightmare for a moment, he involuntarily brought his hands up to his nose and sniffed, half expecting pungent fish slime. He was relieved when all he smelled was his expensive sandalwood hand lotion.

He was, thankfully, jolted back to the present when Brenda walked in (without knocking) and set a mug of coffee on his desk.

"Thank you, Brenda," he said, without hiding his annoyance, as he picked up the mug, wiped up the ring of moisture with a scented tissue, and set it back down, this time on a branded coaster. "Can you please send in Amy?"

"Of course, dear."

Why won't *that woman dress properly for the office?* he wondered again, watching Brenda stride out of the room. He had never seen her wear anything to work except jeans and a plaid shirt.

During his first week as CEO, he'd gathered the staff together and, using an hour-long PowerPoint presentation, outlined the future of Hades Fish Co. under his bold leadership.

Bored with the new logo concepts and office furniture designs, the plant manager interrupted after an hour and asked if there were any plans to offset the recently announced cuts in quota, and whether there would be any lay-offs.

"No lay-offs at all," Adrian answered smoothly, not sure what the man was referring to, having not read any DFO announcements, even though Brenda had handed him a stack of paper to read "to bring him up to speed". He'd binned it all. Luckily, he had Steve Hilstead, his newly appointed director of operations, to deal with that.

Steve cut the staff in half over the next few months, and installed a new part-time employment policy, which meant that Hades wasn't on the hook to pay benefits or holiday pay.

With the budget surplus, Adrian bought a new Audi and employed Amy as his personal assistant and digital marketing manager.

Amy sashayed into the office now, with her brand new company iPhone at the ready. For the next few minutes, Adrian and Amy discussed the social media strategy, and she took a few candid black-and-white photos of Adrian studiously gazing at a piece of paper on his desk, and one five-second video of him striding around the office with a phone to his ear, his brow furrowed in concentration. They mused about the captions for a few minutes and settled on *#leadership* and *#dedication*. Amy glided out the office to update the company's Instagram, and Adrian decided it was time for a late breakfast.

Adrian's father used to be a daily customer at the Steveston Café at the end of the main street. He arrived each day, 6 a.m. sharp, and held court with the steady stream of fishermen who ate bacon sandwiches and drank steaming hot mugs of black coffee, laughing, joking and exchanging fishing tales. Occasionally, when Adrian was little, his father would shake him awake early and take him for breakfast, feeding him fried eggs on toast and shushing the men when the tales got too lewd.

The café was still there, attached to the bar and hotel. The facade was undergoing renovations to fit in with the new trendy vibe of the village. But inside, it was still the same Formica seats, plastic tablecloths and familiar plates piled high with fried food.

Adrian hadn't been in there since his father handed over the business. He knew Nikos still went for breakfast a few times a week, hungry for company since Iris died, but Adrian avoided even looking in the café's direction, disliking the accompanying pang of guilt. He knew that Brenda sometimes joined his father there to tell tales, he assumed, so why would he give them the satisfaction?

He smoothed down his tie and walked in the opposite direction, along Moncton Street, the heart of Steveston Village, then made a turn towards the waterfront. He was always filled with pride to enter the brand new Hades Bistro, with vaulted ceilings, faux-industrial chrome fittings and a gourmet menu. It had been his vision to diversify his father's business and acquire a seafood eatery in Steveston, and opening the bistro was his main focus when he took over from Nikos. His project was a perfect fit with the trendy artisan atmosphere of "new Steveston". These days, the narrow streets were more likely to be blocked by a film crew and movie sets than pick-ups piled with nets, traps and fish totes.

Adrian liked the changes. He'd had several photos of himself taken with various C-list celebrities, which boosted his Instagram following quite nicely, and he regularly invited local politicians and businessmen for dinner at the bistro.

"You are who you surround yourself with," Adrian was fond of quoting.

Adrian was shown to his regular table overlooking the Fraser River by an immaculately dressed, smiling hostess. A cappuccino materialized with an artistic chocolate swirl in the shape of the Hades logo, and the hostess placed a leather-bound menu in front of him. He studied it for a while. It was all good. No sign of pancakes, waffles or greasy fried eggs. The head chef had worked at several international restaurants and had written on his resume that he'd been trained by Gordon Ramsay himself. Adrian wasn't sure if anyone had checked, but he used it for marketing purposes and paid the man more than his entire office staff put together.

Adrian couldn't help but notice that he was alone in the bistro. Just early in the season, he told himself.

Lately, Brenda had been fussing at him about cash flow.

"You have a lunch-bucket mentality," he said, trying to brush her off. "We have to spend money to make money."

But she persisted, asking questions about incoming volumes of fish, sales invoices and payments to fishermen.

"None of this adds up," she said. "We just don't have the quantity of fish delivered to support these sales figures."

He'd sent her out of his office but knew that she'd be ferreting around every chance she could, so he made a mental note as he sipped his coffee to hire a different bookkeeper and move Brenda onto filing or something. Perhaps she'd finally leave.

As he sat waiting for his breakfast to arrive, he decided to make a call. To follow up on another project. One he was convinced would top up Hades' less-than-healthy bank account. Steve was in charge, but lately, he had been leaving Adrian out of the loop. So he called Steve and was irritated when the call went straight to Steve's voicemail.

His meal arrived. He was fiddling with the artistically arranged slithers of smoked salmon over poached eggs when his phone buzzed. He grabbed it.

"Steve, where are you? What's going on?" He stopped as Steve interrupted him.

He dropped his fork and got up from the table and started to pace nervously as he listened. Twice he tried to say something, but the voice at the other end gave him no chance to interrupt. Eventually, he turned the phone off and sat down again. Steve had been reassuring, confident that they were on track.

But Adrian was uncertain.

Had they done the right thing, he thought, as he held out his cup for another cappuccino, wondering if it was too early for something stronger than coffee.

CHAPTER FOURTEEN

Brenda watched Adrian leave the office for breakfast. Amy was watching too, and as soon as she heard the reception door swing shut, she slipped her phone in her purse and grabbed her coat.

"Just off to take some shots of the river," she announced brightly and disappeared before Brenda had a chance to answer.

Brenda rolled her eyes. *Digital marketing manager, indeed*, she snorted to herself. But the empty office gave her some privacy to make a few phone calls. She knew Adrian wouldn't return for hours, and Amy knew that too. So it was a good bet that she'd have a chance to dig a little deeper through the invoices and receipts.

Brenda was loyal to Nikos Palmer. At sixteen, she'd been broke and had a sister to support. Both her parents had died in a car crash. They left virtually nothing behind, just enough for Brenda to pay funeral expenses. She left school and started looking for work.

Nikos Palmer gave her a job.

He was just starting out, a recent immigrant from Greece with his young gorgeous wife. Brenda translated for him when he was dealing with the fishermen, handled all the cash and made sure he wasn't shorted, and did a lot of the heavy lifting as well. They sold direct to local restaurants at first, so Brenda became skilled at filleting and packing the fish in ice, making sure the quality of produce was top-notch. Soon, restaurants were putting in regular orders with "the Greek", and they started to expand.

Nikos paid her well and treated her with respect.

One day, he appeared at her tiny rental apartment and handed her a cheque for $10,000 so her sister could go to college. A gift, he said, for her loyalty.

He had her loyalty, she told him, without the gift. But he insisted.

Adrian was another story. Iris's health had never been good. She lacked the energy to discipline the boy, and his father was working too hard to notice how spoiled and unruly his son was becoming.

Brenda remembered Adrian as a happy toddler, his father sometimes bringing him to work early and having breakfast with the fishermen. Plump and curly haired with long eyelashes, he melted Brenda's heart, and even she, she had to admit, had been complicit in indulging his every whim.

She sighed. All the old man wanted was to pass on the family business to his son. To see Hades Fish Co. prosper under his son's management in his golden years.

Sadly, it happened too quickly. Iris passed away and Nikos's heart wasn't in it anymore. Knowing that Adrian was far from ready, he implored Brenda to help him.

"He'll grow into it, Bee, with your help."

She doubted it. Adrian had none of his father's work ethic and business savvy. He cared little for the fishermen bound to the company or the staff who worked in the processing plant. He was charming and charismatic but often spiteful. Brenda did not understand where he'd learned how to be so callous. Iris was kind and loving, and Nikos Palmer was a gentle man.

Brenda shook herself mentally. She didn't have time to lament her boss's shortcomings. She had work to do. First, she made a call to the fisherman she had put through to Adrian earlier. He'd been waiting for three months for payment. She noted down how much they owed him, reassured him he wouldn't have to wait much longer and ended the call.

It wasn't just incompetence. Adrian, with Steve's guidance, had purposely been squeezing the fishermen tighter and harder, cutting their margins down to the bare bones. They let these hard-working men struggle, waited until they were facing financial ruin, and at the last moment offered to buy their quotas and licenses. It seemed like a good deal on the surface. A chunk of cash to help them out of a hole, and they could still rent back the license and fish for Hades Fish Co. Quick and easy, Adrian explained. "Just to help out."

It came with strings, of course. The fishermen were bound to sell only to Hades, who controlled the price and charged a hefty fee for the license rental. Some fishermen were literally working for free.

Brenda shuffled through the papers and debris on Amy's desk. Amy was responsible for processing all the marketing and PR invoices. Brenda tutted at the extravagance. Adrian had cleared out his father's office and ordered top-of-the-range new furniture — a solid wood desk, leather office chair, two overstuffed easy chairs and a coffee table. He also bought an espresso machine — Brenda couldn't think why, Adrian wouldn't dream of making his own coffee — and he also expensed his thousand-dollar suits to the business. Brenda sighed, but it wasn't why she was rifling through these papers. She found the stack of cheques that Amy had prepared for Adrian's signature. Brenda wrote out a cheque for the fisherman and slid it into the pile. She knew that neither Adrian nor Amy would notice. And although Amy jumped at any opportunity to fawn over the boss, she always dumped the cheques on Brenda's desk to put into envelopes and mail out.

Satisfied that she had made good on her promise, Brenda turned her attention to Adrian's office.

A slight waft of expensive cologne lingered in the air. It was hard not to compare. Brenda was wistful for a moment.

Nikos had an open-door policy. He spent many hours with fishermen and staff, listening to their problems and handing out his own brand of forthright advice. He was the heart of the company, he liked to say, while Brenda was the head.

The office had always smelled of sweat and the ocean back then. A working smell, she thought, and she missed it.

Adrian was careless with paperwork. The top of his desk was polished, and neatly arranged with his iMac and an expensive planner, still in its plastic wrapping. When Brenda pulled out the drawers, they were stuffed with papers. The top one was just credit card receipts, paper clips and old Post-it notes.

But in the bottom drawer, Brenda found two manila folders. She laid them open on the desk and went through the contents carefully. There was nothing unusual about the contents for a fishing company, at first glance. Shipping and packing receipts, export documents, everything that Brenda would expect to find — except that Adrian hardly ever bothered himself with the daily operations of the processing plant. Usually, Brenda would have all this paperwork to carefully record each incoming delivery. So why had Adrian kept this file? She frowned when she saw a note scrawled to Adrian on one of the receipts. It was Steve's handwriting.

Brenda had warned Adrian against hiring Steve. He'd been in the industry for years and had earned his reputation as a cheat and a poacher. He'd fished in unauthorized areas, out of season and with outlawed equipment. He'd sold fish illegally, and one time, he'd nearly killed someone by selling them crab that had been dead for days. He'd been hauled into court at least three times that Brenda knew of. He'd been fined and immediately declared bankruptcy before returning to his shady business. Over the years, Steve had slipped under the radar, and although Adrian insisted that Steve was a changed man, Brenda suspected that Steve had just got better at not being caught.

It was beyond her comprehension, Brenda thought, why Adrian had employed him. It worried her that Steve was becoming more than an employee. He was taking charge of the company, and Adrian was lazy enough to let him. And she knew now that whatever they were up to, it wasn't legal.

Brenda had been suspicious for a while. The volume of paperwork required for incoming fish deliveries, processing and final sales was immense and complex. Just lately, she'd been finding sale receipts for product that Hades Fish Co. had sold, but, according to the paper trail, they had never purchased or processed.

She laid out the contents of the manila file, noting dates and times. Hades had imported salmon. It wasn't against any law to do that. But it was illegal if it was spoiled or if Hades was mixing it with other supplies and passing it off as locally caught.

That would make sense, she suddenly realized. A couple of days ago, she got a call on her cell phone from one of Hades' oldest customers, a restaurant on Denman Street, in downtown Vancouver.

"Brenda, what's going on?" the chef asked. "Twice I've returned a delivery because it's off, and twice it's been replaced with the same shit. I've talked to Steve, but he basically told me to fuck off."

Brenda tried to talk to the plant supervisor, a gangly young man with dirty nails and a pockmarked face who she found smoking outside the break room. He stared at her belligerently and refused to look into the complaint. Finally, Brenda returned the call and told the chef that she too had been told to fuck off.

"I'm sorry," she said. "Things aren't the same around here."

Brenda sorted through the papers again. There was nothing in here that proved her suspicions, but there were still unanswered questions. Lots of these papers had nothing to do with fishing, she realized. Consultancy? Leases? Was Adrian branching into real estate? She thought of the bistro and the cash that had been poured into that failing venture and hoped that Adrian wasn't getting in over his head for a second time. A bankruptcy would break his father's heart. She pondered what to do next. Maybe nothing? After all, it wasn't really her business, was it?

But she had promised Nikos she'd keep an eye on Adrian. He probably didn't think, though, that she'd end up spying on his son.

Time to get out of here. She didn't want Adrian or Amy to find her.

One document caught her eye. It was a receipt, but not for fish. It was a substantial amount of money, and she recognized the name printed at the top, but couldn't place it. On an impulse, she picked up Adrian's phone and dialled the number she found next to the name. No answer. It went through to voicemail, and Brenda hung up without leaving a message.

She rubbed her eyes, suddenly feeling tired.

She gathered up the papers, put them back in the file and replaced it in Adrian's desk.

Maybe it's just time I quit, she thought.

* * *

Steve Hilstead topped up his teacup and added a heaped spoon of sugar. The meeting was over, he supposed, as he noisily stirred his tea and sat back in the armchair.

From his vantage point he could see people were slowly gathering on the boardwalk, attracted by the sounds of sirens. Hephzibah herself had left the café and the fishermen — just like gossipy women — had followed suit, unable to ignore the drama unfolding outside.

He wasn't interested. His phone had pinged a minute ago and now, in real time, he was watching Brenda in Adrian's office, on the small screen. During the office renovation, Steve had taken the trouble (at his own expense) to install tiny cameras in the office, and all around the plant, that streamed directly to his smartphone. They were strategically placed so he could spy on Adrian from every angle and notified him every time someone entered or left the office. Just insurance, he figured. Just in case. But now, he observed Brenda with interest, as she riffled through Adrian's desk and pulled out the very file he'd handed to Adrian for safekeeping.

For safekeeping. Adrian was a fuckwit. He turned his attention back to Brenda as she spread out all the shipping receipts of the Russian delivery of last year's salmon that had arrived the week before.

Brenda had been asking far too many questions lately. It wouldn't take long for her to work out the details of their scheme. Steve knew that he'd have to monitor her.

Luckily, he thought, laughing inwardly, there's an app for that.

CHAPTER FIFTEEN

Andi remembered something. She shoved her hand in her pocket and pulled out a cell phone. She put it on the desk in front of Jim.

"I forgot about this."

Jim picked it up.

"Whose is it? Andi, you didn't . . ." He looked at her, and Andi guessed from his horrified expression what he was thinking.

"No, I didn't take it from the scene. But I do think it belongs to Pierre Mason."

They were both sitting in the office drinking coffee. Jim wanted Andi to go over the events of the morning in detail before they started writing.

"Due diligence," he'd said, and Andi agreed.

This was a scoop, but they had to confirm details first. She knew they couldn't screw it up.

Andi told Jim about Brian McIntosh at Hephzibah's café that morning.

"He dropped the phone when he took off running, when he heard the police sirens."

"He could have stolen that from anywhere," Jim said. "At any time. Doesn't mean it's connected to the body. It isn't significant . . . yet."

"True. It's still got a charge, though, so he must have stolen it within the last day or two."

"Can we see who it belongs to? By looking at the call history?"

"Not unless we have the password. But there was one call that came through . . ." Andi told Jim about the received call from Hades.

"So it could belong to a fisherman. If Hades means Hades Fish Co."

At that moment, the phone vibrated. Andi looked at Jim.

"Answer it," Jim said. "Then we'll know."

"Hello?" Andi took the call. "No, I just picked up the cell phone," she said in answer to the confused caller. "Someone dropped it. Who is this? Who are you trying to get hold of? Oh . . . I see."

Andi lowered the phone from her ear, her gut telling her that now, this was significant.

"The phone," she said to Jim, "belongs to Pierre Mason." Jim looked serious.

"So how did Brian McIntosh get hold of it?" he asked.

There were too many unanswered questions to put anything in print. Jim was adamant about that.

"Hand in the phone," he told Andi, "and see if you can get any more details from the police. I'll see if I can get any information from Mason's posse."

* * *

The RCMP detachment at Coffin Cove was manned by only two officers, who were on call almost all the time. The detachment was locked when Andi arrived with the cell phone, so she headed back to the fish plant, guessing correctly that all available officers would be there.

The coroner had arrived. A forensics team, all dressed head to foot in white overalls, masks and booties, were entering the building just as Andi got there. A white tent covered the car. Apart from the squad cars, Andi noticed several dark-coloured SUVs inside the taped-off area.

IHIT, the Integrated Homicide Investigation Team, or Major Crimes Unit, Andi thought. So she was right: if they were bringing in the heavy hitters, this was no accident.

One of the figures in white stopped and looked in Andi's direction.

"Hey, Silvers!"

Andi saw that he was carrying a camera in his gloved hand.

"Hey, Terry!" she called back. "Thought you were doing weddings these days?"

"Fuck no!" he shouted. "Couldn't deal with fuckin' bridezillas."

Andi laughed. She liked Terry Pederson, a crime scene photographer who said he enjoyed taking pictures of still life. "Very still life," he always added with a smirk.

Andi understood the need for Terry's macabre sense of humour. He captured images that only existed for most people in their worst nightmares.

"Let's catch up," he shouted, making a drinking gesture with his hand.

Andi waved in agreement, as a uniformed officer came hurrying over.

"Please leave the area, you're not allowed to be here," the officer started.

Andi waved the cell phone at him. "I think this is relevant," she said. "I think it belongs to your victim, Pierre Mason," she ventured, hoping to strike up a conversation and get some more details.

"It's a lost cell phone," the officer said dryly, too experienced for Andi's tactics. "I'll pass it on and a member will get in touch with you if necessary."

Andi passed him her business card.

"The *Gazette*," he remarked. "There will be a press conference later. Until then, I must ask you to leave. Please."

Andi joined Jim at the dock. The protesters, who were milling around like scared kids, having lost their cocky swagger now that their leader was likely lying dead in the fish plant, were eager to talk. They told them that, yes, Mason was driving a rental car like the one parked outside the fish plant. No, they didn't know if he was meeting anyone the previous night, they only knew to meet him at the dock this morning to organize their next protest. "But you'd know more about that," one of them said, looking at Andi, "seeing as you met Pierre at the pub last night."

Andi refused to meet Jim's eyes.

* * *

"You met Mason last night?" Jim practically yelled at Andi when he got back to the office. "And didn't tell me? What else haven't you told me?"

"Nothing!" Andi said, irritated by Jim's reaction. If it wasn't for her, they would be in the dark and waiting for the press conference like everyone else.

"You were one of the last people to see him alive, one of the first people to see him dead, and you had his cell phone," Jim stated, his voice back to a normal level.

"What are you trying to say?" Andi asked.

"That the investigating officer will probably want to talk to you," Jim replied. "You're supposed to report the story, not be part of the story."

Andi considered this for a moment. She had to admit Jim had a point.

"I'll turn myself in tomorrow," she said. "Right now, I'm writing my piece for tomorrow's issue, and I've only got an hour before the print deadline."

An hour later, after arguing with Jim about the details she could include in the article without being sued and pointing out for the thousandth time that if the *Gazette* went digital, they could report the news throughout the day instead of having these ridiculous deadlines, Andi checked her email.

"Holy shit!"

"What's the matter?"

Andi swung her laptop round to show Jim.

"'The Bigger Picture'," he said, reading the subject line. "What does that mean?"

"Look who it's from," Andi said impatiently.

"Holy shit." Jim looked at Andi.

"Yes," she said, "Pierre Mason."

"Something else you should mention at that police interview—" Jim looked at her seriously — "otherwise, you'll end up as the prime suspect."

"Funny," Andi said. "There's an attachment to this email, but no message."

Andi printed off the picture. "It looks like Mason scanned an old photo," she said, peering at it. "Looks like a bunch of boats fishing."

Jim studied the photo.

"That looks like a packer," he said, "and that one there is a seiner. It's not very clear."

"OK," Andi said, "explain."

"Oh, a packer is a boat that doesn't fish, it literally goes out to pick up fish, to pack them. That way, the boats can carry on fishing and they don't have to spend valuable time running back to the dock. They can sell their load right away. A seiner is a 'purse-seiner'. The boat makes a big circle with its net around the fish, and then pulls it in, so that the net tightens up . . . like a purse. Hey, give me that picture again."

Jim looked closely.

"I wouldn't swear to it," he said, "but that boat looks like the *Pipe Dream*."

"Harry's boat?" Andi said, surprised.

"Yes, I'm fairly certain. Now why would Pierre Mason send you a picture of Harry's boat?"

* * *

It was just getting dark as Jim and Andi walked down to the dock. The fish plant was flooded with light. Huge lamps, positioned so that the police investigators could work into the night, threw long shadows over the boardwalk. A press conference was scheduled for the next day. A TV crew had already arrived. Andi knew that by the time all the reporters were assembled, the body would be long gone, and the forensics team would be focusing on the painstaking lab work that would reveal at least part of Pierre Mason's story.

Andi knew that she could add to those facts. The email had a time and date, so assuming that Pierre sent the message himself, the police could narrow down the time of death. Brian McIntosh had dropped the cell phone. Did he find it? Steal it? Or (and Andi shuddered at this thought) did he take it off the dead body? And was any of this related to Sarah's death or was it a horrible coincidence? She intended to find out.

Andi didn't believe in coincidences, and wanted to hear from Harry what he thought about Mason having a picture of his boat. Or at least what he was willing to tell them. She didn't share Jim's confidence that Harry could or would tell them anything.

The *Pipe Dream* wasn't tied up in its usual place.

Odd, Andi thought.

"Does he often go out fishing at night?" she asked. "Seems weird — just about the whole town is heading to the Fat Chicken to find out the gossip." They had seen cars parked in the street and people walking to the pub, a distinct excitement in the air.

People enjoyed death, Andi thought, as long as it didn't involve them directly. She had experienced this before, people contacting her, wanting to be interviewed about their third-hand knowledge of the crime or about some small snippet of unrelated information, to make them seem relevant to the story.

The pub would be humming with conspiracy theories. She wondered if Sue and Joe knew that the main suspect in their daughter's death was now lying in a morgue.

Jim shrugged.

"Harry could be anywhere," he said. "We'll catch up with him."

CHAPTER SIXTEEN

Brian McIntosh was cold. He had been hiding in the undergrowth on the road out of Coffin Cove since running from Hephzibah's, crouched out of sight until the day faded into night. The vodka he had grabbed as he left the fish plant sustained him for a few hours, before he drifted into a disturbed sleep. Then he woke up, panicking. He knew it wouldn't be long before the police were looking for him. He thought a few fishermen at least knew he camped at the fish plant. Then all those people at Hephzibah's saw him run when the sirens came. He knew he should have stayed and acted casual, but he couldn't help it.

And he always got blamed for everything.

He cursed as he remembered the phone. He still had the cash from his client, but that wouldn't go far. He was going to sell the phone to a kid he knew who could reprogramme it somehow and sell it on.

But what to do now? Where could he go? He thought briefly about Joe and dismissed that almost immediately. He hadn't seen Joe for years, and the last time he showed up, that bitch Tara called the police. *Keeping me away from my own brother*. A wave of self-pity and anger overcame him for a moment.

Brian wasn't stupid. He knew it was no coincidence that he was paid a wad of banknotes for stealing a gun, and a few days later, somebody was shot.

"I was fuckin' set up," he whined, out loud, "fuckin' set right up. I'm a fuckin' innocent man, I'm innocent," he went on, conveniently forgetting his pride at a perfectly executed theft.

Then he remembered something else.

He hadn't worn gloves.

"FUCK!" He pounded his forehead with his palm.

He hadn't bothered, assuming that the gun would be far away from Coffin Cove by now. He had been so excited about the money that he didn't think—

Wait a minute . . . Had his client worn gloves? He couldn't remember and it had been dark when he handed over the gun. Maybe not? So more sets of prints. That was reasonable doubt, right? Maybe the shooter took the gun. Maybe he wasn't set up after all. His prints couldn't be the only ones on the gun, the owner's were on there too.

Brian began to calm down.

Maybe it was a coincidence. Maybe if he just lay low for a bit they'd catch the shooter. Someone else might have heard the shot. Someone might have seen the killer's truck arrive and leave. There was always some asshole watching everything, nosing in everyone's business in this fucking town.

He tried to concentrate on his immediate situation. He needed food and somewhere to stay. Somewhere he could hide until the cops figured out who did the killing, and then he could come back.

He decided to take a chance and buy some food at the gas station. It was just up the road and it was early. He hadn't heard any sirens . . . Maybe they weren't looking for him yet? Then where to go next?

Brian suddenly remembered a place he could go. A place he hadn't been for years. Nobody would think to look for him there.

He checked the cash in his back pocket, felt in his rucksack for his box of treasures and felt comforted. It would all work out.

Feeling almost cheerful, he headed towards the gas station, keeping his head down, and ducking as far out of sight as possible whenever a car or truck passed him.

CHAPTER SEVENTEEN

Brenda lingered at Steveston Dock. Eight o'clock in the morning, and the marine mist was already clearing. The muddy Fraser River shimmered, disturbed only by a large grey seal, rolling lazily by the fishing boats, and seagulls skating along the surface.

It was too early for tourists in Steveston. Another couple of months and the town would be bustling.

So many changes, Brenda thought. As a child her father had brought her to Steveston to get freshly caught fish from the fishermen who sold their daily catch straight off the dock. She remembered the scream of the gulls circling the vessels as they came in, and the froth of blood and fish guts in the water. The old cannery was still in operation then. In those days, there was a steady stream of boats jostling for position to offload, just where she was standing now. The cannery closed a few years before Brenda started working for Nikos, and now tourists trooped through the old building learning about those historic heydays of the fishing industry, and gulls pounced on discarded junk food rather than rotting fish heads.

Not all changes were bad, Brenda thought. The stench of decomposing fish offal was gone. Brenda's new apartment, built in place of the Imperial Plant that used to grind herring into powdered fish meal, had a spectacular view of the river and a smart new coffee house and boutiques on the ground floor.

She'd always loved living near the ocean and had bought into the new development before all the real estate prices went crazy. She lived a comfortable life and hoped that her current worries about Hades would be short-lived.

In the distance, Brenda could see a small aluminium boat heading up the river. She remembered waiting for that familiar sight with excitement and anticipation.

It's the only thing missing, she thought. *Someone to share my life.*

She watched the boat get nearer and wondered if she had done the right thing. Wondered if she'd been waiting for a reason to make that phone call.

The past is the past, she told herself firmly. This is about saving the future. And she walked down the boat ramp to wait for the *Pipe Dream* to dock.

Brenda had often wondered how she would feel if she ever met up with Harry again. A long time ago, Brenda had hoped that their friendship would develop into something more intimate, but Harry was going through a divorce back then, and didn't want the complication of another relationship while he fought for joint custody of his daughter.

So they agreed to be friends. And then drifted apart. Brenda was sad about that. She didn't think she had waited for Harry, but in her mind, nobody had ever measured up, so most of her relationships had been short-lived.

She felt a mixture of nervousness and excitement as the *Pipe Dream* got nearer, and she saw Harry's outline in the wheelhouse. *Like a silly teenager*, she thought. *Pull yourself together*.

He docked the *Pipe Dream* and hopped down from the wheelhouse. Still agile, Brenda noted, even if he was slightly thicker-set than she remembered. Grey hair and a face creased from the wind and sun — of course, it had been twenty years.

Brenda was suddenly self-conscious. Her hair, once jet black, was greying, and was scraped back in a bun, the same style she'd worn since she was a teenager. She didn't go to the expensive gyms or trendy classes in the village, preferring to get her exercise from brisk walks in the ocean air, but she wasn't as skinny as she'd been last time Harry saw her. And she hadn't been happy either, then, she thought. They had argued — she had been hurt and a little selfish, she admitted to herself.

When they met face to face at the dock, she held out her hand. Harry laughed and gave her a hug. There was no trace of resentment or anger in his eyes, just the same kind twinkle, Brenda saw with relief, and she hugged him back.

"How have you been, Bren?" he asked.

"Good. And you?"

"All the better for seeing you," he smiled. He used to say that to her every time they met. She was glad he hadn't forgotten.

Brenda felt warm inside. *I was right to call him.* This would all be sorted out now.

Harry had fished for Nikos and Hades Fish Co. until he sold his licenses. His timing was good, Brenda thought, because the industry had waned since then. Nikos always liked Harry. He called him "the Gentleman Fisherman".

"He never forgets that he's only as good as his next catch," Nikos used to say. "And he never steps on anyone else to get it."

Brenda knew that Harry could talk to Nikos about Adrian without upsetting him or insulting his son. She knew how proud Nikos could be.

Yesterday, Adrian arrived back from breakfast (surprisingly early, Brenda thought) looking worried. He shut himself in the office, even telling Amy curtly after signing the cheques that he was too busy to be bothered with the social media strategy. He didn't emerge for the rest of the day.

Brenda left early. She rarely did that, but Amy was still too busy sulking from being dismissed from Adrian's office to notice. So Brenda gathered up the mail to take to the post office, making sure that the cheque she had written was included. The worried fisherman would receive payment, at least. Then she hurried home to think over the day's events.

As she sat in her tiny apartment, alone, she made a few notes about what she had discovered in Adrian's desk. She wished she had taken a few pictures with her phone, but she could remember enough to make some realistic assumptions about what was going on.

Brenda was certain that Hades Fish Co. was buying illegal fish and that Steve Hilstead had either arranged it or was heavily involved. She didn't know what to do next. If she ignored it and Hades got caught, Adrian would face a fine and possibly jail time. If they didn't get caught then Steve Hilstead, she was sure, would get more brazen. She wondered what *he* was getting out of it. He didn't strike her as particularly selfless. And he was part of the reason that Hades was struggling. He'd encouraged Adrian to refurbish the offices and open the bistro. Adrian had needed little persuading, though. He loved luxury and hadn't begrudged a penny of the thousands he'd spent on that ridiculous hipster place.

Thousands of Nikos's hard earned cash, Brenda thought, and now they wanted to make a quick buck by selling substandard illegal fish and squeezing the fishermen who'd always been loyal to Nikos.

Brenda briefly considered quitting in disgust. But she was too young to retire, and wouldn't get much of a pension. She'd hoped to have more savings before she stopped work. She'd been with Hades for her entire working life — who else would hire her now?

Besides, she owed Nikos Palmer a lot. He'd asked her to stay on and help his son. He deserved her loyalty. Maybe if she could persuade the old man to talk to his son, get rid of Steve, maybe, she fantasized, he might come back temporarily . . .

She needed some help. So she picked up her phone and called the only person she trusted, other than Nikos, to give her good advice.

Harry listened. If he had been surprised to hear from Brenda, he said nothing. He agreed with her. Nikos had given them both a chance and now they owed him the respect of at least laying out the truth. It would be Nikos' decision, Harry said, what to do next, before telling her that he would come over.

"It's a bit crazy over here," he told Brenda, but didn't say why. "I could do with getting out of Coffin Cove for a bit."

And seeing me? Brenda hoped so.

She would have to lay out her case. Be factual, not accuse anyone of anything, but suggest that Steve wasn't a good influence on Adrian. She grabbed her laptop and googled Steve Hilstead. Three articles popped up, one only dating back a year. He'd been charged with harvesting abalone. Brenda was astonished. Abalone, a shellfish that once had been plentiful on the West Coast, was now on the endangered list. The delicacy had been practically wiped out back in the nineties.

It was well known in the industry that organized crime syndicates paid large sums of money for the illegal shellfish. Poachers who got caught with abalone usually got massive fines, but Steve Hilstead was acquitted. There wasn't much information, but Brenda read that Hilstead's lawyer had put forward evidence that the DFO officers had conducted an illegal search.

Digging back further, Brenda found Steve had been charged several times for violating the Fisheries Act, but he had never got more than a fine.

He must have a good lawyer. In any case, the information was scant, and she wasn't sure what she was looking for, anyway.

The omelettes at the Steveston Hotel were Brenda's favourite. She ordered from the waitress who had worked the breakfast shift forever and thanked her for the coffee.

While she and Harry waited for Nikos to arrive, she told Harry again, this time in more detail, about her suspicions about Hilstead and what she had found in Adrian's desk.

She coloured a little and stumbled over her words as she described her snooping, but Harry touched her arm.

"You did the right thing, Bren. Nikos and Adrian will thank you. Hilstead is bad news."

Before Brenda could ask what he meant, Nikos Palmer arrived at the café. As he shuffled towards them, Brenda hoped her face didn't show her shock at seeing how frail her former boss had become. Nikos wasn't ever a big man, but his personality used to fill every room he was in. Now, he seemed shrunken and small — fearful, even, Brenda thought.

If Harry was surprised, he didn't show it.

"Nikos!" He stood up and grabbed the old man's out-stretched hand.

"Harry. Good to see you, man. And Brenda. You two ask me here to invite me to your wedding?" Brenda was pleased to see the humour in his eyes, and she hugged him.

"No way, Nikos, I'm holding out for someone better!" she laughed.

"Ah, did you hear that, Harry? You'd better smarten up!" Nikos, a first-generation immigrant, had never lost his accent. He was full of energy and drive and swept everyone along with him.

Remembering that enthusiasm, Brenda felt twenty years fall away as she listened to Nikos and Harry retell old fishing stories and exchange banter.

After they had eaten, Harry ordered another round of coffee. Nikos slapped his hand on the table.

"So! If you two are not getting married, why did you drag an old man out here this early in the morning, eh? What's going on?"

Brenda looked at Harry and took a deep breath. She told Nikos her concerns about numbers that didn't add up and the file of receipts and documents she'd found in Adrian's office.

"I'm worried about Steve Hilstead, Nikos. Maybe Adrian doesn't know what's going on," she added, gamely attempting to shield the old man from his son's involvement.

Nikos patted her hand.

"Brenda. I asked you to keep an eye on my son. Not to cover up for him."

He turned to Harry.

"This Steve Hilstead. What do we know about him? Why would Adrian trust him?"

Harry shook his head.

"I don't know why he would trust Hilstead. Remember that year I delivered the biggest catch of my life?"

Nikos nodded and laughed. "Remember? You never let me forget." He puffed his chest out and pretended to swagger, imitating young Harry.

Harry smiled. "OK, maybe I was a bit cocky back then," he admitted, "but do you remember the packer that was buying fish for cash? It was even called *King of Cash*, remember? They were buying directly off us and then selling to the processors."

Nikos bent his head for a moment. "I'm getting old, Harry, I don't remember."

"Well, remember what you told me then?" Harry persisted. "You told me that if they were buying a fish for a dollar and then selling it for a dollar, they were washing cash, remember?"

Nikos nodded slowly. "I do remember that."

"Well, that was Steve Hilstead. And his father, I think. He wasn't just washing cash, he was selling coke. He even paid some of the guys in coke. Rumour was that he was paying off a DFO guy, because he never got busted."

"And this same guy is working with my son?"

"Same guy. But it was years ago, Nikos. Things might have changed."

Brenda interrupted. "I'm not sure he has changed." She told them what she had found the night before.

"And that's not all, Nikos. Adrian is paying the guys less and less. Some of them are really struggling, so Adrian has bought their licenses and quotas and sometimes shares in the boats. They have to rent the quotas back, and now, if they have to pay Hades a share to cover boat costs, some of them are literally fishing for nothing. They can't even cover their fuel bill."

Nikos nodded.

"I hear things still, Brenda. Some old guys still phone. I know that Adrian has been squeezing them. I don't know why." He sighed. "But I suspect he's spent his way into trouble. I warned him against opening the bistro. Makes no damn sense!" Brenda could see Nikos was agitated.

"It's my fault," he said, shaking his head. "I guess I should have spent more time with him when he was young. Iris spoiled him. He wanted nice things, fast cars. He doesn't love the work, not like I used to."

"We just want to protect your legacy, Nikos," Brenda said. "For you and Adrian."

"Ah, Brenda." Nikos had tears in his eyes. "Hades is not my legacy. My son is. I must help him."

The three of them sat in silence for a moment while Nikos composed himself.

"I will talk to my son," he said at last. "But I must have proof, not just suspicions. Can you get that for me, Brenda?"

She nodded. "I can do that. But I don't know what to look for."

"It's not illegal to import fish," Harry said. "It's only illegal if the fish have come from a closed area, or if they are being passed off as something else."

"How will I know?" Brenda asked. "All I have is paperwork and numbers that don't match up."

"The only way to know for sure is to have the fish tested in a lab. You would have to get scale samples. And you'll have to do it fast, before it's sold. Hilstead is not stupid, he won't want illegal fish hanging around."

"It won't be his neck on the line," Brenda pointed out. "It'll be Adrian that takes the fall if they get caught."

Harry nodded. "It's a sweet situation for Hilstead. He gets a backhander, I'm sure, for taking the fish, and Adrian takes all the risk."

"I'll do it," Brenda said. "I'll find a reason to get into the storage unit, and I'll get samples. Then we'll know. Hopefully, we can stop it before Adrian gets into trouble."

"You sure, Brenda?" Harry asked. "Steve Hilstead is a nasty piece of work. Where he goes, trouble happens." He told them about the suspicious death at the fish plant the day before.

"You don't think Hilstead is involved?" Brenda said, feeling worried.

Harry shrugged.

"I'm not saying that. I just know that he's bad news. So be careful."

"You would do all this for Adrian?" Nikos asked.

"Of course I will," Brenda said, squeezing his hand, knowing that she was doing this for Nikos, not his son.

"Thank you, Brenda. I must go," Nikos said, struggling to his feet. "Please be careful. And you—" he turned to Harry — "make an honest woman of her, will you? You've left it far too long!"

Harry laughed and got up to shake Nikos' hand. "Oh, she can do much better than me, Nikos."

Brenda hugged the old man, and she and Harry watched him walk away, his shoulders stooped, as if he were shrinking inward with age and worry.

"I should go," Brenda said, "I'm late for work."

Harry paid the bill, and they stepped outside.

"One thing," she said. "Who was it they found dead in the fish plant? Do you know yet?"

When Harry told her, Brenda looked at him wide-eyed. "That's the name on one of the receipts in that file!" She told Harry how she had found the name and on impulse called the number.

"Well, you know now why you didn't get an answer," Harry said. "You were calling a dead man. But I wonder how Mason was involved with Hades? Maybe they were paying him to protest and screw up the Herring fishery."

Brenda let that sink in as they walked back to the dock. Harry jumped on his boat and started her up. Brenda helped untie the lines and threw him the ropes, same as she had done years ago. Above the throaty roar of the idling engine, she shouted, "Thanks for coming over, Harry."

There was something else at the back of her mind, that she wanted to ask, but she couldn't grab it out of her recesses of her memory. She shook her head.

Never mind, she thought, *I'll get it.*

Harry waved and shouted back, "I'll call you when I get back," and with a last smile, he climbed up into the wheelhouse, and the *Pipe Dream* chugged away from the dock.

Brenda watched as the boat slowly made its way beyond the breakwater, and then heard the engine kick into gear as the boat gathered speed and slipped away on the horizon.

It had been wonderful to see Harry again, she decided. And they could surely help Nikos and Adrian get Hades back on track. But as she slowly walked towards the office, she couldn't shake a weird feeling that there was something more ominous going on.

As she reached the doors of Hades and entered the familiar lobby, decorated with black-and-white photos of the glory days of the fishing industry, she caught the thought that had been eluding her.

She remembered where she had heard the name Pierre Mason before.

And she knew what she needed to ask Harry.

CHAPTER EIGHTEEN

Andi waited impatiently at the RCMP detachment. The previous evening, she had gone to the press conference and listened as the official press liaison officer confirmed that the deceased was Pierre Mason and that his death was under investigation. Andi hadn't expected to get any more information. The press conference was sparsely attended, but she knew that it wouldn't be long before the media arrived. Pierre Mason was a controversial figure. Sure enough, on her way to the detachment, she saw a couple of media vans just arriving into town.

A young constable told her that someone would be along shortly to speak to her and showed her into an interview room, where she sat on a plastic seat at a desk in the middle of the room. He offered her some coffee, and Andi accepted.

It was horrible coffee, lukewarm and served in a styrofoam cup, but she drank it anyway. Half an hour passed. She was about to leave and make an appointment for another time when the door swung open, and a tall man in jeans and a sports jacket came into the room, holding a notepad and a file.

He was youngish — forty, maybe, Andi guessed. Dark hair and complexion, with brown eyes. Mediterranean or Middle Eastern, she thought.

"Hi, I'm Inspector Vega." He held out his hand. "Andrea Silvers, isn't it?" he said, smiling. "Sorry to keep you waiting, but you'll understand that we're pretty busy at the moment."

"Andi," she replied, and smiled back. She understood.

"So you have something to tell me about the deceased?"

Inspector Vega took a seat, grabbed a pen from his inside pocket and waited for Andi to tell her story.

She told him first about her encounter with Mason at the Fat Chicken, two nights previously. Vega listened, making notes. He waited until she was finished before asking questions.

"Why do you think he felt the need to threaten you with legal action?"

"Well, I guess he wasn't happy with the articles that Jim did last time," Andi said, shrugging.

"Mason was cleared completely of any involvement with Sarah's death. Why would you be pursuing the same story?"

Andi was irritated. "I'm not pursuing the same story, I'm pursuing the story of why he is — was — in Coffin Cove."

Vega checked his file.

"Yet you and Jim went out to interview Sarah's mother and grandfather?"

"Yes." Andi felt herself redden.

"Why would you do that, if you're not pursuing the same story?" Vega asked, fiddling with papers in his file. "Could be upsetting for them, couldn't it, having someone ask painful questions about the past?"

"Well, I am curious about who might have killed Sarah — you guys still haven't solved the case, right?" Andi shot back. "They might be glad that Sarah hasn't been forgotten."

Vega ignored her.

"OK, do you know the significance of the picture Mason emailed? Recognize any of the boats?"

"No, I don't," Andi answered. Technically it was true. *She* hadn't recognized any of the boats, Jim had. But she wanted the chance to investigate further, maybe get an interview with Harry to get a head start on the police investigation.

115

"And the cell phone you turned in, did you see this, er . . . Brian McIntosh drop it?" Vega looked up from his notes.

Andi nodded. "Yes, I saw it hit the ground when he ran off."

"Were there any calls? Before you turned it in?"

"Just one," Andi lied again. "I answered it, and that's how I found out the phone was Mr Mason's."

"Sure?"

Andi shrugged. "It was the only one I heard."

"Right then, Miss Silvers . . . Andi. Thanks for all your help. And if you think of anything else, please let me know." Vega handed her a card and got up, indicating that the interview was over.

Andi shook his hand and Vega showed her to the detachment entrance.

"Oh, Miss Silvers," he called after her, as she walked away, "be careful about digging up old stories. Don't want you to lose another job, do we?" He smiled and disappeared back into the building.

Andi stared back at his disappearing figure. She was getting tired of people investigating *her*.

She checked her phone. She didn't feel like going to the office just yet. The interview with Inspector Vega had left her feeling unsettled. He had an unnerving way of looking through her, she decided. She hadn't exactly been untruthful, she'd just omitted a couple of details, and it wasn't her job to do their investigation for them.

She needed to clear her mind, so she went back to her apartment to work on her story wall.

She had two victims now. Two violent deaths in the same town, and connections between the two victims. Even if Mason hadn't killed Sarah, he was seen with her before her death, and she had been to the forestry protests at least once, according to Hephzibah.

Andi pinned up the picture that Mason sent her. Why would Mason send her a picture of Harry's boat? She squinted at the picture again. He'd obviously scanned an old photograph, because the edges were ragged and there were crease marks through the centre. But Andi could see not two, but three distinct vessels. They knew that one was the *Pipe Dream* — they would have to identify the others.

Talk to Harry re: picture, she scribbled in her notebook.

Ask Hephzibah/Jim about Brian M.

Talk to Tara McIntosh.

Check Mason's background — Black OPS.

Find out about Hades.

She thought for a minute and then wrote:

Find out about Slippery Steve.

She had a weird feeling in her gut about that guy.

* * *

Jim wasn't alone at the office. Andi could hear his voice and another man's, a voice that was vaguely familiar, when she pushed open the door.

Fuck, she nearly said out loud.

Instead, she forced herself to smile.

"Gavin. What brings you here?"

Jim smiled at her — sympathetically, she thought. Gavin got up and strode towards her, and for a second, Andi thought he might try to hug her. She stiffened, but he held out his hand.

"I'm here for the murder," he said cheerfully. "How are you, Andi? You look well. Small town life must agree with you."

Andi took the outstretched hand, and as she felt the warmth of his skin and looked into his eyes, the last months fell away. She remembered how much she'd missed his touch.

"I'm fine," Andi muttered, not wanting Gavin to detect how she was feeling.

"How did it go at the detachment?" Jim asked, to Andi's relief.

"You've been talking to the police?" Gavin asked. "Find out anything about Mason?"

Andi sighed inwardly. Jim didn't know how devious Gavin could be when he was after information. She straightened up and shot Jim a look which she hoped would stop him divulging any information.

She needn't have worried. Jim just shrugged. Of course, Andi thought. Jim was a professional. He wouldn't fall for Gavin's charm. She gave herself a mental kick.

She'd wondered what she would feel if she ever saw Gavin again. And now she knew. Disgust. With herself, for practically swooning like a teenager, just because he touched her hand. How ridiculous.

"Just returning some lost property," she managed, and then turned to Jim. "Do you have that DFO contact? For the sea lions?"

Jim looked at her, not understanding.

"I'm going to interview the DFO officer about those dead sea lions," she explained.

"Dead sea lions?" Gavin laughed. "Sounds important. Don't let me hold up the investigation."

He reached out and took Andi's hand again. "It really is good to see you. I'll be here for a while, following up on Pierre Mason's murder. Perhaps when you've done with your wildlife piece, we could get a drink?"

Andi pulled her hand back.

"We'll see," she said.

Jim scribbled a number on a piece of paper and intervened with perfect timing.

"Here," he said to Andi, "DFO contact." He turned to Gavin. "Nice to meet you. Feel free to use a desk if you need to during your stay."

Gavin politely acknowledged Jim's offer and, to Andi's relief, left the office.

"Sorry," Jim said. "Didn't have a chance to warn you. Seems strange for an editor to cover this story. You'd have thought he'd send a staffer."

Andi shrugged. "I don't know," she said. "But he won't be getting any information from me."

"Certainly not your sea lion scoop," Jim said, with a straight face.

Andi laughed.

"How did it go with the RCMP?"

Andi told him about her interview with Inspector Vega, not telling him she had withheld details, or that Vega had done some checking up on her.

"We're not likely to get much information from them," Andi said. "Although I do have a connection with the investigation." She told Jim about Terry, the photographer.

"Good. But let's try not to get him fired," Jim said.

Andi pulled a face and then showed him the list of questions and interviews she'd put together earlier.

"OK, add to that list an interview with the DFO," Jim said. "Come and have a look at this."

On Jim's laptop screen was a grainy but enlarged image of the picture Mason had sent Andi.

"See," Jim said, "that's the *Pipe Dream* for sure. That's a packer and I've got the first three letters of the name, K-I-N. But *that there*," he said, pointing at the screen, "is a DFO vessel. I can't see the name but I've got a registration number. And now you have a contact. According to my friend at the department, Gerry Roberts was the enforcement officer in charge on that vessel around the time the picture was probably taken."

"How do we know the time frame?"

"To a certain extent, it's just a guess. But if you look at the photo of the *Pipe Dream*, you'll see the wheelhouse is above the cabin? Harry built that, but only had a couple more fishing seasons after that. He often says that he spent all that money for no reason. That narrows the time frame down."

"So how does this help us?" Andi asked.

"Honestly, I don't know," Jim replied. "But Mason sent that picture for a reason. And if you really intend to talk to the DFO about their sea lion policy, then you might as well follow up on this too."

"Good idea. What about Harry? Is he back?"

"Not sure, I'll check while you're at the DFO. Might as well drop into Mason's office while you're there." Jim smiled at Andi. "Chance to get out of town while you-know-who is around, right?"

Andi smiled back, grateful for Jim's understanding.

She got up to go, but a question had been nagging at her since last night. She just wasn't sure of Jim's reaction.

"About Harry," she started, "it seems strange that he disappears right after Mason is found dead . . . and I get a picture of his boat on my email from the dead guy."

She waited while Jim leaned on his desk and clasped his hands at the back of his head. Finally he said, "You know, it is odd. But I've known Harry for a long time. He's never taken much notice of what people might think if he does something. He just does it."

"Should we keep an open mind, though?" Andi asked. There was something about Hephzibah's enigmatic older brother that intrigued her, and she hoped he wasn't involved. But she'd been wrong about men before.

"Yes." Jim was serious. "We go where the facts take us, Andi. That's our job."

CHAPTER NINETEEN

When Brenda got to the office after breakfast with Harry and Nikos, she waited until Amy was huddled in Adrian's office before making a surreptitious call to the Department of Fisheries and Oceans' laboratory from her own cell phone. For a few hundred dollars, Brenda discovered, she could find out exactly where a fish had been caught, just from a tiny scale sample. Brenda made a few notes about the procedure and was relieved that the lady on the other end of the line hadn't bothered to ask why she needed the samples analysed.

That's the easy part, Brenda thought. The next evening, she would have to find an excuse to wander around the cold storage.

Steve Hilstead did not appear at the office, but news of Pierre Mason had filtered back.

"A dead body in Coffin Cove!" Amy said. "The only exciting thing that's ever happened there, I bet. It's a dump. Have you ever been there?"

Brenda nodded. "A long time ago," she said. "A lot of our fishermen live there. It's quite pretty, actually," she added, but Amy had lost interest.

Curious, Brenda googled Pierre Mason. She found a brief article posted by the *Vancouver Mail*. It was sparse on detail: Mason's body had been found in the old fish plant. He had apparently died by a gunshot wound. Suicide had been ruled out by the coroner and the Integrated Homicide Investigation Team had been called in. Inspector Vega, the senior investigator, stated that they had "one person of interest" they were actively seeking, but apart from that, no leads. The article summarized Mason's controversial career.

Brenda remembered Mason from a Greenpeace campaign against commercial fishing — overfishing, they contended. Mason was all about the publicity. He ran the Greenpeace vessel, the *Ocean Crusader*, and made headlines by firing water cannons at the fishing boats. He had nearly rammed the *Pipe Dream*, and hot-tempered Harry had aimed his rifle at Mason, threatening to shoot, until the crew calmed him down.

Wanting to milk the last drop of media attention, Mason insisted on pressing charges. Finally, Harry had to go to court, and luckily got a judge who was quickly weary of Mason and his supporters' grandstanding. Nikos and all his crew had been ready to testify but the judge dismissed all charges. Mason didn't care. He got what he wanted — publicity and donations.

It bothered Brenda a little that Harry hadn't mentioned it that morning. Now Mason was dead, after leading a protest in Coffin Cove, and somehow Hades was involved with him, according to the paperwork she'd found.

Was it possible that this was all coincidence? Was she getting paranoid in her old age?

The rest of the day passed without incident, and Brenda was glad she didn't have to talk to Adrian, and that Steve Hilstead was nowhere to be seen. Finally, Adrian left the office — early, of course — and Amy trotted out less than five minutes after.

Brenda, too, went home.

I have to get Nikos some concrete proof, she thought. This was on her mind all evening.

She didn't sleep well. She lay awake, agonizing over whether she had done the right thing by making a big fuss and calling Nikos and Harry. Maybe she had overreacted.

Maybe there was a simple explanation. But if there was, then the lab tests would prove it. And if she had been wrong all along — well, maybe it was time to quit. She'd manage. Just tighten her belt. The apartment was just about paid for, maybe she would get a part-time job in a coffee shop . . . but she was sure that she was right. She had been in this business a long time.

Brenda's stream of thoughts swirled round and round. To think about something else for a moment, and maybe get some rest, she focused on Harry. *What do I feel about him?* She tried to analyse her feelings. She'd been glad to see him. It felt . . . comfortable? Was she too old to think there would be any more than just the warm familiarity of old friends after all this time?

She adjusted her pillow, turned on her bedside lamp and read a few chapters of her book.

Brenda finally drifted to sleep in the early hours of the morning, but only slept for a while. She woke with the book on her chest. She felt heavy and apprehensive but dragged herself out of bed.

Just get this over with, she thought.

But by the time she had showered and dressed and stopped in the coffee shop on the ground floor of her apartment block, she felt better.

How ridiculous, she thought, *it's my job to look into these things.* She almost felt cheerful by the time she got to the office.

But Brenda's confidence evaporated during the day.

Adrian's mood was uncharacteristically dark. He snapped at Amy, causing her to slouch in her seat, scowl at Brenda, and refuse to answer the phone. Brenda fielded calls from suppliers who had not been paid and two irate head chefs who had received incorrect orders. By lunchtime, her head was pounding, and she left her desk to go for a walk. As always, she was drawn to the water, and she sat on a bench on the boardwalk looking out to the breakwater, to the other side of the river.

In the early spring sunshine, her worries seemed ridiculous.

Did it matter, she thought, if Hades did process a bit of illegal fish? *Is it such a big deal? Is my ego bruised because Adrian doesn't need me the way that Nikos did?*

Brenda looked around at the familiar yet forever changing waterfront, and wondered if she was just stuck in the past.

Her lunch hour was up. She walked back to the office, her steps purposeful. She sat in front of her computer, opened a new document and started typing, and then pressed print. She folded the paper into an envelope, gathered up the notes from her morning calls and walked over to Adrian's office and knocked on the open door.

Adrian looked up, but didn't invite her in.

"Yes, Brenda?" He sounded tired.

"Adrian, I had two calls this morning about deliveries that were wrong."

"And?" Adrian looked up but seemed uninterested.

"Do you want me to look into them?" she asked.

"OK, do that," he said.

"Right, I'll check with the plant later on," she said, stepping into the room. "Adrian, there's something else I'd like to talk about."

"Well, it will have to wait," he said, "I've got a meeting."

"OK, well, later it is, then."

Brenda forced herself to concentrate on her work for the rest of the afternoon. Adrian's office door was shut for a meeting with the plant supervisor. Amy took the opportunity to grab her purse and slink out, to Brenda's relief.

Just before five o'clock Adrian's office door opened, and the plant supervisor walked out, followed by Adrian.

"Adrian?" She half got out of her seat.

"Brenda, I've had a long day and I'm done. Can whatever it is wait until tomorrow?" Without waiting for a reply, he left the office. Brenda sank back down in her seat, disappointed. She had wanted to get this over with today.

She waited until she heard the reception door click shut. She was alone, and she sat for a moment, listening only to the soft buzz of electronics around her.

She looked over at Adrian's office. He never locked his door.

This is the last thing I'll do for Nikos, she thought, *then I'm out of here.*

Brenda walked into Adrian's office and behind his desk and pulled open the bottom drawer. Exactly as before, she found the manila file. Working quickly, in case anyone came back, she photocopied all the documents and replaced them in the file and put it back in the drawer. She folded up the copies and shoved them in her purse, apart from one packing slip.

She was about to close Adrian's office door and leave, when she hesitated. She groped around in her purse and found the envelope she'd tried to give Adrian earlier and placed it on his desk.

Satisfied, she took one look around, stepped out and closed the door behind her.

One last thing, she thought, and walked briskly to the processing plant entrance.

The supervisor was still there.

"Can I help you?" he asked, when Brenda stuck her head into his office.

"I've got a problem with some paperwork. I need to match up some items on this packing slip with the invoice we received. Could you help me?"

He gestured to the pile of paper in a tray on his desk.

"Leave it there. I'll get to it when I can."

"Actually, I need an answer tonight." Brenda was firm. "If you like, I'll look myself. I used to spend a lot of time in the plant, I know my way around."

"I'm just about to leave."

"Not a problem, you go ahead, I'll make sure the door is locked behind me."

He looked at her for a minute, weighing her request, and then nodded. "Suit yourself. Put on those overalls and a bonnet, please. When was the delivery?"

Brenda told him.

"OK, that's been processed, it will be in the freezer. There are jackets hanging outside."

"Thank you."

"Whatever."

Brenda put on the overalls and a bonnet and walked to the back of the plant. She grabbed one of the padded jackets and gloves and pushed open the heavy steel door to the freezers. The ice-cold air momentarily paralyzed her lungs, and she gasped for breath.

Rows of shelves containing boxes of processed fish of all different species were lined up in front of her. Each delivery was given a batch number and a date so anyone could trace the fish back to the fishing boat that had caught them. It was the law. She walked up and down the rows checking dates until she found an area that had boxes that matched the packing slip.

Already Brenda could see that something was wrong. The boxes were all marked *Wild BC Salmon* and were ready to be delivered. Yet the season didn't start for at least three more months. Wherever this fish was from, it wasn't British Columbian waters.

Brenda heaved one box off the shelf. It was heavy, and she couldn't manage to get the lid open while she balanced the box with her other hand, so she slid it onto the floor and tugged off the lid.

It was salmon, she could see. Russian, probably, she thought. Not illegal to buy salmon from Russia, but it was a complete gamble when it came to quality. Nikos had built his reputation on the quality of his product. Fish, looked after and frozen properly, could be thawed out and cooked a year later, and taste just as good as the moment it came out of the ocean. Nikos demanded that his fishermen look after their catch too, paying a top price to get the best product. But fish that had been in a sea container for a week? That had probably thawed slightly and been refrozen? And then passed off as Canadian-caught?

No wonder they had been getting complaints, Brenda thought, shaking her head. She bent over the box, shaving a few scales from the frozen fish with a tiny knife she had brought with her, wiping the silvery flakes into small plastic bags.

She put that box back and pulled another four from the shelf at random.

When she heard the door to the plant creak open and slam shut, she relaxed a little, relieved for once that the plant supervisor was disinterested in his work.

No way would Nikos let anyone poke around the plant, she thought, crouching down on her knees to take more scales from another box.

Brenda finished her delicate task, taking care not to damage the frozen fish. She struggled to her feet, and bent down to pick up a box, to replace it on the shelf.

As she raised her head, she felt a rush of air behind her.

"Wha—"

Brenda didn't finish. She felt an instant and searing pain on the back of her head. The pain was so bad that vomit rose into her mouth, making her cough and spit and sink back to her knees. As she hit the concrete floor, everything went black.

CHAPTER TWENTY

Steven Hilstead ordered some iced water from the waitress. He watched appreciatively as she walked away, a trim figure in a sleeveless black dress.

The one thing that Adrian got right was this place, he thought. *Although he never would have dared without a push from me.*

The bistro had been his idea, Steve decided, shaking his head with contempt. Adrian was still tied to the past, under Nikos's shadow.

Born with a silver spoon in his mouth, never had to work for anything.

Nevertheless, he conceded, Adrian was definitely becoming more responsive to taking the odd risk.

The waitress returned with the water. Steve waved away her offer of a menu. He purposely avoided ordering alcohol. He'd seen Adrian getting loose-lipped after a couple of cocktails. He'd been embarrassed for him. That wasn't the proper way to conduct business, he thought.

He tugged at the sleeves of his new suit and adjusted his cufflinks.

This is the real me, he thought, *a businessman. Dressed properly.*

One thing he admired about Adrian was his style. Steve liked the bistro. Upmarket. The perfect place to entertain powerful clients.

Hilstead checked his watch, pulled his phone from his inside pocket and turned off the ringer. His client was due any minute, and he didn't want his phone ringing during the meeting. Everything must be entirely professional, he thought.

He had taken care of everything. He'd made sure that Adrian was in a meeting with the plant supervisor for at least two hours. By the time he appeared, the main business would be done, and they would be on to phase two. Adrian would be irritated, but that was no problem. When he hinted at the money to be made, he'd have Adrian eating out of his hand again. Steve smiled to himself.

A few small hitches, but everything was going to plan.

A small bald man dressed in mismatched pants and jacket, wearing horn-rimmed glasses and carrying a shabby attaché case, came in and waited for the concierge to greet him.

After a few words, the concierge showed him to Steve's table.

"Hello?" Steve said, surprised. "Can I help you?"

"I believe we had a meeting scheduled?" the man said with a pleasant smile. "May I sit down?"

"Er, I was expecting—"

"Yes, I know you were," the man said smoothly. "I'm his lawyer, Jonathan Dunn, from Dunn and Grant Associates. I believe my colleague Duncan Grant represented you recently, correct?"

"Yes." Steve tried not to show his annoyance and managed a smile.

"May I sit down?" Jonathan Dunn didn't wait for a reply, he took a seat and gestured "no" with a polite nod to the waitress who was hovering to take an order. "Now, Mr Hilstead, we are here to discuss the matter of your debt to my client and our mutual acquaintance."

"Well, actually, I thought we were here to discuss my business proposal." Steve interrupted, no longer smiling. This wasn't what he'd expected. How dare he send this shabby little lawyer?

"More of a business idea than a proposal, don't you think?" Jonathan Dunn replied, irritating Steve further.

"It's an opportunity to make . . . to make a lot of money." Containing his anger, Steve lowered his voice and spoke urgently. "Has Mr Nguyen read my proposal?"

"Indeed he has, Mr Hilstead. But he has some concerns, the first being that he makes it a policy not to go into business with someone who owes him money. He simply feels that it's bad energy when there is such a wide power differential. And second," he continued, raising a finger as Steve opened his mouth to object, "second, your proposal involves Hades Fish Co. When I did a cursory search, I found that you are not even on the board of directors, Mr Hilstead. How do you propose to partner with Mr Nguyen, when you do not control any business assets at all?"

"Mr Palmer is about to make me a partner," he replied with more conviction than he felt.

"I see. Mr Nikos Palmer or Mr Adrian Palmer? Because it seems that Mr Nikos Palmer still holds a substantial amount of shares."

"At the moment," Steve conceded.

"I see. Well, Mr Hilstead, I can tell you that my client was not convinced of the value of your proposition. He believes that it will be a very long time, if ever, before your debt is fully repaid, should he decide to go forward. However . . ." Jonathan Dunn paused. "However, Mr Hilstead, I do see some value for Mr Nguyen to consider it. He has some considerable . . . let's say *exposure* with his current business model and I have been encouraging him to diversify into more mainstream activities. There are some advantages in pursuing your proposal, I believe."

"That's right, I—"

"But," Dunn stopped him, "there are hurdles to be overcome. I've detailed our counterproposal in this document." He produced a manila envelope from his attaché case and laid it on the table. Steve reached out to pick it up. "Please don't read it now, Mr Hilstead. I should tell you it's non-negotiable. You have one month only. After that time, the debt will be payable in full, with the interest that has been accruing and continues to accrue. And Mr Hilstead," he leaned forward and lowered his voice, "I need not tell you it's very rare for Mr Nguyen to allow any extensions to his debtors. Please don't let him down."

He leaned back and snapped shut his attaché case, then smiled.

"That concludes our business, Mr Hilstead. Enjoy the rest of your day." Dunn got up, pushed his chair under the table and walked out of the restaurant without waiting for a reply.

Steve sat there for a moment, feeling his chest pound as adrenaline flowed through him.

What the fuck? One month?

He rubbed his palms on his thighs, calming himself down and trying to think coherently.

He knew that Nguyen was tough. But they had a history. Just one bad deal, and it hadn't been his fault.

He took a deep breath. *Well, if I'm going down, then I'm not going alone.*

He picked up the thin envelope, folded it up and shoved it in his pocket. He knew what he had to do.

Overcome obstacles, he thought grimly, *and here comes the first one.*

* * *

Adrian flopped into the chair that Dunn had just vacated.

"I've just spent two hours doing your job for you," he said, waving with irritation for the waitress to bring him a drink. "That fuckin' supervisor has got to be the most goddamn . . . where the fuck did you get him, anyway? And what have you been doing all afternoon — I don't pay you to sit in here."

"No, you don't," Steve agreed, and was about to remind Adrian exactly why he was around, when he felt his phone buzz.

He pulled it out of his inside pocket, looked at the screen and cursed.

Steve got up and, without bothering to explain to Adrian, started to walk out of the bistro.

"Where are you going?" Adrian called after him.

"To do what you pay me to do," Steve shouted back, without turning round. "My fucking job."

CHAPTER TWENTY-ONE

Andi was glad to get out of town. She promised herself a Starbucks coffee after discovering that Hephzibah's café was heaving with customers. Coffin Cove was vibrating with gossip about the death of Pierre Mason. Everyone seemed to have a theory about the crime, each one less plausible than the last.

Nothing like a murder to invigorate people, Andi thought, a touch cynically.

She saw Terry through the window, drinking coffee, and she noted with irritation that he was chatting to Gavin. She wasn't concerned about Terry handing Gavin a scoop — he was too professional for that — but Gavin's presence in Coffin Cove was getting under her skin.

All this time I've been desperate to hear from him, she realized suddenly, *and now he's here, I wish he would just piss off*.

She felt strangely protective of Jim and the *Gazette* and knew that Gavin would enjoy mocking the local paper when he was back on the mainland. She'd seen him appraising the tired office with its outdated panelled walls and worn carpet. She knew that Gavin would have fun entertaining his well-heeled staff with tales of the old man trying to keep a local rag going with undercover investigations into fraudulent bake sales. Andi had seen his performances before. Gavin despised local newspapers. He described them as "nothing more than advertising rags and 'what's on' listings for local businesses, nothing to do with real investigative journalism". Andi knew, because she'd laughed along with him.

She felt ashamed now. And determined to chase down this story.

She turned her thoughts towards today's missions and felt a little better as she drove towards the highway. Andi had plenty of time. She planned to grab a coffee near the Ocean Protection Society's office and then pay a visit and see if she could glean any information about their campaign against the fishermen in Coffin Cove. After that, she had an interview with Jim's contact at the Department of Fisheries and Oceans.

The official purpose of her interview was background on the DFO's protection of sea lions and the recent shooting of the mammals in Coffin Cove. The real reason was to find out more about Pierre Mason's mysterious photograph. Could she ferret out any connection between the DFO, the Ocean Protection Society and Pierre Mason's death? Andi felt certain there were connections, she just couldn't see them yet. And when she could, the real work would be following up each lead and verifying every fact.

Andi took the first turn off the highway into Nanaimo, the Harbour City, towards the downtown core. Nanaimo sprawled over several miles, from the southern airport to the mall district at the north end.

Andi had wandered around the Nanaimo malls once since she moved to the island. She found them a little depressing. She'd been a teenager when it was cool to hang out in malls, eating junk food in the food courts and spending hours browsing in the multitude of cheap clothing stores and over-perfumed makeup counters of the big department stores. Now, many of these stores had disappeared, replaced by dollar emporiums or boarded up completely as online purchasing took over the retail industry.

In her mind, she started mapping out an article about how small communities were navigating economic disruption.

Like Coffin Cove, the outskirts of the downtown core of the city of Nanaimo were a patchwork of dilapidated residences, pawn shops and thrift stores. Jim had warned her to be careful where she parked.

"Lots of homeless people, and plenty of drug problems," he said. "We had our own tent city spring up in Coffin Cove before — it's an epidemic."

Another symptom of economic change, Andi thought, and sighed. *No kid decides to grow up to be poor, homeless or addicted*, she thought. *But we all treat them as if their lot in life was all down to poor decisions.*

The Ocean Protection Society HQ, which sounded a lot grander on the website, was one, possibly two, cramped rooms — a storefront and back office — beside the Salvation Army soup kitchen. Andi could only verify that the society had once been here from the sign in the window. Apart from that, the door was locked, and it appeared that the headquarters was closed down. Peering through the window, Andi could just see a few brochures on the floor and a door at the back propped open with packing boxes.

Strange that the office had closed down so abruptly. It had been just a few days since Mason was killed, and it looked like the entire Ocean Protection Society had disappeared. Andi had expected to at least find someone manning the office and issuing press releases.

She stood for a moment, undecided what to do next, when she caught sight of a small sticker in the corner of the window. It was peeling off, but she could still see a phone number and a partial name. Andi punched the number into her phone and waited. A man answered.

"West Island Property Management, can I help you?"

"I'm interested in one of your properties," Andi answered, and described where she was.

"Oh yes, that one has just come available again," the man replied.

"Who was in it before?" Andi asked, hoping that her question didn't sound too suspicious. The manager was happy to chat, and in a few minutes, Andi discovered that the Ocean Protection Society had rented the office space and paid six months in advance, but refused to sign a long-term contract. They had only been there for a couple of months and had not given notice that they were leaving. The first the manager had learned of anything amiss was when he heard about the suspicious death on the news and had recognized the name. But the next day when he checked the property there was no sign of the Ocean Protection Society, and no forwarding address.

"I haven't even advertised the property yet," he was saying. "What did you say your name was?" But Andi wasn't listening. Through the grimy window, she caught sight of something moving at the back of the office.

"Thanks, I'll get back to you."

A thin woman with close-cropped grey hair was bending down, picking up documents. She hesitated when Andi banged on the front door, but didn't look up or move to answer.

"Hey, can I speak to you for a moment?" Andi called out.

The woman finally looked up but still didn't move. Instead, she tossed documents and files into a cardboard box, stuffed it under her arm and hurried towards the back of the building, then disappeared.

"Shit!" Andi looked around to see if there was access to the back of the building. Three storefronts down, there was a narrow alleyway. Andi jogged down it, side-stepping garbage and gagging on the smell of urine. At the back of the building was a small parking lot, but it was empty.

"Damn," Andi said out loud. The woman could have useful information. Or, Andi considered, she could just have been an office worker cleaning up.

Either way, she wouldn't find out now.

Andi made her way back through the alley and checked her phone for the time. Still two hours to kill before her interview with the DFO officer. She was still on the hunt for coffee, so she wandered through Nanaimo's Old City Quarter.

An hour later and she still hadn't had any coffee, but she'd bought a book in the tiny Window Seat Bookstore and some clothes from a small boutique. Jim wasn't paying much but Andi's rent was cheap, and living in a town where there were virtually no shopping opportunities, unless you wanted bait or a hunting knife, had its financial advantages.

Feeling the glow of retail therapy, but mindful of her sparse bank account, Andi passed on the expensive branded coffee and walked past the Coast Bastion Hotel, a Nanaimo landmark, towards the waterfront. She found a tiny coffee shop, Java Time, that had the same feel as Hephzibah's and settled down at a table overlooking the harbour. After a few months in Coffin Cove, Andi found that she wrote best in sight of the ocean. Today was all about research, though. She programmed her phone to buzz in an hour, flipped open her laptop and googled the Ocean Protection Society.

The website looked professional and had some spectacular West Coast photos, but very little information. There were some blog posts, a mission statement all about protecting the oceans and wildlife from overfishing, poaching, pollution, the tourist industry — just about everyone who spent any time on or near the ocean, Andi thought. Nothing new here, same as multiple environmental organizations. Apart from making half the planet and all the oceans protected zones, there was lots of pointing out the problems and apportioning blame, and little in the way of constructive suggestions. Andi had come across organizations like this before. Someone looking for an opportunity to cash in on environmental issues, organizes a few protests and puts up a website with a donation button.

She kept scrolling and found a few press releases but, interestingly, nothing about Coffin Cove.

Maybe Mason was just trying to make himself relevant again? Or looking to make some cash? It would be impossible to get any financial records. Mason was basically a private individual, and although Andi found the Ocean Protection Society registered as a non-profit corporation, it had only existed a few months, so had not filed any financial statements. That fit with the information she'd got from the property manager. Was the OPS a legitimate organization? If so, why wouldn't it continue even after Mason's death? Why the abrupt departure? Andi sighed and wished she had caught up with the woman in the office.

There was nothing here that might explain why Mason was killed, Andi thought. Did he interrupt a drug deal or some other crime? Or maybe someone in Coffin Cove decided to exact revenge for Sarah McIntosh, believing that Mason was responsible?

Andi checked out the *About Pierre* page on the website and found a few photographs of Mason in his Greenpeace days, addressing crowds with a megaphone and waving placards. Andi noted with amusement that Mason had written this section. It was self-aggrandizing, to say the least. Just reading this, Andi thought, you would think Mason was single-handedly saving the planet, fighting against big corporations and big government all on his own. The reality was so different. Andi knew from articles she had researched that it was the daily grind and work of faceless volunteers writing court briefs and constantly lobbying politicians that got legislation passed.

There was nothing here.

She clicked off the website and googled Pierre Mason. A list of references came up — top of the list was Gavin's article in the *Vancouver Mail*, Andi noted with irritation, again resolving to pester Jim about bringing the *Gazette* into the twenty-first century. There weren't many recent articles about Mason, mainly references to his exploits twenty years ago. He had been controversial and occasionally dangerous in his quest for media attention. Greenpeace made little mention of him except a reference to his "tireless fight for the planet" and how they had decided to "part company and continue the mission, albeit in different directions". On the second page, Andi found a *Vancouver Mail* editor's article that mentioned Jim's investigation into Sarah McIntosh's death. There was only a brief mention of Mason, but Andi smiled at the picture of a much younger Jim, with an older man, standing outside a much smarter-looking *Gazette* office. The older man must be Jim's father, Andi guessed. Scanning it briefly, Andi realized that the angle was all about the importance of local journalism. *Oh, how things have changed*, she said to herself, thinking of the way Gavin mocked struggling local newspapers.

She found some references to court proceedings involving Mason — nothing a protester loves more than getting arrested — but the Google references were drying up, and she was just about to abandon her search when she saw a link to another court case. She clicked the link and found that Pierre Mason was the plaintiff. Then Andi read the defendant's name.

"Holy shit!" she said out loud. Her heart sank.

Her phone buzzed. She had to leave to get to her interview, and she didn't have time to phone Jim either, so she quickly saved the link and snapped her laptop shut. This would have to wait.

CHAPTER TWENTY-TWO

The Department of Fisheries and Oceans' office, which also housed a Marine Biology Unit, was located on prime waterfront real estate overlooking Nanaimo Harbour. Despite meticulous landscaping and the spectacular ocean view, Andi couldn't help thinking that the box-like building resembled a hospital. It also appeared to be deserted.

There was no security officer at the gate, and only one notice pointing towards reception. After trying several doors that looked like they could be the entrance, Andi found one that was unlocked. She walked into a small lobby, painted institutional grey. There was no reception desk, just a door with an electronic lock.

Andi rummaged and found the contact number and name that Jim had given her and called it from her cell phone. A bored-sounding lady answered, and after describing where she was and who she was scheduled to meet, Andi heard her sigh and finally agree to walk down, collect her and show her to the right office.

Andi thanked her and waited.

After ten minutes, Andi was just about to call again when the door swung open. A young woman with a bored expression to match her tone asked Andi to follow her.

The building was a maze of corridors lined with closed brown office doors and narrow staircases that all looked the same. Andi wondered if she should drop breadcrumbs so she could find her way out after the interview. A couple of times, she caught a glimpse into an office with an open door, and saw desks piled high with files, dusty shelves full of bank boxes and people huddled silently in front of computer screens.

It was eerily quiet.

"How long have you worked here?" Andi asked her guide in an attempt to make conversation. The woman ignored her completely and stopped in front of a glass door. A brass plaque to the left read *Department of Fisheries and Oceans, Enforcement Division, Pacific Region*. The woman pressed a button on the right-hand side, and another young woman with an equally bored expression opened the door. At least, Andi thought, this young woman was rebelling against the beige interior of the building, with a pink streak in her hair and a nose piercing.

She took Andi's business card and asked her to sign in.

"Take a seat," she said to Andi. "Captain Roberts will be with you in a moment."

Confused, Andi checked the note that Jim had given her. *Gerry Roberts*, Jim had scrawled, plus the phone number.

Inwardly, Andi groaned. It had been a while since she'd interviewed a government bureaucrat. Some of them had been institutionalized for so long, insisting on the importance of rank and seniority, that they had completely lost touch with the real world. And they tended to talk a lot.

Andi tried again to make conversation, this time with the pink-haired secretary.

"Could you give me an idea about what you guys do in this department?" she asked.

Pink Hair looked up and pointed to the plaque on the door.

"Enforcement," she said, and looked back down at her desk.

Another twenty minutes went by, and Andi got up and wandered around the reception area, looking at the pictures on the wall. They were mainly posed photographs of men in uniforms receiving awards or standing to attention on government vessels. Andi imagined that this government department would attract military types, used to a regimented environment.

"Miss Silvers?"

On first impressions, Captain Gerry Roberts met most of Andi's expectations. He stood straight, towering over her. A pot belly that sank over the belt of his pants marred the military bearing and slightly puffed chest. He was about sixty, Andi guessed from his thinning white hair. He had a reddish face, and because he was standing close enough to Andi to invade her personal space, she got a whiff of coffee breath — maybe a hint of alcohol?

Overall, Captain Gerry Roberts was dishevelled. Andi noted a button missing on his white shirt and yellowing sweat stains seeping out from his underarms. His dark pants were creased, and his shoes were scuffed.

Interesting, Andi thought. Most military men and women she met, even if they were now civilian, still dressed impeccably, a habit that was drilled into them during their military career.

Captain Gerry Roberts, from his appearance, seemed to have abandoned those standards.

Andi shook Captain Roberts' outstretched hand.

"Thank you so much for taking the time out of your busy schedule for me," Andi gushed.

It worked. Captain Roberts' previously unsmiling face relaxed a little. "Well, not sure what all this is about, but if I can help . . ." he said grudgingly and indicated a door behind his secretary's desk. "Come into my office."

Captain Roberts' office was a small windowless box. Stark fluorescent lights exposed a worn, mud-coloured carpet and scuffed paintwork. The only decoration was a large nautical chart stuck to the wall by peeling tape. On the desk was a chipped coffee mug and papers scattered haphazardly.

Who had Captain Roberts pissed off to get shoved into a shitty office like this? There were no family pictures, she noticed, and none of the award-type photographs that hung on the reception walls.

"Sit." Captain Roberts gestured to the one metal chair available, and he settled into the office chair behind his untidy desk.

"Coffee?" he asked, and before Andi could reply, he bellowed "Christina!"

The pink-haired secretary appeared at the door. "Yes?"

"Get us some coffee, would you?" Captain Roberts barked at her.

"Right . . ." She walked away without bothering to collect the dirty mug from the desk or asking how Andi took her coffee.

Andi felt sorry for Christina. Andi had only been in Captain Roberts's company for a few minutes and already she knew that he was an arrogant, overbearing boss.

Retrieving her notebook and pen from her bag, she surreptitiously tapped the voice record app on her phone. The notebook was mainly for show.

"Thank you again for your time," she said brightly. "I'm writing a piece for the *Gazette* on the important work that the department does, enforcing the rules and regulations that protect our oceans. I'm sure you know we had quite an upsetting incident in Coffin Cove recently. Two sea lions were shot."

"Yes, of course, very upsetting," Captain Roberts agreed, as Christina barged into the office, plonked down two mugs of black coffee on the desk and exited without a word.

"Shut the door!" Roberts shouted, flushing even redder with irritation.

The door banged shut and Andi carried on.

"Before we get to that, Captain," she said with a winning smile, "I'd love to hear about your career and how you ended up being in charge of the Enforcement Division?"

Andi had no idea if he was in charge or not, but she figured a little ego-stroking on her part would eventually tease out the information she wanted.

Captain Roberts responded as Andi had expected. He droned on for about forty minutes, prompted occasionally by Andi, as she sat forward in the uncomfortable metal chair, interrupting every so often with an appreciative, "Oh, that's interesting, could you expand a little on that?" and scribbling notes in her book.

Despite the act, Andi was listening attentively. The long, boring (and probably exaggerated) tale of Gerry Roberts's rise through the coast guard ranks was interesting, not because of what he was telling Andi, but because of what he was leaving out.

Why was he stuck in this tiny office? How did he fall from grace? Andi wondered.

She steered his monologue to the dead sea lions.

"The fishermen think the sea lions are destroying the fish stocks," she said. "What's your opinion?"

"Well, let me think," Captain Roberts said, clearly enjoying Andi's attentiveness. He leaned back in his chair and sipped his coffee. "I have to say," he said, leaning forward again, in a conspiratorial way, "I have to agree with them! But you can't print that!" He wagged his finger at her.

"Wow," Andi said, sitting bolt upright, as if Gerry Roberts had handed her the scoop of the century.

"Yes, the sea lions are bloody parasites. We should have a cull, but the 'scientists'—" he made air quotes — "they say the data doesn't support the theory, and it's all anecdotal evidence they're wiping out the stocks."

"Hmm. Well, of course I won't quote you, but that is really interesting," Andi said, and decided to push him a bit more. She felt that he was letting his guard down.

"What about the environmental groups? There was a group protesting in Coffin Cove. I hadn't heard of them, but maybe you have, the Ocean Protection Society? They call themselves the Black OPS because they wear black — it's a bit theatrical, if you ask me." Andi wasn't certain, but she thought Gerry Roberts flinched.

"No, I haven't heard of them," he answered abruptly, the confiding tone all gone.

"Yes, I did a bit of digging, and the group had only existed for a short time, but . . ."

"Just kids — rich kids with nothing else to do. We don't bother with them as long as they keep out of the way." Captain Roberts shifted in his chair, clearly uncomfortable with this topic.

"But their founder was Pierre Mason, you must have heard of him? He's quite famous," Andi pushed.

"No, no, can't say I have," Roberts answered quickly. "I'm really out of time, Miss Silvers, I'm sure you have enough for your article?"

"Mr Mason was murdered a few days ago in Coffin Cove, I'm surprised you haven't heard?"

"I heard something, but as I said, it's not a name I recognize." Captain Roberts stood up. "I'm very busy, Miss Silvers. We're done here."

"Just one more thing, Captain Roberts." Andi ignored his tone, which was now angry. "Just before Mason was murdered, he sent me this picture. Do you recognize any of the vessels? Or know why he might have sent it to me?"

She pulled a copy of the photo from her bag and set it on the desk in front of Roberts. He was flushed bright red and breathing heavily but bent forward to look at the picture.

"No," he said after a moment's pause. "No, to both your questions, I don't know the vessels, and I don't know why this Mason would send you anything, so if you don't mind—"

"That's weird," Andi said quickly, knowing she was just about out of time. "That vessel belongs to the DFO. You should recognize it, you were captain on that vessel. Are you sure you don't know Pierre Mason?"

"What the hell do you think—? Get the fuck out of my office! Christina! CHRISTINA!" Roberts bellowed, losing control.

A wide-eyed Christina opened the office door.

"Show this woman out! Now! Make sure she leaves the building — and Miss Silvers, I'm warning you—"

Andi didn't wait to hear the warning. Grinning to herself, sure now that Captain Gerry Roberts was caught up in this story somehow, she clicked the voice recorder off on her phone and followed Christina out of the office.

"So what was all that about?" Christina asked curiously, as they made their way back through the maze of corridors and staircases to the reception area. "I've never seen that pompous prick so mad."

She had perked up considerably, Andi thought — the drama must be a welcome reprieve from her dull job.

"I guess he didn't enjoy the interview," Andi laughed, and Christina giggled.

"That guy you were asking about," she said, "my friend knew him. She was a member of that protest group."

"Really?" Andi was instantly interested. "Could I talk to your friend?"

Christina shrugged. "She might talk to you. But she was a bit freaked out when he got killed."

"Could you ask her for me? Here's my card." Andi handed it over. "Do you know anything else about the Ocean Protection Society? Or Pierre Mason?"

"There was one woman from that society who tried to talk to the captain the other day, but he wouldn't see her. He made me come down to reception and tell her to go away."

"What was her name? What did she look like?" Andi tried not to let her excitement show.

"She was thin and had short grey hair. Looked like she was older than you," Christina said, chewing her fingernail. "I don't know her first name, but she said she was Pierre Mason's wife."

CHAPTER TWENTY-THREE

This was the time when Sue felt close to God. Out here, it was just her and Him, on equal footing.

The mist hung low over the valley, obscuring her vision, but she knew her way. The dampness muffled sounds. Sue paused every few footsteps to listen for cracks and snaps in the undergrowth. They didn't need any more meat. She and Fred had finished butchering the deer and had filled their freezers. But this was where Sue felt most at peace, where everything made sense. And lately, she'd been on edge. Unsettled.

Fred's customary rage ebbed and flowed. Sometimes, his fierceness was replaced by fearfulness. Several times a day, he laid down his tattered Bible and his magnifying glass, and struggled from his chair to stare intently out of the grimy windows.

"Girl, there's somethin' out there, I know. The Devil jus' waitin' for a chance."

Sue didn't answer, but she sensed it too. These days, though, she felt little distinction between God and the Devil.

God had taken her girl. With a rifle in her hand, and the ability to take a life with a squeeze of a trigger, Sue felt for a few fleeting moments that there was some equality of power, some reckoning of the debt she was owed.

"An eye for an eye" — wasn't that what the Bible said?

Growing up with Fred, the certainty of God's rules reassured Sue Harding. Every Sunday, her father's preaching had mesmerized her. The thunder and roar, the conviction that sinners would perish in the fires of Hell and only the righteous would be welcomed into Heaven. It was simple. *Follow the rules. Avoid temptation.* And for years, she had done just that.

The Devil sent Joseph McIntosh to tempt her.

Joe was charming and courteous. Sue was tall, awkward and a loner. She knew that boys avoided her because they were afraid of Fred. She didn't mind. She had no idea how to talk to boys. Girls didn't bother with her either. Sue plaited her long dark hair and covered her head with a scarf, just as her mother insisted when she was a little girl. She wore old-fashioned skirts that nearly touched the ground while the other girls were experimenting with bell-bottoms and miniskirts. She still had no idea why twenty-year-old Joe McIntosh, who could go with any girl in town, wanted her. Sue refused to speak to him. But Joe persisted, and she finally allowed him to drive her home in his new truck one day.

Sue had expected Joe to leave her alone when Fred burst out of the house in a rage. He pointed his gun at Joe and roared at him.

"I'm good for a headshot for 200 yards, boy. After that, I'll shoot you in the gut if you ever come near my daughter again!"

Joe stood his ground.

"I meant no disrespect, sir," he said, and to Sue, "I'll see you again soon."

And he did.

Joe McIntosh always got what he wanted, Sue thought. And eventually he got her. He made promises.

"I'm a hard worker. I'll be a good provider," he said, and Sue believed that God had sent him, despite Fred's warning that Joe was a wolf in sheep's clothing.

When Sarah arrived, she held out her sweet angel as proof that God had blessed her union with Joe. Surely this innocent soul could not be the Devil's work?

And then it all started to go wrong. Joe was at home less and less. The big house on top of the hill he had so proudly built was isolated. She wandered from room to room, touching the furniture, afraid to scuff the polished wood floors. Sarah was a difficult baby. Sue was exhausted and depressed after she was born. Her mother refused to help, afraid of Fred and his fists.

Joe became more distant. He loved the baby, Sue could tell, by the way he cuddled her and hummed soft tunes to her when he arrived home late in the evenings. Joe couldn't understand why his young wife wasn't happy. He asked her what she needed. Sue missed God. She missed the familiar structure, knowing that the rules would keep her and Sarah safe. She persuaded Joe to drive her to church in Coffin Cove. It wasn't the same as Fred's strict scripture teaching, but Sue liked the soft-spoken pastor who spoke kindly to her and made a fuss of Sarah.

For a while, Sue felt at peace. The constant worry she carried in the pit of her stomach, that she had angered her God and was on a path to damnation, subsided. Fred was wrong. The pastor was right. God was all-forgiving. He had blessed her.

When Sarah was four years old, Ruth, Sue's mother, was waiting when Sue and Sarah left church. It was time, she said, for Sarah to go to school.

Fred's granddaughter would not grow up a heathen. Not like the McIntosh family, Ruth said. They were drunkards and sinners. Sarah would attend Fred's church school.

Joe was at first opposed to Sarah having anything to do with her grandfather, who had turned his back on his own daughter. But Sue was firm. It was an olive branch to her family, she said. Sarah should know her grandparents. Besides, she insisted, maybe her father was right. Sarah was being exposed to sinful behaviour. It was a low blow, Sue knew, but effective. Joe was struggling to deal with his younger brother, Brian, who would turn up at the house late at night, intoxicated and demanding money. It was not always a godly environment for a child, she argued. Joe relented. He was distracted by work anyway, working longer and longer hours.

Sarah met her grandfather for the first time when she was five years old. Wide-eyed but unafraid, she clutched Fred's outstretched hand and the fierce preacher led the tiny child into his Bible school.

Sue seldom ventured into Coffin Cove. She divided her time between their house on the hill and the valley. Fred barely acknowledged his daughter but had formed a bond with Sarah. He hung a swing in the garden and pushed her higher and higher, the little girl laughing with delight. He took her for long walks along the riverbanks, pointing out wildlife and explaining the changing seasons and nature's laws. The salmon in the river, he told Sarah, were God's blessing.

Sue, comforted a little that her father had accepted Sarah so readily, could still not shake her feeling of doom. She tried to bridge the widening gap between herself and Joe. She made an effort. She asked questions about the business, waited to eat dinner with her husband, and even reached out for him in the middle of the night. Maybe another baby would help?

What a fool she had been! God was just waiting to punish her for her sins.

Joe took Sarah to work with him one Saturday morning. Sue watched them leave, heard Sarah giggle at one of Joe's silly jokes, excited to be spending time with her daddy. Sue drifted around the house, unable to settle without Sarah's presence. She stood on the deck, waiting to hear the rumble of Joe's truck coming up the track. Early afternoon, Joe and Sarah came back. Sarah ran towards her mother, but avoided Sue's outstretched arms, her hands balled into fists, and her blonde hair pulled loose from her ponytail and hanging round her tear-stained cheeks.

Joe grabbed Sue's arm before she could go after her daughter.

"Eight years old!" Joe's face was contorted with anger. "Eight years old and she can't write her own name! Or read one damn thing! What the hell are they teaching her at that damn school? Nothing except the damn Bible?"

Sue shrank back from Joe, appalled at his blasphemy. She had never seen him so incensed.

"That's it, Sue. Sarah's going to the Coffin Cove Elementary. I'm going there on Monday to register her for the new term. And until then, she's coming to work with me. Tara says she'll help with her reading and writing until she starts school."

Sue stared at Joe. Who was Tara?

God had made the first move. Sue lost. She moved back to the valley, taking Sarah with her. Joe retained a lawyer from Nanaimo. Sue could not afford legal representation, and the court was unmoved by Fred's insistence that Joe and his Jezebel would corrupt his granddaughter. They awarded Joe joint custody, and Sarah would go to Coffin Cove Elementary.

Sue paused, her hand gripping the rifle. The fog had lifted, and she could hear the roar of the river. Each step she made in the mossy ground left a pool of water, and she trod carefully, aware that the river had eroded the banks and the ground was unstable. She was at the old hatchery. Since Jim Peters and that woman reporter visited, Sue had felt the old unease return. God's ominous gaze was on her again, she could tell.

For the last few days, on her morning hunt, she had gravitated towards these crumbling structures. Sarah had loved the hatchery. She defied her grandfather and volunteered here rather than attend church. Fred had bellowed his disapproval, but Sarah had refused to budge. Sue allowed herself a small smile as she remembered Sarah's calm response to her grandfather.

"The salmon are a blessing, Grandpa. You told me that. God wants me to help."

Sarah got her stubborn streak from Fred, Sue thought, and her drive and passion from her father. The thought of Joe made her palm sweat as she gripped the rifle tighter. The last time she saw Joe was at Sarah's funeral. It was late October. Maple leaves blanketed the ground as Sarah's coffin slipped gently into the earth. Joe had collapsed, wailing, as his Jezebel tried to comfort him.

Joe divorced Sue, but although she signed the legal papers, she knew they were still married in God's eyes. Nothing would change that. So now here they were, still husband and wife, at their daughter's graveside.

Sue stood beside Fred and Ruth. She held her mother's hand, and it felt shrivelled, claw-like. Fred was stooped and withered, his thunder smothered by the shovels of dirt that hit the coffin with a rhythmic thud. Sue allowed their grief to swirl around her. She felt nothing but rage. It engulfed her. People seemed to sense it, as they clasped Joe's hands and hugged him tight, but moved past Sue quickly, just murmuring their respects. She stood at the graveside, long after the mourners left. She was at war now. It would never end.

The police promised justice. But their justice did not interest her, and the police stopped driving out to give her updates. Until Jim appeared the other day, it had been years since she'd heard Mason's name spoken aloud.

She clenched her hands, one clutching her rifle, the other digging in her fingernails to try to eliminate the thought of Mason from her mind.

Maybe Sarah was rebelling, they'd said. It's normal for teenagers to sneak out. Lots of parents don't know where their kids are half the time. Drinking and smoking, right? Isn't it possible Sarah went to meet Mason?

Sue had felt sick. She had sat on the edge of the couch, looking at a police officer, trying to grasp what he was saying. She had said nothing, staring blankly at him. But inside she was screaming, *Not Sarah, not Sarah.*

"Not Sarah," she whispered to herself. "Not Sarah."

Sue glimpsed a movement in the corner of her eye. Not an animal, she knew. It had been the same for the last few mornings. Sue felt she was being watched. The first time it happened she imagined it was Sarah's presence. If she stood still enough, she might be able to stretch her hand through the misty veil that separated their souls and touch Sarah's soft spirit. She came back again the next morning, but the feeling was gone. And now, she was sure that her watcher was human.

"Who's there?" she shouted suddenly, and startled ravens took flight into the rising fog, seeming to echo her voice with their cries.

Nobody answered. Maybe she was going mad. Maybe this was God's final punishment, taking her sanity. After Sarah's death, she had felt her grip loosen on reality. She was grocery shopping in Coffin Cove, months after Sarah's death, lining up with her basket of items waiting for the cashier to serve her, when she caught sight of blonde hair cascading over a bright sweater out on Main Street. She dropped the basket and ran, pushing her way through the checkout, looking wildly from left to right in the street before she saw the blonde hair bobbing down the road towards the boardwalk.

"Sarah!" she screamed, but the blonde hair kept moving. Before she could move, concerned shoppers surrounded her. "It's not Sarah. Sarah's dead," one lady was saying. "I'm so sorry." They were staring at her, as if she were a madwoman. "I'm so sorry," they repeated. What were they sorry about? Sue wondered.

It's not Sarah, Sue told herself now. *Sarah is gone, Sarah is dead, Sarah is gone, Sarah is dead*, the ravens called. God's messengers mocking her from high in the treetops.

Sue tucked the rifle under her arm. The old Nissan hut that used to be the hatchery office was overgrown with brambles. The old wooden steps were rotting, and they sunk under Sue's weight. The door was open. The hut used to be locked, but the rusted screws were torn out of the frame. The door, swollen with damp, had scraped across the faded linoleum floor, leaving a clear half-circle in the green mildew.

Sue stepped in.

There was nobody here.

Sue realized that she was holding her breath and exhaled, allowing her shoulders to relax.

She walked around the hut. There was no furniture left. The hatchery had been cleaned out long ago. Sarah had been heartbroken. It was one of the few times Sue could remember her daughter uttering angry words about her father. The river burst its banks that year. The water ripped apart undergrowth and hurled mud and silt in its ferocious current, unleashed by clear-cutting on the mountain. Sue and Fred frantically dug ditches and built dams to keep the house from flooding. In the end, they only lost a woodshed, but the hatchery was washed out by the torrent.

There was no money to rebuild, and no point, because the damage had been done. The river took control of the valley, pushing out all the inhabitants except for Fred, Sue and Sarah. Ruth had passed, and Fred had mellowed a little since the death of his wife, accepting without argument Sarah's choice to join the protesters against the forestry workers.

Sue never questioned Sarah but knew that her relationship with Joe had become strained. A part of her was glad. She hated when Sarah stayed with Joe and that Jezebel. She was jealous when Tara befriended Sarah and introduced her to a new friend, Hephzibah, the daughter of some hippie, and Ed Brown, a local drunk. Sue knew that someday Sarah would leave the valley and she would be left alone with Fred. She said nothing when Sarah chatted excitedly about studying marine biology at college, and in her heart was relieved when Sarah arrived home from Joe's one day, vowing never to take a penny of his dirty money.

She wished she had talked to Sarah. Not the perfunctory queries about homework and chores and reminders to take a jacket. No, the questions and conversations that Sue had believed there would always be time for. She'd never asked Sarah how she felt about anything. Did she blame Sue for her broken home? What was she afraid of?

I wish I'd asked you. I wish I'd protected you.

Sue had known that something was wrong. Sarah arrived home one evening quiet and white-faced. She had refused food. Gone straight to bed. The next morning she went to the hatchery. She had left early, the other volunteers said. Gone to see her father, they thought. But she never arrived at Joe's house. After, someone told the police they saw Sarah with Pierre Mason.

It had never made any sense.

Sue shivered. The Nissan hut was wet and cold. Mould was growing on the walls, and brambles forced their way through cracked windows.

This place had been where Sarah spent most of her free time. Chatting to visitors about salmon. The epic journey, fraught with danger, from river to ocean and back again to reproduce. The fight for life. It had fascinated Sarah from the time she could walk and squeal with delight at the swish of silver and red of the spawning salmon. When she was old enough to volunteer at the hatchery, Sarah would arrive home, spilling over with infectious excitement, sharing every detail of her day. Sue smiled at the memory. She had listened silently, nodding with encouragement, and wondering how she had produced this fearless, passionate individual.

There was nothing left here. Not a hint of hope. The building groaned as Sue moved, as if burdened by the same weight of grief. Sue could smell human urine. Just a poacher out here, maybe, taking refuge from the rain. She turned to leave and caught sight of a pile of rags on the floor. She flinched and pulled her gun into position as the bundle moved, and then relaxed as a rat scurried across the floor, disappearing into the gloom.

Sue walked over and prodded at the pile with her foot. Looked like an old sleeping bag and a rucksack. An empty bottle of vodka rolled across the floor. She sighed. Her watcher must be some homeless person camping here. A strange place to shelter, Sue thought. A long way from food and warmth, unless you knew how to hunt and build a fire.

She shrugged and pushed the bundle back into a pile. She'd have to clear up the yard and lock away their tools, she thought. Homeless, hungry people made bold thieves.

Her foot touched something solid. A tin box. Without thinking, she kicked it and the lid came off, the contents spilling onto the floor.

Definitely a thief, Sue thought, looking at a curious collection of trinkets scattered on the ground. She bent down to scoop them back into the box.

And then she saw it. A glint in the gloom. Sue reached out slowly to touch it, holding her breath again. She knew what it was instantly. But her hand trembled. Disbelieving, and half expecting that this was just a trick of the light, she touched it. Her fingers closed around this tiny glittering connection to the past.

And in one moment, Sue knew that Sarah had guided her here.

CHAPTER TWENTY-FOUR

Brenda laid her head back on her pillow. Every so often, nausea welled up and she felt a bead of sweat form over her upper lip. She tried not to move, and clenched and relaxed her hands until the feeling passed.

She breathed deeply and focused on the view of the Fraser River from her apartment window.

The doctor had been reluctant to discharge her from the hospital.

"You were lucky," the doctor said, as he conducted his final check-up. "If you hadn't been found when you were, severe hypothermia would have set in."

Brenda nodded weakly. She still only had fuzzy fragments of memory. She remembered being very cold, her cheek pressed against a hard frozen surface. Her head hurt. The back of her neck hurt. She'd tried to open her eyes and when she did, she was aware of a shoe, a man's shoe near to her head. She was afraid. She felt like she should lie still, not call out or speak, even though she was chilled to the bone. She forced herself not to shiver . . . and then it went dark again.

When Brenda woke up, she was in hospital. The nurse who coaxed her awake from her deep sleep patted her hand. "Brenda? It's alright, hun, you've had an accident, a bit of a bump on the head, but you'll be fine. Not to worry, just rest." Before Brenda could grab her arm, tell her she was frightened, she felt a prick on her arm, and the smiling nurse faded from sight.

Next time she woke, the same nurse explained what had happened. A young man had found her, she told Brenda, collapsed in a heap in a freezer, of all places! Brenda had a nasty bump on her neck where a large box of frozen fish had hit her, and a smaller bruise on her forehead, probably from her head hitting the concrete floor. She had a concussion, had suffered very mild hypothermia, but would be fine with plenty of rest. They were keeping her in for a night, maybe two.

Brenda nodded and tried to smile her thanks, but tears rolled down her face instead.

"Oh, don't worry, you've had a nasty shock to the system. Tears are normal," the nurse reassured her. "Try to get some sleep."

Adrian had visited her in hospital. Brenda had woken to find him pacing at the bottom of her bed, whispering urgently into his phone. He had brought her flowers, which she acknowledged with a slight nod of her throbbing head.

He was agitated, and she soon realized why.

"You know, Brenda, you shouldn't have been in the freezer. I know you were only trying to sort out that delivery problem, but still, you weren't supposed to be there . . ." His voice trailed off, and he paced back and forth again. "But look, everything worked out. I know you had a bump on the head, but no long-term harm done, right?" Again, he flashed her an anxious smile. "And maybe it's for the best if I just accept your resignation? Pay you some severance pay? And a bit extra for the holiday you're owed? We can sort it out in no time, if you just sign here . . ."

Brenda was too tired to argue. She'd forgotten about her resignation letter. And now she'd given Adrian the perfect excuse to terminate her employment. She knew why he was nervous — what if she sued? She didn't care about the severance or the holiday pay, what she wanted right at that moment was a sip of water to soothe her parched mouth and for Adrian to leave.

"Leave it there," she croaked.

"Sure, sure, not a problem, when you're ready. OK, then." Adrian's phone rang, and he grabbed it thankfully. "OK, Brenda, get well soon, and let me know about that letter, OK? It's the best thing, the best thing . . ."

The next day she discharged herself. She needed to be home.

And now it was late afternoon. The sun was sinking out of sight, leaving purple and pink streaks in the sky and illuminating the river. Brenda had got up late, pulled on some sweatpants and picked up some coffee from the shop at the bottom of her apartment block. She didn't feel like eating or talking. The nurse had asked her if there was anyone they should contact. Brenda realized that apart from her sister in Ontario, there was no one. No one apart from Adrian and the other people she worked with — or used to work with, she corrected herself — had any idea she was in hospital. Or even alive, or dead. Was that the sum of her life? Nikos used to tell her that nobody was indispensable. *When we leave, it's like pulling your foot out of a bucket of water. Apart from a few ripples, it's like we had never been there at all.* Brenda used to think this was such a cynical view of the impact people make on the world, but now she believed him. All those years, for what? An undignified end to her career. Not even a career. Just a job. And now she didn't even have that.

Brenda hadn't read Adrian's letter until she got home. He'd got legal advice, she guessed. It was written in formal language and made it sound like her fault.

"Against safety protocol . . . not authorized . . . breached the rules . . . Unfortunate that she placed a box back on the shelf insecurely, resulting in it slipping and banging her on the back of the head—'

She stopped when she got to that part. She shut her eyes. She remembered crouching down over a box, but then? The memory was just tucked out of reach.

The letter described the supervisor returning because he'd forgotten his phone, and finding the freezer door unlocked, and Brenda lying unconscious on the floor. She'd been there for two hours. The rest of the letter laid out the terms of her termination. Quite a generous severance — Adrian was probably advised to do that, Brenda thought — her holiday pay and a month's pay in lieu of notice.

At first, she was angry. What if she didn't sign? She contemplated phoning a lawyer herself. But just as quickly as her anger flared when she read Adrian's letter, it dissolved. She would sign it.

Later, while she was trying to get comfortable and take a nap as the doctor ordered, her phone rang. The sudden noise in her silent apartment made her jolt, and her head hurt all over again.

"Brenda? How ya feeling?" Amy trilled, and without waiting for an answer, she went on. "So sorry to bother you, but the new girl can't find your Accounts Receivable file? Do you know where you put it?"

New girl? Brenda wished she was the type of person to tell her where to go, but she wasn't and she didn't. She told Amy where to find the file, then clicked off her phone, pulled herself up from the sofa and signed the letter. She found a stamp and padded down to the lobby of her apartment in her slippers and dropped the letter in the mail.

She could have walked it round to the office. But she never wanted to go to Hades Fish Co. again.

For the rest of the evening Brenda sat at the window, watching darkness engulf the water and listening to the night sounds of the harbour. She tried not to obsess about the questions swirling around in her mind and to just enjoy the familiar night sounds and sights of Steveston, but she couldn't settle. Should she phone Nikos? Had it really been an accident? And why hadn't she heard from Harry? She couldn't shake the feeling that had gnawed at her since she arrived home from hospital. Was it fear? Or loneliness?

CHAPTER TWENTY-FIVE

Steven Hilstead smiled approvingly at the new girl.

"Good morning," she chirped with a wide, lipsticked smile that showed perfect teeth. Apart from her consciously arranged auburn hair, the new girl looked exactly like the other one, Steve thought. Still a vast improvement on that frumpy old woman, in the same old sweatshirt and jeans, who just scowled at him.

No, he wouldn't miss Brenda and her meddling.

Adrian was still fretting.

"She hasn't signed the letter yet," he said as soon as Steve appeared at his office door. "What if she sues?"

Steve shrugged and sat in one of the comfortable armchairs.

"What if she does?" he said calmly and then shouted, "Can I get a coffee in here, please?"

"Look, Brenda was a pain in the ass, but she knew how to work things round here," Adrian practically shouted. "That new girl doesn't know anything, and this morning I've had three calls from pissed-off customers because their order was screwed up." He came out from behind his desk and stood over Steve. "What am I fucking paying you for?" he snarled, pointing his finger in a stabbing motion. "You're my fucking operations manager, and in the last week I've had to deal with an accident in the plant and customers freaking out about their orders — what are you gonna do about it?" His voice had got louder.

Steve ignored Adrian and gestured to the new girl, who was standing at the door, holding a mug of coffee in her hand. The Instagram smile was gone, and her eyes were wide as she witnessed Adrian's outburst.

"Put the coffee here, dear," Steve said pleasantly, "and then, if you don't mind, close the door behind you."

She complied and left quickly, keeping her head down.

Steve breathed deeply and reached for his coffee. He took a sip, savoured the expensive blend which Adrian always purchased, and replaced his mug on the table in front of him, with exaggerated care.

He knew that silence rattled Adrian. He was like a yappy little dog, always needing attention.

It worked. Adrian flopped down into the other armchair and ran his hand through his hair.

"What am I going to do?" he said miserably. "My dad will be mad about Brenda when he finds out—"

"Fuck Brenda," Steve interrupted, "and fuck your precious daddy." He leaned forward and picked up his coffee again.

"What the—?" Adrian spluttered, his face going bright red.

"Listen to me," Steve said quietly, and Adrian must have noticed his menacing tone, because he shut up and listened. "It's time Nikos Palmer moved on from Hades Fish Co." Steve said this conversationally, but inside he was tense. Time was running out.

"It's time he signed over his interest in the company," he continued. "Business has changed. We'll be running things differently from now on."

"What are you talking about?" Adrian held his hands up in confusion. "We're already doing business differently — we have the bistro, we're taking over quotas, my dad's already pissed off, and the fishermen are calling him to complain, and some restaurants too. There's no way he'll sign the business over to me, and when he finds out about Brenda . . ." Adrian was babbling.

"I told you to listen," Steve said, suppressing his frustration. *Why can't this privileged little shit just do what he's told?* "Forget the fucking fishermen, there's no future in fishing, we're in the export business now."

Adrian stared at him. "What are you talking about? We're a seafood company! What will we export if not seafood?"

"We're already exporting other . . . products," Steve said, looking at Adrian, waiting to gauge his reaction. *This has to work. This has to work.* He felt his phone vibrate in his pocket.

"What other products?" Adrian said, his voice lower now, his face registering some understanding of what Steve was telling him.

"Let's just say, if Brenda hadn't had her little accident," Steve leaned forward, "you and I would be totally fucked by now."

"Why would I be fucked?" Adrian seemed to regain some of his arrogance. "This is the first I've heard about your . . . your side business!"

Steve settled back in his chair and steepled his fingers together. "Of course you'd be fucked, Adrian. It's your business. You pay the bills, you sign the paperwork, you enjoy the benefits. How else do you think you could afford the bistro? Look at this office." He spread his hands out. "You think anyone will believe you knew nothing?" He smiled. "You worry too much, Adrian."

Adrian sat still and said nothing. Steve watched him, knowing that he must be processing all of this, assessing his options.

This has to work.

Finally, Adrian spoke. "How much does Brenda know?" he asked.

"She suspected. Look." Steve pulled out his phone and showed Adrian the video of Brenda rummaging through his desk.

"You have cameras in my office?" Adrian said in shock, looking around the office wildly.

"For our own protection." Steve replaced his phone in his pocket, noticing as he did that he had two voicemails. "If we didn't have them, I wouldn't know about Brenda's snooping, in here or in the plant."

"You have cameras in the plant too?" Adrian threw his hands up in panic, realizing what Steve was saying. "You knew Brenda was in the freezer? That wasn't an accident? Are you fucking insane?"

"She has a bump on the head, no big deal. She didn't find anything, maybe a few illegal salmon, but I got rid of them. And she's resigned. Now, if she says anything, she's just a disgruntled ex-employee who broke safety rules in the fish plant. Your problem, Adrian, is not Brenda." He leaned over and brought his face very close to Adrian's. "This is the problem you need to focus on now. I need you to listen to me very carefully and then do everything I tell you."

Half an hour later, Steve left Adrian sitting at his desk. He smiled at Amy and her new colleague, who both beamed back at him, and went to the bistro to get another coffee and make some phone calls in private.

He hoped that he hadn't underestimated Adrian. One useful thing about Adrian, Steve thought, was his attachment to money and the nice things it could buy. Greed was such an easy character flaw to manipulate.

He sat at the bistro, once again admiring the decor. All paid for with a combination of poaching and drug running, a fact he'd left Adrian slowly digesting. He'd explained, as if to a five-year-old, he thought, rolling his eyes, the next steps that had to happen. Adrian had listened, for once without interrupting, and nodded his agreement when Steve told him that Nikos could no longer own any part of Hades Fish Co. "Myself or my associates will be the new majority shareholders," Steve had told him.

Adrian was smart enough not to ask about the associates. He didn't need to know yet. Steve needed Adrian to get

Nikos in line before he knew who his new business partners would be.

Steve checked his phone. He still had two voicemails. He listened to the first one and swore under his breath. This was what you got for dealing with fucking idiots. Why the fuck would anyone talk to reporters?

His hand shook a little as he sipped the coffee the waitress had just put in front of him. It wasn't the caffeine giving him the jitters, he knew that. One more obstacle he'd have to deal with. He checked the time. If he hurried, he could get the lunchtime ferry. It would be quicker to take a floatplane to the island, but he could pay with cash if he took the ferry. Cover his tracks.

Steve drained his coffee and ordered a sandwich to go.

He listened to the second voicemail as he waited.

"Mr Hilstead, this is Jonathan Dunn of Dunn and Grant Associates. There has been a change of plan. Our mutual friend requires the transfer of assets in Hades Fish Co. to be completed no later than a week from today. This is quicker than first discussed, but our friend has a large contract that needs to be fulfilled and he is keen to funnel this business through his new company. We drew the paperwork up for your convenience. Please pick it up from my office and get the necessary signatures. One week, Mr Hilstead, one week."

Steve closed his eyes. *Focus*, he thought, *breathe*.

"Mr Hilstead?" The waitress was standing in front of him, holding a cardboard box. "Your sandwich?"

He opened his eyes.

"Thank you," he said, "put it on Adrian's tab."

One thing at a time, he thought, *one thing at a time*.

CHAPTER TWENTY-SIX

"Christina!" Gerry Roberts shouted from behind his desk. "Christina!"

Nothing. She'd gone home.

Gerry got up and walked to his office door and opened it.

He was alone in the office. Nobody popped their head around the door to say goodnight these days or invite him for an after-work drink. How had he fallen this far?

Gerry Roberts looked down at his hands. They were trembling slightly. He needed a drink. He thought of the empty vodka bottle back at his apartment, and even though he'd promised himself that it would be the last time, he knew he would stop at the liquor store on the way home. Not the liquor store in his neighbourhood. He would drive to the other side of town, even though it was fifteen minutes out of his way.

Last time he picked up a bottle from the usual place — was it yesterday? The day before? He couldn't remember. But he recalled clearly the comment from the fat woman behind the till who always asked too many questions. "Back again, eh?" she said, with a wink. "You know you can buy a bigger bottle? Right there," and she held out a flabby arm and pointed at the Supersize Saving option for his preferred brand. He'd grabbed the bottle in the brown paper bag and slammed down the exact amount of cash. He'd left the store clutching his booze and muttering under his breath, humiliated. Sat in his car, he hesitated for a moment, then unscrewed the cap from the bottle and took a fiery swig. Then he backed the car out of the parking bay, still angry enough to jam his foot on the gas but aware that being stopped by traffic police with alcohol on his breath would be his undoing.

When he got home that night, like most of them, he didn't bother to take off his shoes or jacket. He sat in the small living room, which was as impersonal and gloomy as his office. He didn't get a glass, he just took swigs of vodka straight from the bottle and festered about the unfairness of his life. It had been so good at first. Where had it gone wrong? He'd been top of the heap! Now he was in this cruddy apartment and pushing fucking paper around all day long. This wasn't what he signed up for, no sir, and it wasn't what he deserved either, not by a long shot. As the booze took hold, so did the self-pity, and he started to blubber a little, not bothering to wipe away the tears or mucus that dripped from his chin.

He'd started his career with such high hopes, and he was good too. He'd joined as a second mate and soon been promoted to first mate, then relief captain and finally captain. He was so proud. He'd risen quicker than most through the ranks of the Canadian Coast Guard and soon took a move to the Department of Fisheries and Oceans. He'd had a pretty young wife who loved being married to a captain. They were members of the prestigious Yacht Club and had their own little cabin cruiser that they took out on weekends, just putting around the Gulf Islands, mooring for lunches and cocktail hours. Life was good.

Just one bad decision changed everything. He moaned slightly as he remembered and took another gulp of vodka, hoping to dull his memory. But no matter how much booze he drank, that afternoon was still clear in his mind.

It was the first salmon opening of the season. Back then, the fishing fleet was over a thousand purse-seiners, all competing for the largest hauls of the prized sockeye salmon. There were no aircraft in those days to monitor the fleet and make sure that fishermen stayed in their boundaries and didn't fish over the scheduled time.

"And they were bloody cowboys," he said aloud in the dark.

How were they supposed to make sure all those fuckers followed the rules?

He'd decided to check on a packer vessel. The packer was buying fish for cash straight off the fishermen. It was useful when there was a short opening. They could offload their catch to the packer, get cash immediately and carry on fishing. The packer transported the fish to the processors and made their money selling it.

At least, that was how it was supposed to work. Roberts had got a tip-off that there was something not right about this vessel.

The *King of Cash*. He watched for most of the day. Fishing boats, their hulls low in water, loaded with salmon, pumped their precious catch into the hatches on the packer and headed back out to the fishing grounds to do it all again. An hour before the opening was due to finish, he ordered his vessel alongside the *King of Cash* and told the skipper he was coming aboard, and to have his tally slips ready for inspection.

Roberts had heard rumours about the skipper, Stan Hilstead, and his son. Some said they were working for the bikers. Stan was a short man, with large forearms covered with faded tattoos. When he grinned at Roberts and said, "Welcome aboard, Captain, what can I do for you?" and then laughed as if he'd told a hilarious joke, Roberts could see the glint of a gold tooth.

Roberts ignored him. He stepped into the galley and found Steve Hilstead, Stan's son, sitting behind the biggest stack of cash Roberts had ever seen. For a second it mesmerized him. Then he saw white bundles piled up beside the cash. He must have looked startled.

"What's the matter, Captain?" Steve Hilstead drawled. "Never seen top-grade coke before?" and he too threw back his head and laughed. Gerry Roberts had replayed that moment over and over in his head all these years. Hilstead must have been high. But Gerry was stone-cold sober, and there was no excuse for what happened next.

"So what'll it be, Captain? Coke or cash? We've got lots of both." Hilstead grinned brazenly, making no attempt to hide.

Gerry Roberts said nothing. He was trying to process this. He knew what he should do, of course, but the cash . . . His wife liked nice things. She wanted a bigger boat, a golf course membership and a motorhome so they could winter in Arizona. And the problem was, despite the badge on his arm, his salary wasn't enough.

As if Hilstead was reading his mind, he tossed Gerry an envelope.

"Have this on me, Captain, no questions asked," he said, and tapped the side of his nose. "Buy the wife something nice, eh?"

The rest of that day was a blur. The envelope contained thousands of dollars. For weeks, Gerry kept the envelope under his mattress at home, worried that he'd get called into the office. If he didn't touch it, he could just say he was gathering evidence, right? Just about to hand it in, report the matter. He'd get away with it. No harm, no foul. But weeks passed and then a month, and nothing. He began to relax.

One evening, he took his wife out to dinner at the golf club. He presented her with membership documents. As she flung her arms round his neck, he murmured, "Christmas in Mexico this year?"

He spent all the cash.

A few months later, as the fall fishing season started, his phone rang.

"Captain Gerry Roberts, how are ya?" a familiar voice drawled.

And that was it. Just a few favours at first. Make sure his enforcement vessels avoided *this* area at *this* time. Turn a blind eye. Make sure that discrepancies on paperwork were overlooked. Nothing big, Gerry told himself. Nobody gets hurt. And to reward every small favour, an envelope would appear, sometimes on the front seat of his car, sometimes hand-delivered to his home and left in the mailbox. A thank you and a veiled warning.

We know how to find you. Keep your mouth shut.

Gerry Roberts came to rely on the cash. By now he had twin daughters. His wife wanted them enrolled in a private French immersion school. She wanted a sports car and *expected* two foreign vacations per year.

Sometimes he didn't hear from Hilstead for months. So he borrowed money to make up the shortfall.

Some nights he couldn't sleep, worrying about paying bills and getting caught. He got the sense that he was being sidelined a little. Paranoia set in so he started having a few drinks in the evening.

Just to help me relax, he told himself.

One day he was called in to talk to his superior.

His hands went clammy. His neck felt constricted in his shirt. He was sure that this was it. He would be fired, or worse, turned over to the police.

But he was wrong. His superior officer told Gerry curtly that he was being transferred to a desk job.

His first reaction was relief. Then horror. Pushing paper? And more importantly, no more money?

Gerry Roberts was smart enough not to argue. He felt certain that the department managers had an inkling about his lucrative side business. After all, it was hard to keep a secret in this town. His wife openly boasted about their wealth, and it wouldn't take a genius to put two and two together. He decided it was probably a blessing. They had given him an off-ramp and he should take it. He'd had a good run.

"Ah well, Captain," Hilstead said in that mocking tone when he told him, "I guess our business is concluded." He took it well, Roberts thought. His wife did not. Especially when Gerry told her that their household budget would be severely curtailed.

Gerry and his wife argued. Her spending habits remained the same. Gerry's credit card debt soared and his drinking increased.

He couldn't remember when he started taking a mickey of vodka to work. It just happened. He only intended to have the odd shot at the end of a busy day — to unwind, he told himself. But soon he was filling up a water bottle with booze and taking regular sips during the day.

He was sure nobody noticed.

Then he arrived at work one morning to find the manager of his department and two of his colleagues waiting in his office. His secretary was nowhere to be seen.

"Well, what's going on here?" Gerry asked. "What can I do for you gentlemen?"

His colleagues shuffled their feet awkwardly and refused to look at him directly. Finally, his manager told him. His secretary had requested a transfer because of his drinking. He smelled of booze most days and slurred his speech. He often fell asleep in his office and she was tired of covering for him.

"Go to rehab," his manager said. "Get help."

Gerry Roberts denied it angrily. "Bullshit!"

His manager handed him a letter. "You have no choice, Gerry. Get help or be fired. You are suspended as from today."

Gerry's bravado deflated. He snatched the letter and drove home.

His wife was playing golf, and she arrived home to find him passed out. She read the letter, and when Gerry came round, he found another letter. She was leaving. She was humiliated. He had humiliated his family. He was a loser and a disgrace. She wanted a divorce. He staggered out to the car and drove to the liquor store and bought another bottle of vodka.

For a few months, he tried. He refused to go to rehab, but he went to AA meetings. He hated them. He looked around the room, the earnest faces clutching plastic cups of coffee, taking turns to air their dirty laundry, he thought. He refused a sponsor, refused to speak, and grudgingly held hands and muttered the prayers and phrases that were supposed to cure him, he supposed.

After a month, he went back to work. He found himself in a tiny windowless office with a new secretary.

After a bitter divorce, he sold the house, the boat and the new car. It covered his debt, but not the financial settlement to his wife and children. So he took out a new loan and moved into a basement suite.

And this is it, he thought. *This is how it's going to be. For fucking ever.*

He didn't hear from Steve Hilstead again. He turned up for work, put the hours in, paid his wife every month and saw his daughters less and less. The only change to his dismal routine was the occasional new secretary seated outside his office.

Until a year ago.

Gerry's cell phone rang that day, and the display showed only *Unknown Number*. He answered.

A voice he hadn't heard in a long while said, "Captain Gerry Roberts, how are ya?"

"I can't do anything for you," he said abruptly and pressed the *End Call* button. The phone rang again an hour later. And then again in the evening and twice the following day, before Gerry finally answered. "Look," he said angrily.

"Now, now, Captain," Hilstead said pleasantly. "I don't need you to do anything. All I need from you is some information. And I'll be paying you, of course."

Gerry was silent. He needed cash.

"What information?" he asked at last.

Hilstead explained that he and a very good friend had got themselves in a spot of bother. Mr Nguyen, his friend, would be *grateful in the usual way* if Captain Roberts could provide a heads-up on an operation that the department was currently conducting.

"I don't have access to that information," Gerry said.

"Sure you do." Hilstead's voice turned hard. "I need that information, Captain. Or . . ." He didn't finish. He didn't need to. Gerry shivered, imagining further humiliation, if that were possible — no job, no pension, maybe even a conviction.

"I'll try," he said and scribbled down Hilstead's instructions.

The department emptied promptly at five every evening. Nobody paid attention to Gerry. He sat at his desk, sweating slightly, waiting until he was sure that nobody would rush back to pick up a forgotten phone or car keys.

He must have waited for half an hour, he thought, before he could muster the courage to push open the door to one of the few open-plan offices in the building. The bullpen, as the department called it, was a maze of cubicles, divided by flimsy partition panels. The office was noisy during the day and Gerry avoided entering unless he really had to.

Now it was silent and dark except for the blue glow of desktop monitors.

At the far end of the bullpen was a bank of filing cabinets. Gerry hurried over and rummaged in his pocket for a set of keys. He'd had the keys for years. Nobody had bothered to check or ask for them back when he went to rehab. They kept all the active investigation files in the last cabinet. They'd had this system for years. Occasionally, the department hired a new manager who got fired up about replacing the paper files with a software program. But this was a government agency, and after a flurry of meetings, the proposals usually died in the face of overwhelming disinterest, leaving operations personnel to complain about the constant paperwork.

Gerry was relieved that his key still fit, and his hand trembled as he unlocked the cabinets and pulled open the top drawer. Hilstead had only given him the name of the vessel he thought was under surveillance.

Gerry cursed when he saw the contents of the drawer. It was divided up by species and types of violations, not by vessel. There were thousands of manila files, and without more information, he could take hours or days to find the right file.

Gerry smacked his hand on the top of the cabinet in frustration. He couldn't fail, he couldn't.

His instructions were clear. Find the file. Make a copy. Leave it on the front seat of his unlocked car, parked a block from his apartment, no later than 7 p.m. Walk away from the car and pick it up an hour later.

He tried to think logically. For Hilstead to call and sound so desperate, he must be involved in something big. If the Fisheries officers spied small violations like fishing in a closed area or out of season, they acted immediately. To spend some of the precious department budget on a full-scale surveillance operation, this must be major.

Gerry's hands moved over the files. He pulled them out one by one, checking and shoving them back, until finally his fingers found a thick file. He flicked through the documents. This was it. In line with protocol, the file didn't mention names of individuals. But it had the vessel name he was looking for printed at the top of one page. Gerry whistled to himself as he leafed through the rest of the file. Photographs, details of dates and times and multiple vessels. No wonder Hilstead was worried. He was poaching abalone. There had been a complete moratorium on fishing abalone in Canadian waters since 1990. The sea snails were an endangered species, but highly prized by Asian consumers. Gerry had eaten them once or twice and couldn't understand what the fuss was all about. But there was a thriving black market for the rare shellfish. With the promise of large sums of cash, there were people, like Hilstead, prepared to gamble in that high-risk arena.

And it looked like his gamble would not pay off. This was a thorough investigation, Gerry realized. The department would gather enough evidence to be certain of a conviction. They would seize assets, including boats, Hilstead's truck and fishing gear, and impose fines. There was even the possibility of jail time.

He didn't have time to read it all. Gerry quickly took the file over to the photocopier, praying that it wasn't out of toner. It was working fine, so he carefully copied each document, making sure the file was in the same order when he finished. He dropped the file back into the drawer, locked up and walked back to his office.

With his heart pounding, he placed the copies in a large envelope, grabbed his jacket, car keys and phone, and left the office.

Gerry hung around in the coffee area more than usual the next day. He listened for snippets of gossip. He had collected his car at 8 p.m. and found an envelope stuffed with cash. It had been a long time since his last payment, and he was nervous. He pushed it under his mattress, thinking he would leave it for a few days. See what happened.

He jumped every time his cell phone rang, but Hilstead didn't call.

A week later and Gerry was beginning to think maybe Hilstead and his cronies had had the good sense to lie low. If the surveillance didn't produce any results, sometimes the department would drop the investigation. They were short-staffed and underfunded, so they needed quick conclusions. He began to breathe a little easier.

But he was wrong.

"Have you heard?" his new secretary said, plonking his coffee on his desk, causing some of it to slop and run down the side of the mug and pool on some documents.

"Heard what?" he said, irritated, scrabbling around his desk for a tissue.

"Those guys in there," she said, nodding her head in the bullpen's direction, "they got a result. Arrested some gang diving for shellfish or something. Something banned, anyway."

"Abalone?" Gerry asked, holding his breath.

"Yep, that's it. Do you want a cloth?" she said, looking at Gerry, who had become very still.

Gerry heard nothing from Hilstead. He followed the case as much as he could. Finally, it went to court. The gossip was that the lawyers expected it to be a slam dunk. So Gerry was surprised and a little hopeful when he arrived at work one morning to a despondent atmosphere.

"Fucking lawyers," one of the enforcement officers told him, "they got off on some technicality."

"Oh, that's unfortunate," Gerry agreed, trying hard not to clap his hands in relief.

Back in his office, he rejoiced inwardly and stretched back in his chair. Now, finally, he could have some peace. Just keep his head down and make it to retirement. He began to feel optimistic. His new secretary, Christina, stared at him, as he hummed under his breath and thanked her for her hard work.

That was two months ago. Gerry's warm feeling of relief ended when Hilstead finally called.

"Captain, not good news, I'm afraid to say. Not good news at all."

Gerry gripped the phone, feeling his world collapse around him again.

"You got off!" he said, almost pleading with Hilstead. "How can that not be good news?"

"Well, that's the problem, Captain," Hilstead said. "I got off, but I owe my good friend a considerable amount of money. The Fisheries confiscated our product, and then there are the lawyer fees to deal with on top of that. The thing is, Captain, when I'm doing good, you do good, right? And if I'm not doing so good . . . well, it's only fair that you help me out. That sounds fair, doesn't it?"

"I can give you back some money," Gerry said quickly. "I haven't spent much of it." It was true. For once he was being careful, just taking the odd few notes here and there, so as not to arouse suspicion. His ex-wife was always looking for evidence of income, accusing Gerry of hiding money from her.

Hilstead laughed, without humour.

"No, Captain. After everything I've done for you, you owe me. You're going to help me out." He told Gerry what he needed.

"I can't do that!" Gerry gasped. "I'm not in the same department anymore, you know that! I'm behind a desk!"

He pleaded with Hilstead, but Hilstead just said, "You're going to pay, Captain. Somehow, you must pay."

Tonight, Gerry Roberts stood at the door of his office and wished he could crawl into a dark room and wait for the mercy of death. This would never end. And now he had reporters sniffing around.

He heard the distant hum of a janitor's vacuum cleaner. He wasn't sure of the time, but it must be late. He'd lost all track of time. He walked to the men's washroom and splashed some cold water on his face.

He'd shaved in a hurry this morning, sleeping through the alarm and having to propel himself from sweat-drenched sheets into the shower. He couldn't remember getting to bed or undressing himself. He found the empty bottle of vodka on the floor beside the armchair.

He did remember that he'd been dreaming again. It was the same dream, over and over. He was crawling through the darkness, keeping low, hiding. He was being hunted. He'd woken in his usual fog and hadn't taken care with his razor, the dream still real and vivid in his mind. He knew he'd nicked his neck, and although he'd stopped the bleeding, there was a raw patch that had chafed against his collar all day.

At work, he'd sat at his desk knowing he couldn't go on like this. He called the number that Hilstead had left him and waited for him to answer. When Hilstead didn't pick up, he left a message. Told him about the reporter and the picture. "I think she knows something," he said, trying not to sound desperate.

All day he'd taken papers out of his in tray and put them back in again, unable to concentrate until he heard back from Hilstead.

He stared at himself in the mirror, red-faced from the booze and red-eyed from lack of sleep. He wished he had the courage to slice that razor across his neck and end his miserable existence. *I can't even do that right.*

He walked slowly back to his desk, picked up his jacket and shoved his phone in his back pocket. His ex-wife had called several times today, but he couldn't face that conversation. He owed her money too, and there was no way he could deal with her until he had a good half a bottle of vodka inside him.

Outside, he felt the cool breeze from the ocean, and it occurred to him that the happiest days of his life had been on the water. On an impulse, he walked away from his car and down towards the sea. He crossed the manicured lawn and stopped at the edge of the stony beach. The tide was coming in and he breathed deeply, taking in the scent of the seaweed and feeling calmed a little by the rhythm of the waves, lapping nearer and nearer.

He pulled out his phone and turned it over and over in his hand, wondering if he should phone his wife and apologize. Tell her everything. Clear his conscience. Maybe a fresh start?

Or maybe he should just turn himself in. Would it be so bad? Maybe he could cut a deal, give them Hilstead, and avoid prosecution. He mulled this over. In his mind, he pictured himself as the hero, conveniently forgetting for a minute all the bribes he had taken over the years.

He heard a footstep crunch behind him.

Gerry turned around, expecting a groundsman. He probably shouldn't have walked on the grass.

It wasn't a groundsman.

"Hello, Captain."

Gerry stared in surprise and held out his hand as if to defend himself.

Before he could speak, he saw a flash, and stared in horror at Hilstead.

Gerry crumpled wordlessly to the ground.

As his eyesight faded, Gerry saw Steve Hilstead walk away from him. It all got fuzzy, but he thought he saw Steve stuff something into his jacket pocket.

A seagull landed beside him, and Gerry watched as it pecked at wisps of seaweed. He felt something warm trickle down the side of his face, and then the ocean lapped over his feet just before Gerry felt nothing at all.

CHAPTER TWENTY-SEVEN

Inspector Andrew Vega was irritated. He needed space and privacy to do his work. The RCMP detachment had one small conference room, and his team had squeezed in, bumping elbows and tempers as they perched laptops on the corner of shared desks and tried to keep the noise at manageable levels.

The building was old and badly insulated. Brown stains had formed on the white ceiling panels from previous roof leaks, and Vega's assistant had driven to Nanaimo to purchase an electric heater to counteract the damp. The result was akin to a sauna, especially when they were all gathered for a briefing.

That was another thing that irritated Vega. Day four, heading into day five of the investigation, and he had virtually nothing to report to his superintendent. Logically, he knew that it took time to thoroughly process a crime scene and gather and analyse the data. He and his team had worked twenty hours straight after being notified of Mason's murder. Vega's job was to coordinate and guide his specialized team toward a prosecutable conclusion. The time didn't matter as much as the end result.

Still, the longer it took to get answers, the harder it would be.

Refusing to think about the department budget, he'd requested a police diver. They hadn't found the murder weapon yet, and he was hoping that the killer had discarded it in the area. A thorough land search turned up nothing, so Vega was betting on the ocean bed around the fish plant. It was a long shot, he knew. But he needed to move this investigation along, before it went stale.

Vega was trying not to feel the pressure. He'd joined IHIT three years ago and had risen through the ranks to inspector and operations officer, overseeing the investigation units.

Every officer recruited to IHIT felt some pressure to get speedy results, he knew that. The Integrated Homicide Investigations Team had been formed in response to the RCMP's spectacular failure to apprehend one of Canada's most notorious serial killers, Robert Pickton, before he had butchered nearly fifty women. Vega shivered. He wasn't even out of college when the Pickton Pig Farm killings were taking place, but still, he felt the responsibility of never allowing such an atrocity to happen again. The motto of the unit was "Justice for Those Who Have Died Unfairly", and Vega was driven to be worthy of this mission.

His job was to coordinate seven investigative units from the mainland office. He didn't like to be chained to a desk, so he often visited crime scenes and incident rooms, trying not to interfere or undermine his officers but offering the benefit of experience and making sure they had the resources they needed.

This time, he'd opted to come to Coffin Cove and head up the investigation himself.

Vega was familiar with the town, having worked a homicide here a year ago — a joint operation with the US Drug Enforcement Agency. They'd got a good result, but he'd battled to get information from suspicious residents.

"Coffin Cove is . . . er . . . unique." He'd struggled to find the right words to describe the tiny isolated fishing town to his superintendent, Sharon Sinclair.

"How so?" she asked. She was a veteran of a major crimes unit. She liked procedure but knew how to be flexible, if the results were worth it.

"The residents are slow to trust outsiders," Vega said. "They prefer to turn a blind eye, not get involved."

"Aren't many communities the same? What makes Coffin Cove different?"

Superintendent Sinclair was hesitant but knew that Vega got results. She also knew that most of their successful investigations relied on help from communities. Somebody usually had a key piece of information that cracked open a case — even if they didn't know it. It took gentle professional persistence to tease out all the relevant facts of a homicide case.

Vega tried to explain. "They have their own . . . code, I suppose. They dislike authority. It's isolated, just one road in and out. Back in the seventies, Vietnam draft dodgers hid there, and they still have the same mentality of 'don't ask, don't tell'. Also, this particular homicide will rake up an unpleasant past." He explained why Pierre Mason was significant to the town.

"You think maybe Mason's homicide has something to do with the cold case?"

"Maybe." Vega shrugged. "I'm keeping an open mind. But even though Mason was cleared, it's possible he still had enemies in Coffin Cove. Plus, he was a controversial figure for the forestry industry and fishermen. We'll need to get people who are willing to talk. Otherwise, it will be an uphill battle if we don't get slam-dunk forensics."

"OK," Sinclair said, "I'll authorize it. But don't fuck up. I want to retire gracefully in a year or two, with my reputation intact." She smiled but Vega knew she wasn't joking.

Vega needed to clear his head. The claustrophobic atmosphere of the detachment was clouding his thinking. They were still waiting on forensics from the old fish plant building, and Vega knew that would take some time. They had one person of interest: Brian McIntosh. Local fishermen told them that McIntosh was likely living in the disused building, and the forensics team spent hours sifting through debris and bagging evidence, even human faeces. The reporter, Andrea Silvers, had handed in the victim's phone, and they obtained a warrant to search contacts. Vega was satisfied that each team member was working diligently on their assigned tasks. It was his job to pull all the data together and analyse the story it told.

Vega wrinkled his nose. The room smelled of grease and sweat. He wandered round the small room, gathering up sandwich wrappers, discarded coffee cups and a pizza box. In most circumstances, he would blast the team for a dirty, disorganized work area. He hated clutter. But they had all been working long hours in cramped conditions, so for once, he was letting it slide.

He decided to go back to his motel room and work there for a few hours. He needed to focus. His colleague from the Cold Case Division of IHIT had sent over the files for the Sarah McIntosh homicide. Vega had only found enough time to scan them quickly, and he wanted to read them thoroughly. He also had a pile of research on the victim, Pierre Mason. He had been a controversial figure, especially in Coffin Cove. Vega had promised Superintendent Sinclair to keep an open mind, but his gut was telling him that somehow the two cases were connected. Vega didn't believe in coincidences. Mason had been linked to Sarah McIntosh and Coffin Cove all those years ago, and now he'd been killed in the same town?

Vega never ignored his gut feelings, but he knew he needed data.

He took a brisk walk from the detachment to Hephzibah's café, intending to grab a coffee and head back to his motel room. It was mid-morning, and a steady drizzle of rain soaked his jacket. He didn't mind the dampness against his face. The cool air eased the headache that had started to form, and he looked forward to a decent cup of coffee to sharpen his mind.

He'd expected the café to be empty at this hour, but the condensation on the windows and hum of chatter told him otherwise. Every available seat was taken, mostly by fishermen, the steam rising from damp rain gear strewn across the backs of chairs. The noise level abated a little when Vega entered the café. Everyone knew who he was and why he was here, Vega supposed.

He nodded to a couple of familiar faces. He'd sat in on some of the preliminary interviews with fishermen who had been in the vicinity when Mason's body was discovered.

Vega ordered coffee from the tall woman behind the counter, who greeted him with a smile.

"Morning, Inspector! Any news yet?"

He smiled back at her directness.

"No, not yet. But we are working hard. Could I get a large black coffee, please?"

Hephzibah Brown. Who could forget a name like that? He had also interviewed Hephzibah to corroborate the reporter's story about Brian McIntosh and the phone she handed in. Hephzibah had confirmed Andi Silvers' statement and was also able to give more details about McIntosh's background. Seemed he had a reputation for petty theft.

Vega wasn't sure why, but Hephzibah Brown was ringing a bell far in the recesses of his mind. He filed the partial memory away for later.

Hephzibah handed him the coffee and a small paper bag.

"It's a muffin," she explained. "Morning Glory. I make them myself. On the house."

"Oh, I . . . er . . ." Vega was caught off guard for a second.

"Oh God, are you not allowed?" Hephzibah clapped her hand across her mouth in horror. "It's not a bribe or anything! You just looked hungry!"

Vega laughed out loud. "No, it's fine. Thank you very much."

Back at the motel room, he munched on the muffin and sipped coffee as he read through the files. Occasionally, he scribbled notes about lines of enquiry that his team could explore. He was looking for patterns. Small pieces of detail that would thread the investigation together, names that stood out.

The McIntosh family featured in both case files. Vega and one of his female officers, Sergeant Fowler, had visited Joe McIntosh and his ex-wife, Sue. He hated interviews with cold-case victims. He felt he'd personally let them down. This was the part the media and public didn't see. Murder is like dropping a stone into a perfectly still pond. The moment the stone breaks the surface, ripples fan out, disrupting the calm waters again and again. The pain never stops.

He saw in a moment that Joe McIntosh was a broken man. The loss of his daughter had consumed him. Alcohol had done little to deaden the pain but was certainly hastening his death. The man didn't react at all when Vega asked about his whereabouts at the time of Mason's murder.

"Here," he said. "I'm always here."

Tara, Joe's second wife, confirmed this. "He rarely leaves the house," she explained. "Neither do I. I make sure he eats something and he gets to bed. Otherwise he would just sit out here on the deck all night long, drinking whiskey."

"Have you tried grief counselling, ma'am?" Vega asked. Tara had shown him into the house and made him some tea, while Sergeant Fowler had a surreptitious walk around the property to see if there was any sign of Brian McIntosh.

Tara sighed. "No, Inspector. Joe wouldn't go to counselling. You see, he thinks he deserves this. He blames himself for Sarah's death." She continued, "Sarah and Joe argued a lot before she was killed. She was angry about Joe's forestry operations. They blamed the clear-cutting for the flooding in the valley. Joe wouldn't hear it. He just thought Sarah's mother and grandfather were poisoning her mind against him." She paused. "And I have to say, Inspector, he was probably right about that. Sue never forgave Joe for their divorce — in fact, she still doesn't accept that Joe and I are married." She smiled slightly. "Sue still refers to me as a 'Jezebel'."

Vega thought nobody looked less like a "Jezebel" than this tired-looking sixty-something woman, with her sensible haircut and large framed glasses.

"It's been hard, Inspector," Tara McIntosh said suddenly, her eyes full of tears. Vega wondered if this lady ever got to talk to anyone about her feelings.

"When we lost Sarah, I lost a stepdaughter who I loved very much, and I also lost my husband and my marriage."

Vega nodded in sympathy. The ripples, he thought. Destroying more lives than just the murder victim's.

"What did you and Joe think about Mason returning to Coffin Cove?"

Tara shrugged. "We wouldn't have known about it, except that Harry came to tell Joe."

"Harry?"

"Harry Brown. His father, Ed, was a friend of Joe's once upon a time, and Hephzibah, his sister, was Sarah's friend. Sarah's only friend," she added. "Harry went out on all the searches when Sarah disappeared, and he was the one to break the news when they found her body. I guess he feels an obligation to let Joe know if there are any developments. Not that there have been many over the years." She said it in a non-accusing way, but Vega acknowledged her point anyway. Again, he felt a flash of recognition at the name.

"I know," he said, "I'm sorry."

"I never really believed that Mason did it, you know," Tara confided suddenly. "I didn't ever believe that Sarah was involved with him. She was very . . . innocent," Tara tried to explain. "She'd led a very sheltered life with her mother and grandfather. Fred's a religious zealot. He's a mean old man," she said fiercely. "Sarah had a very difficult childhood. We tried to make sure she did all the normal things that children do, but Sue and Fred would just go at her, refuse to let her dress like other teenagers or have fun. Everything was 'the Devil'. She was even afraid of going to the movies, terrified that the roof would cave in because God was angry with her.

She would never have gone with Mason. She would have been too frightened."

Vega pressed her gently to continue. "But she did go to the protests, though. Wouldn't Fred and Sue have disapproved of that?"

Tara shook her head. "I don't know. Maybe they hated Joe more? The protests were hurting his business. Or maybe they didn't know she was going? Hephzibah would have encouraged her. All the kids joined the protests back then. They didn't even know what they were protesting about, not really. It was just something different, something to break the boredom."

"But Sarah wasn't there out of boredom?" Vega asked.

"No. She was passionate about the environment. She volunteered at the hatchery every spare minute she had. It was the only time she defied her grandfather, I think." Tara smiled at the memory. "We even encouraged her to think about university. A degree in marine biology or something. She was smart enough. But after she argued with Joe, she refused to listen."

Tara took off her glasses and rubbed her eyes.

"I've been over it a million times in my head, Inspector. I know that people around here still think Mason had something to do with Sarah's death, but the problem with this small town is the gossip. People here love a bit of drama. We don't have many outsiders, not like other parts of the island, so everyone knows everyone else's business. And once a story takes hold — well, it's hard to change people's minds."

Vega nodded. He understood this phenomenon. He'd seen people's reputations ruined forever when they were falsely accused of crimes. Even after they were cleared, people still clung to the notion that there was no smoke without fire. It was one reason he strove to get every detail verified. It was imperative that they arrested the right person.

"You think someone in Coffin Cove knows what really happened to Sarah?" Vega was curious to hear this woman's opinion.

"I think so," Tara admitted. "I can believe that Sarah had some sort of crush on Mason, or a schoolgirl fantasy. He was quite charismatic, and the protests were a bit of excitement. Sarah may have felt some kind of connection to him because of their shared passion for the environment and all that, but I don't think there was any kind of affair. She just wasn't sophisticated enough. And she wasn't a liar either. I wasn't surprised when they cleared Mason. And you know what, Inspector?" She looked directly at Vega. "I don't think Joe was surprised either."

Vega finished his interview with Tara with one last question.

"Have you seen Brian McIntosh in the last few days?"

Tara shook her head. "No, Inspector, I haven't. He knows better than to come here. I . . . well . . . we told him he wasn't welcome years ago. And I promise you, if he does show up, I will contact you without hesitation," she said vehemently. Vega believed her.

Tara laughed — an odd, almost disrespectful sound in a house shrouded in grief. "You know, Inspector, Brian McIntosh is probably the only thing that Sue and I agree on. We both wanted him away from Joe."

A slight shake of the head from his sergeant who was waiting for him in the driveway confirmed that Brian McIntosh was nowhere to be seen on the property. Vega wasn't surprised — he'd assessed Tara as a forthright woman with nothing to hide.

They drove away, leaving Tara standing with her hand on the hunched figure of her husband, watching them leave.

Vega swallowed a mouthful of the now lukewarm coffee as he processed his interview with Tara McIntosh and the subsequent visit to Joe's first wife, Sue McIntosh. It had been a completely different experience.

Tara had given him directions. Sergeant Fowler drove their vehicle down the rutted track from the main road to the valley. She'd stopped briefly and pointed out the washed-out remnants of the hatchery.

"Do you want to have a look around, sir?"

It was raining steadily, and Vega looked at the sagging buildings, partially swallowed up by brambles, and reminded himself that he wasn't investigating the death of Sarah McIntosh. He was pursuing the killer of Pierre Mason.

"No, that won't be necessary," he said.

Sue McIntosh wasn't nearly as forthcoming as Tara. She sat on the edge of an old sofa, after moving several boxes to make room and finding two empty chairs for Vega and Sergeant Fowler. Fred Harding struggled to get up from his rocking chair. He looked Vega up and down, leaning on his cane, before holding out a withered hand.

Fred still had quite a grip, Vega thought, as he shook the old man's hand.

Vega's throat had constricted as soon as he entered the house. The mould must be at dangerous levels. Sue McIntosh and her father Fred seemed unaware, even though the old man was wheezing from the effort of leaving his chair.

Sue said nothing, watching them suspiciously, as Vega explained why he was there.

"You think one of us blew Mason's head off?" Fred asked and cackled with laughter. "She could, you know," waving his arm at Sue. "She's a good shot."

"Is that right, Mrs McIntosh?" Vega asked.

Sue met his gaze but fidgeted with the frayed cuffs of her faded plaid shirt.

"I just shoot deer, Inspector," she said quietly.

"You knew that Pierre Mason was in town?" Vega asked.

"Jim Peters and some reporter girl came all the way out to tell us," Fred snorted. "Why would we care? God took our Sarah. Ain't nothing we can do about it now. And we wouldn't waste a bullet on Mason, neither. He has to face God's judgement now."

Vega said calmly, "I understand, Mr Harding. But we have to check, you understand."

"My Sarah had nothing to do with that man," Sue blurted, looking up. Her voice was emotional. "Those were all lies! I know what they were saying, but it wasn't true! She was just a child." Fred Harding thumped his cane on the ground, as if in agreement.

"I understand, Mrs McIntosh," Vega said gently. "We'll leave you in peace."

Thinking about Sue's outburst now, Vega realized that Tara had been wrong. There was one other thing that the two women agreed upon, apart from their mutual dislike of Brian McIntosh. Neither of them believed that Mason had anything to do with Sarah's death.

He drained the last of his coffee just as his phone started to vibrate.

"Vega," he answered. The constable on the other end sounded excited. Vega listened for a minute, then realized that another call was coming in. He checked the phone display and quickly said to the constable, "I have to take this call. Good work. Get everyone together. Briefing in twenty."

He then answered the incoming call from his headquarters.

"Vega here. I see. I'll be there right away."

Vega hurriedly gathered up his documents. He thought about checking out, and then decided to keep the room. Chances were that he'd be back here soon, maybe even tonight.

Another murder on the island? Coincidence?

As Vega locked his motel room door and walked back to the detachment, he reminded himself that he didn't believe in coincidences.

CHAPTER TWENTY-EIGHT

"I definitely touched a nerve," Andi said. "Roberts just lost it when I showed him the photograph."

She and Jim had opted to meet at Andi's apartment, and he was studying her story wall with interest. Andi made them both a coffee. Hephzibah's café was busy, and Gavin with his team from the *Vancouver Mail* had taken Jim up on his offer of office space.

"How's that sea lion story coming?" Gavin had asked in mock seriousness. There were giggles from the team of reporters, and Andi felt her face heat up. Jim stepped in before she could answer, showing them how to work the anti-quated photocopier and writing down the Wi-Fi password.

Gavin's new assistant, a sleek, meticulously dressed woman, wrinkled her nose and made a show of wiping down a desk and her seat before she set up her laptop.

Andi watched as Gavin stood over her with his hand on her shoulder and murmured something in a low voice that made his assistant beam up at him, showing perfect white teeth.

Andi recognized the move. She bit her lip as Gavin called his team around him and rolled up his sleeves. Andi had seen this countless times before. Gather the troops, make an inspiring speech and send them off to do the work he would ultimately take credit for. She knew she was being bitter, and she turned away to gather up the files she and Jim needed.

"OK, folks," she heard Gavin say. "We'll just need to make the best of it. I know you're missing a decent cup of coffee and proper workspaces, but I'm sure we're all grateful to the *Gazette* for making room for us and putting up with the disruption of a full-on investigation. And just remember folks, if you don't do a professional job, this is where you'll be if you fuck up. OK, what have we got?"

Andi heard another ripple of amusement from Gavin's team and she wanted to punch him. She took a step forward and opened her mouth to call him out, tell them all what a lying treacherous bastard Gavin really was, but she felt Jim's hand on her arm.

"Come on, we haven't got all day," he said kindly.

As they were leaving, Gavin's assistant called out, "Oh excuse me, Andi?"

"'Fraid not," Andi answered cheerfully as she could, when the assistant asked if there was a separate ladies' washroom. "Just the one. And you'll have to hum loudly while you're in there because the lock doesn't work."

Feeling a little better, Andi had walked with Jim to her apartment. As she unlocked the door, she'd been relieved that for once, she'd cleaned up and remembered to get fresh milk. She told Jim to make himself at home and he'd dumped his box of files down in the dining room area that Andi had converted to her workspace.

"This is fascinating," Jim said, taking a mug of coffee in one hand and gesturing to the story wall with the other.

"It's all from your original files," Andi said. "I just work better if I can see the story in front of me. I can't explain it." She stopped and smiled at Jim. "Gavin used to say I was 'playing detective'. I dunno, maybe he was right." She paused, horrified to feel tears coming. The humiliation she'd felt back at the office was overwhelming.

"Tell me about Roberts," Jim said, to Andi's relief, pointing to the blown-up picture of Captain Gerry Roberts that Andi had copied from the DFO website and pinned to the wall.

"Well, there's definitely a connection between him and Mason, judging by his reaction. Listen to this." Andi played back the voice recording of the last few minutes of her meeting.

"Wow. You're right. Quite the reaction," Jim agreed.

"Apart from that, I found him to be . . . well, a bit pathetic, really." Andi described his appearance. "He came across as angry with his lot in life, as if he was owed something. But he came completely unglued when I mentioned Mason."

"He didn't say anything about the *Pipe Dream* or Harry Brown?"

"No. He just got mad when I pointed out the DFO boat."

"Hmm."

Jim and Andi sat in silence for a moment. Jim got up and took a few steps back so he could view the wall in its entirety. He studied it for a minute more. Andi kept quiet, knowing that Jim was processing all the information — trying, as she had, to make sense of it all.

"You still think there's a connection between the two murders?" Jim asked.

"I'm not sure," Andi admitted. "Now I see the connections in front of me, it's showing a pattern. See here—" Andi pointed at the wall — "this is new information. Mason has more overlapping connections in Coffin Cove than just the McIntosh family. He's connected to Hades Fish Co. somehow, and the DFO. Plus, he has an old connection with Harry." Andi showed Jim a printout.

He sighed. "Yes, I remember. They charged Harry when he threatened Mason with a gun. But in fairness, it was after Mason had rammed his boat and nearly caused a deckhand to go overboard. Look, you can see from this there were multiple witnesses supporting Harry."

Andi stared at him. "Jim, I get it, I do. Harry's a friend, Hephzibah too. But this is a significant connection, right? Mason sent a picture of Harry's boat to me just before he was killed. And—"

"I see where you're going with this," Jim interrupted, "but we're missing Harry's story. I've known him a long time, and yeah, he has a temper, but killing Mason over something that happened years ago? I don't buy it."

Andi looked down and took a deep breath. She wanted to believe Jim, more than she'd realized. But not chasing down every lead had got her fired before. "OK. I'll keep working on it. But it was you who said we go where the facts take us, remember?" She met Jim's eyes, challenging him.

He nodded.

"I said that. I meant it too. So, what's next?"

Andi grabbed her notebook. "Try to find Mason's wife. I've searched the marriage registry in Quebec, and I've even joined one of those ancestry sites, but I can't find anything."

"She might be common law, or they may have got married in Mexico or something," Jim suggested.

"Yes. So I've left a message with Captain Robert's secretary, Christina. Her friend was one of the Black OPS protesters. If she'll talk to me, she might have contact details for the mysterious Mrs Mason. And in the meantime, I thought I'd poke around Hades Fish Co."

"OK." Jim smiled. "Good work. I have to put some calls in to advertisers so we can pay some bills, but I'll wander down to the dock later and see if I can chat with Harry. Over a coffee."

Jim's phone rang.

He listened for a moment. "Thanks, we'll get down there."

Andi looked at him expectantly. "Well?"

"Vega brought in a diver. And it looks like they found something."

"You go on ahead, I'll catch up."

Jim nodded. "OK, meet me down there."

He stopped before opening the door to leave.

"You know something Andi? This is good work. Great work. You'll get through this."

After Jim left, Andi sat in her apartment with her head in her hands. Jim was right. This was a good story. She was a good journalist. Working for him and the *Gazette* wasn't punishment for her fuck-up, it was a second chance. She saw that now.

She had to move on. She couldn't allow Gavin to waltz in to her life and destroy her all over again.

Andi's face burned as she remembered her encounter with Gavin's wife and then felt tears at the back of her eyes. Why had he lied to her? She'd loved him so much. Maybe she still did, a little bit.

But then she heard his mocking words echoing in her head, and remembered the smirk on his face as he belittled her in front of his colleagues, and this time, instead of being reduced to tears, she felt anger. How bloody dare he? Who the fuck did he think he was?

Andi got up and marched out of her apartment, letting the door slam behind her.

Gavin and his assistant were alone in the office. They were sat beside each other at Jim's desk, their heads close together as they studied the laptop screen in front of them.

Andi faltered for a moment and nearly turned to leave, but Gavin looked up.

"Andi," he said, without much enthusiasm. "Did you forget something?"

"No," she said, keeping her voice level, "I wanted to talk to you, Gavin."

His assistant stared at her but Andi kept going.

"If you don't mind, this is a personal matter. Maybe you could get a coffee or something?"

"Andi . . ." Gavin began, but Andi held her hand up to stop him.

"Gavin, I'm going to say what I want to say, whether we are alone or not."

He glared at her, and Andi felt something new. Confidence.

Gavin nodded at his assistant, and she flounced past Andi, before pausing at the door. "Can I get—"

"No!" he almost shouted, and Andi saw with surprise that he was agitated.

"Look, Andi, I know what you're going to say." Gavin got up and started pacing back and forth in front of the desk. "I know I signed off on that story, and I could have pulled it when I found out that source was suspect, but it was a damn good story and—"

"What?"

"The story. I know I shouldn't have let it run, but at the time—"

"You knew?" Andi felt her stomach tighten, as if she had taken a blow. "You let me take the fall? You bastard!"

"Andi . . ." His voice had taken on a patronizing tone. "Look, you should have checked, but you didn't. It *was* your story, and as it was, I did get a bollocking."

"I lost my job! I got blacklisted!" Andi knew she was shouting, but didn't care. "You piece of shit."

Gavin came towards her, his arms out, a smile on his face. "Come on, Andi, shit happens in our world, right? And you'll do OK, a couple of years and everyone will forget. You can leave this shithole and come back to the mainland. No harm, no foul, right?"

"You wanted to get rid of me. So you threw me under the bus. Why, Gavin? Why didn't you just break up with me? Ask me to leave?" Andi's voice shook a little. "You never cared about me at all, did you? I was just another bit on the side. Your wife said as much."

Gavin's face lost the smile.

"You were out of line, coming to my house! Upsetting my daughter like that."

"Yes, Gavin. I *was* out of line. And I'm sorry. Sorry for that poor woman and your child — they both deserve better. And I'm ashamed of myself. But what you did to me was despicable, you lowlife piece—"

Andi heard a cough from behind her. She swung round to see Gavin's assistant holding a cup of coffee, but she didn't care. She carried on, her voice steady.

"This isn't over, Gavin. One day, all your lies and bullshit will catch up to you. You know what? You did me a favour. Maybe the *Gazette* is only a local newspaper but I'm still a better journalist than you'll ever be—"

"This is damn well over," Gavin interrupted her. "We'll be out of this office in a few days, Andi. Good luck with your wildlife piece."

He turned and walked back to the desk, and his assistant hurried to his side.

Andi stood for a moment. She'd been dismissed, but it didn't matter. She'd said what she needed to say, and it felt good.

She turned and left the office. She walked down the stairs and out into the street and took a couple of deep breaths of fresh air.

She wasn't sure she was "over" Gavin, but it was a good start. And now, she had work to do.

CHAPTER TWENTY-NINE

Finally, some progress. The team was feeling it too. The mood was upbeat as they filed into the briefing room.

Vega now knew why the name Hephzibah Brown had been taunting his memory. It was her brother, Harry. Harry had more than one connection to their victim.

He let Sergeant Fowler brief the rest of the team, and he settled in a chair at the back of the room.

"Brown was charged back in the eighties for threatening Mason with a gun. Mason was working for Greenpeace, and Brown's defence at the time was that Mason had just deliberately rammed his boat, putting his crew in danger and causing damage to his property. He admitted that he'd lost his temper, but the case was dismissed. Then when Mason was here in the nineties protesting the clear-cutting, as we know, Sarah McIntosh disappeared and was washed up on the beach, her arms and legs tied. She was the daughter of Joe McIntosh, owner of the biggest lumber business in the area, and the subject of Mason's protest." Sergeant Fowler paused and looked around at her colleagues.

"It was a big deal for the community. A witness implicated Mason, but a full investigation cleared him. Trouble was, the community decided that Mason had something to do with it. Harry Brown's younger sister, Hephzibah, who now owns the café on the boardwalk, was Sarah's best friend, and Harry was involved with the initial search. Also, Tara McIntosh, second wife of Joe and Sarah's stepmother, confirmed that Harry recently took the trouble to inform Joe that Mason was back in town."

She looked at Vega, who nodded for her to continue. Fowler pointed to the board on the wall, which now had Harry's picture pinned next to Mason's.

"Nothing concrete here connecting Brown to Mason until this morning. The diver found a rifle. We don't know yet if it's the murder weapon, but it seems probable. The rifle is registered to Harry Brown. We've sent it over to the lab for testing. This is all coincidence so far—"

"But as we know," Vega interrupted, "there are no such things as coincidences in this line of work. I have one other piece of information. Pass this around, please." He handed out copies of the picture Andi Silvers had given him.

"As you know, Andrea Silvers is a reporter for the *Gazette* in town." He broke off and looked around the room. "Some of you might know the name. She used to work for the *Vancouver Mail*, but they dropped her like a hot brick after she fucked up a case for the Financial Crimes Unit last year. Well, she ended up here and she's been digging around. I guess she still thinks of herself as an investigative reporter. So far she's kept out of the way, but she handed over the picture you are now looking at, plus Mason's cell phone — dropped, as you know, by Brian McIntosh, who is still in hiding."

He walked to the front of the room and pinned a copy of the picture to the board.

"Forensics went over the cell phone — nothing interesting, except a call from Hades Fish Co. They're based in Steveston, and we have someone following up on that. But it is worth noting Harry Brown used to sell fish to them throughout his fishing career."

Vega let that sink in and then pointed to the picture.

"The fishing boat — the one with the big drum thing on it — is the *Pipe Dream*. It's Harry Brown's boat and it's parked in the harbour, here in Coffin Cove."

"Moored, sir," someone called out. "A boat is moored, not parked."

Vega waited for the giggles to calm down, and carried on, ignoring the comment.

"Harry Brown lives on the *Pipe Dream*. Pierre Mason emailed this picture to Andrea Silvers the same night he was killed. He also met her in the pub earlier that evening. She claims Mason was still upset about the Sarah McIntosh investigation and went so far as to threaten legal action if she wrote anything about it. The subject line on the email from Mason says, 'The Bigger Picture'. Now, I didn't give this much weight." He paused for a second until he was sure he had everyone's attention. "I didn't give this much weight because I thought Mason was just trying to get an interfering hack off his back. That's on me. That's my responsibility. But this morning, another murder victim was found in Nanaimo. He's been identified as Captain Gerald Roberts, and his body was found on the beach beside the Department of Fisheries and Oceans, where he worked. He was shot."

Vega waited for the murmurs to quieten.

"Two things. First, as we know, I don't believe in coincidences. Murder is very rare on this island, so to have two within a few days . . . Well, we have to consider whether they're connected. And there's this picture." He held it up. "There are two other vessels in this picture. One is a DFO enforcement vessel. We don't know yet, but if Captain Roberts was in any way connected to that vessel, we have another killing that's not only connected to Mason but also to Harry Brown. So, Sergeant Fowler, next steps?"

"Bring Brown in for questioning," she said promptly.

Vega nodded. "Yes. Ask him about his gun, obviously, but don't show him this picture. Ask him if he knows Captain Roberts and watch for his reaction. We don't have enough to arrest him . . . yet. But let's keep an eye on him. And keep searching for Brian McIntosh. It's imperative that we find him."

One of the team put his hand up. "Should we question Andrea Silvers? See if she's found out anything?"

Vega considered this for a minute. "Not yet. I don't want the press finding out anything about the investigation, except what we want them to know. I don't need Miss Silvers fucking up another case."

* * *

Harry had seen and heard the commotion on the beach. A police diver had shown up in the morning, and Harry had watched with interest as he struggled into his black wetsuit, pulled on a weight belt, dive tank, fins and mask, before dropping into the water beside the crumbling fish plant pier.

Hephzibah was chattering animatedly with customers when Harry arrived at the café for a late lunch.

"They've found something," she said, before he could order a sandwich. "They think it's the murder weapon."

"They?" Harry couldn't help smiling. "Did Inspector Vega drop by and announce it himself?"

Hephzibah rolled her eyes at Harry's sarcasm. "No, but that diver found something. And they were pretty excited about it."

An hour later, as Harry was leaving the café, a young female RCMP officer stopped him at the entrance.

"Harry Brown?"

He nodded.

"We'd like to ask you some questions, sir," the officer said pleasantly. "Would you mind coming with me to the detachment?"

Harry hesitated. "Sure," he said. "I'll meet you there."

"No need, sir," the officer said, "I'll drive you."

They drove the two blocks to the detachment.

Quicker to walk, Harry thought, and couldn't help wondering if the officer was making sure that as many people as possible in Coffin Cove saw him get into the police car.

Harry cursed under his breath when he saw reporters from the *Vancouver Mail* loitering at the entrance. He ignored them as he followed the officer inside and she showed him to the interview room.

Harry waited for twenty minutes. He checked his phone several times as he sat at the table in the middle of the small room. He considered leaving but decided against it. He didn't need another scene. The café had gone quiet when the officer stopped him this afternoon, and he'd felt all those interested eyes on him. He didn't need to feed the gossip machine.

The female officer finally came into the interview room and identified herself as Sergeant Fowler. She sat down at the table opposite Harry, placed a file in front of her and thanked him for being there.

Not like I had much choice, Harry thought, but he acknowledged her pleasantries and refused coffee.

Sergeant Fowler opened the file and took out a piece of paper. She placed a picture in front of him. "Is this your gun, Mr Brown?"

Harry looked at it for a long moment. He was startled but didn't want to show it.

"It looks like a gun I own," he said finally. "But I can't be certain from a photo."

"We have the serial number," Fowler told him.

"Then you can check the registration," Harry said impatiently. "You already know if the gun is mine, Sergeant. Ask me what you need to know. We don't need to play guessing games here."

Fowler nodded. "Our diver pulled this gun — your gun — out of the ocean this morning. Do you have any idea how it got there?"

Harry felt his heart sink.

"No. But I didn't put it there. So the only way it could have got there was if someone took it off my boat," he added. "I live on my boat, the *Pipe Dream*."

"You didn't notice your gun was gone? Or that someone had been on your boat?"

"No. But I lock away the gun. I don't check it every day."

Sergeant Fowler sighed. "Mr Brown, you know what my next question is going to be, right?"

Harry nodded. "I keep my gun in a drawer under my chart table. It's locked all the time." He looked at Sergeant Fowler and closed his eyes for a moment. "I do leave the keys on the boat when I go out." Harry was feeling like an idiot.

"Who knows where you leave your keys? And have you been aware of anyone on your boat? Anything else missing?" Fowler asked.

It was an obvious question, Harry knew. He shook his head.

"Not that I'm aware of. Nothing missing, and I leave my laptop out. Probably a lot of people know where to find my keys. There's a cubbyhole above the door to the galley," he tried to explain. "Fishermen know that keys are usually within an arm's length of the door. It's kind of a custom, I suppose."

"Not very secure," Fowler noted drily.

"Apparently not," Harry agreed.

"And how would this intruder know where to find your gun?" asked Sergeant Fowler, a little sarcastically, Harry thought.

"If you have ever been on a boat, Sergeant Fowler, you'll know that there isn't much storage space. I kept my gun under my chart table. It wouldn't take long for someone to find it."

"When was the last time you checked on your gun? Or fired it?"

"I have no reason to 'check' on it. I fire it occasionally — but not out of hunting season. That's why I have the gun. I go hunting." Harry reached into his pocket and pulled out his wallet. "Here's my hunting license. It's up to date."

He handed the card to the sergeant, who studied it for a moment and handed it back.

"Again, Mr Brown, when was the last time you fired your gun?"

Harry hesitated. "I don't know exactly — a couple of weeks, maybe?"

Sergeant Fowler looked at him for a long moment and nodded.

"Mr Brown, would you be open to our team having a look at your boat? We might find something that corroborates your, er . . . 'theory'. Of course, we could get a search warrant . . ." She let her sentence tail off.

Harry shrugged. "Be my guest. I'll stay at my sister's place."

Fowler nodded her approval. "Thanks for your cooperation. Did you know Pierre Mason well, Mr Brown?" She opened her file and ran her eyes over a document while she waited for Harry to reply.

It rattled Harry a little.

"Not really. I remember him from a . . . legal matter years ago, and he was investigated for the murder of Sarah McIntosh."

"He was cleared though, correct?"

Harry nodded.

"Maybe you still think he was involved?"

Harry could feel Fowler looking intently at him, waiting for a reaction, he thought.

He answered truthfully. "Mason may not have been directly responsible for Sarah's death. But if he hadn't been here, hadn't stirred up all that trouble with protests and whatnot, I'm certain that Sarah would be alive today."

"I see. The legal matter you mentioned, it was a bit more than that, wasn't it, Mr Brown? You threatened Pierre Mason with a gun, I see from the court records."

"That case was dismissed," Harry said, feeling himself flush a little. He knew where Fowler was headed with this. And he knew to say as little as possible.

Fowler obviously decided that she'd unsettled Harry enough, because she closed her file and smiled at Harry.

"Thank you." Fowler got up. "That'll be all for now, Mr Brown, thank you for your time."

Harry couldn't help himself. "Did my gun kill Mason?"

Fowler didn't miss a beat. "We'll know that very soon, Mr Brown. Any more questions? Or anything else you'd like to tell me?"

Harry got up. "No, nothing," he said and walked toward the door.

"Mr Brown?"

Harry stopped.

"Mr Brown, do you know a 'Gerald Roberts'?"

Harry shook his head. "No, don't think so."

"You might have known him as Gerry? Or Captain Roberts?"

"No, never heard that name before."

Fowler nodded. "Thanks again, Mr Brown."

Harry left the detachment. He found Hephzibah waiting anxiously outside. But he was surprised and relieved to see she was on her own.

"Are you OK? What did they want?" Hephzibah bombarded him with questions as soon as she'd hugged him. "I didn't know whether I should call a lawyer or what to do."

Harry hugged her back. "I don't need a lawyer, Hep, I haven't done anything wrong. But I could do with a drink."

CHAPTER THIRTY

Jim sniffed the air in his office. Expensive aftershave lingered after Gavin and his team had hurriedly left. He'd assumed that they were at the detachment after word leaked out that Vega's team had found a gun. But a short while ago, Jim had seen the whole of the *Vancouver Mail* get into their vehicles and head out of Coffin Cove. Jim was pleased to see them go.

He was glad to get the office back, he thought. Even if it did stink. "Lady Lure", his father used to call it, teasing Jim when he was younger and getting ready to go out on the town.

The memory made Jim smile. "Out on the town, in Coffin Cove," he chuckled to himself. That made him think of Andi. He'd seen her look at Gavin and the other reporters from the *Vancouver Mail*, with their smart suits, Bluetooth earpieces and expensive laptops, and he wondered if she missed her former life.

He leaned back in his chair and looked with fresh eyes at the litter of paper on his desk, yellowed files and documents wedged down in places with chipped coffee cups. It had been twenty years or more since he'd moved into this cramped office. The mould stain in the corner of the ceiling from the leaking roof was still there, as was the wastepaper basket underneath that caught the drops of water during these wet winter days. The office was sparsely furnished. Jim didn't need space or equipment these days — he had long since contracted out the actual printing of the *Gazette* to a modern facility on the mainland. All he needed was his laptop. He had reluctantly invested in a new sleek model a few months ago. It looked out of place on the heavy oak desk. Gleaming high-tech perched on a piece of history. The desk used to belong to his father, the only relic from the *Gazette*'s more prosperous days.

An observant reporter would look around this room and *know*, Jim thought, noting the worn path on the cheap carpet from door to desk, the dated faux wood panelling and the few framed newspaper cuttings arranged haphazardly on the wall. They would know that the *Coffin Cove Gazette*, the last independent new organization on the island, was in its death throes.

Without a miracle, *some divine intervention*, Jim could not fight off the corporate media organizations that regularly sent smiling, suited salesmen from the central island highway down the one, potholed access road to Coffin Cove, to promise that they were *absolutely committed* to providing a local news service to the population of Coffin Cove. Each time they came, the dollar offer got a little less, as if they sensed that Jim couldn't hold on for much longer.

Hiring Andi was his Hail Mary. A last attempt to breathe some life back into the *Gazette*. Make Jim feel like it hadn't all been a complete waste of his life.

He had invited Andi for an interview on impulse. And, he acknowledged to himself, because she had been the only applicant. A few phone calls — he still had connections — revealed her likely motivation.

Andi had changed a lot from the dispirited woman he'd first interviewed. He remembered how she'd blustered through the interview, saying all the things she thought he'd wanted to hear, but in all that bravado, she had no confidence in her work. She was a good writer, Jim thought. She had a good instinct for a story, and she knew how to listen to people, to coax out information. It was a talent. But somewhere along the way, she'd stopped paying attention to those instincts and started to behave like she thought she should. She'd stopped trusting herself.

Andi took the job because she had no other choice. Jim knew that. She'd assumed, like many outsiders, that Coffin Cove was a dying town. Her work would be limited to reporting on the mundanity of community life, happenings important to the inhabitants of the town, but lacking the — what was the word? Significance? Prestige? — of investigative journalism.

But Andi had impressed Jim. She was thoughtful, observant. If she had preconceived ideas about small-town life, her work didn't show it. She listened to people, and they trusted her.

Jim wanted to ask Andi about her career-ending incident at the *Vancouver Mail*. What had really happened? He'd heard the rumours, knew that Andi was professionally toxic and had seen the full-page apology to the businessman that Andi's unsubstantiated article had targeted. He'd wondered at the time why Andi had taken the full brunt of the fallout. Sure, she should be accountable for her work, but what about the editor's responsibility?

And then he met Gavin.

Gavin. That's what happened, Jim was sure. He'd been in the newspaper business long enough to meet people — mostly men, he had to admit — just like Gavin. Short on talent, long on bullshit, but smart enough to use other people to further their own career.

What was Gavin doing in Coffin Cove? Why did he bother to make the trip? Sure, it was a big story for this town — a murder. It doesn't get much bigger than that. But the *Vancouver Mail* was a big-city paper. Gavin could have dispatched a junior reporter, so why hadn't he?

Still pursuing Andi? Jim dismissed that thought. He'd watched Gavin sniffing round his young interns and strutting around like it was rutting season, and doubted that he gave Andi a passing thought.

So he either had a lead on a story they knew nothing about, or it was the same old thing — business.

Jim knew Andi had confronted Gavin. He hoped she had given that idiot his marching orders, once and for all. She deserved better. He was certain Andi would still make her mark as a journalist. But would it be with the *Gazette*?

Jim sat at his desk and turned on his laptop. He opened a spreadsheet and studied a cash flow statement intently, as if he could improve the numbers by sheer force of will.

Things had improved over the last weeks. That was the good news. The bad news? The *Gazette* was still far from turning a profit. Jim wondered for the umpteenth time how long he could continue to support the failing business from his savings — and for the first time, if it was worth the effort.

Maybe he should just sell out to the media corporation that had swallowed up all the independent publications all over the island. He noted again that the same corporation also owned the *Vancouver Mail*, so maybe Gavin's presence wasn't really a mystery at all.

Why was he doing this? Jim sighed and rubbed his eyes. He didn't want the *Gazette* to be part of a big conglomerate, with only the odd short article about his hometown. He had long resisted the full conversion to a digital version of the publication, hating the pop-up advertisements and sensational clickbait headlines. Local newspapers used to mentor fledgling investigative journalists. Now they employed website designers and content writers.

Jim was gazing at the laptop screen without focusing, as his same old dilemma occupied his thoughts again. He was startled when he heard the floor creak and looked up to see Sue McIntosh standing at the door of the office.

"Come in, Sue — sorry, I was just lost in my thoughts for a moment."

Sue didn't answer but walked over and placed a twenty-dollar bill on his desk.

"For the diesel. The other day, when you were out at the house."

"Oh, I'd forgotten about that. Thanks." Jim knew better than to protest. Sue and Fred were proud people.

We only need God's charity, Fred used to say. In the aftermath of Sarah's death, well-meaning people had driven out to the valley, offering baked goods and cooked meals, only to have Fred order them off the property, sometimes with his rifle tucked menacingly under his arm.

Sue stepped back but didn't leave the office. She looked hesitant and bowed her head for a moment, as if mustering courage.

"Is there something I can help you with, Sue?" Jim asked gently. "Take a seat for a moment. How's Fred doing?"

Sue accepted his invitation.

"I know you think I'm crazy," she started, ignoring his question. "I know what the people in this town think of me." She looked at Jim defiantly, almost daring him to contradict her.

Jim didn't.

"Go on, Sue. What's happened?"

"Somebody is watching me. Following me." She paused for a moment, and then again drew her breath in as if steeling herself to continue. "At first I thought it was Sarah. Not . . . not . . . her in person, but her spirit. Her soul." She stopped for a moment and then asked Jim, "Do you believe in God?"

"Sometimes," Jim answered truthfully, wondering where this was headed. Sue had never seemed to change over the years, he thought. She was always a well-built woman, striking when she was younger, with jet-black hair. She'd been unaware of her beauty, hadn't known that she'd caught more eyes than just Joe's. Grief aged her almost immediately when Sarah died, but more recently, Jim thought, she'd become fragile-looking, vulnerable. Her eyes were tired, her skin was pale, despite all the time she spent outside. Jim thought the physical challenges of living in the valley and looking after Fred were taking a toll on Sue's health.

Sue seemed satisfied with Jim's answer.

"I've been drawn to the hatchery lately," she said, almost dreamily. "My morning hunt. I don't mean to go there. It's . . . painful. But I always end up there." She stopped again. "I know I sound crazy to you. I feel like I'm going mad sometimes. But I thought if it was Sarah taking me there, if I could . . . could feel her spirit, then maybe I could forgive God."

Jim could see that Sue was fighting tears.

"You see," Sue said in such a low voice that Jim thought she was talking to herself, "if I cannot make peace with God, then I have nothing left."

Jim was silent for a moment. Then he said, "But now you don't think it's Sarah? At the hatchery?"

Sue straightened in her chair, seeming to pull herself together. "No. I've hunted the valley all my life. I know the sounds animals and birds make. I know their smell. Somebody human is watching me."

Jim nodded. "OK, Sue. Who do you think it is?"

"I don't know for sure," she said, "but I found this."

* * *

After Sue left, Jim couldn't concentrate on his spreadsheets. He'd listened to Sue and knew that she wasn't mad or crazy.

She tried to tell us in her own way, Jim thought. *But we'd made up our minds.*

If he was honest, Jim thought, he'd always had an inkling of doubt. Parts of the story didn't fit well. How was it possible for shy, unsophisticated, childlike Sarah, who rarely ventured into Coffin Cove, to strike up a relationship with Mason? And what would have motivated him to kill her? They — he — had been so certain that this evil couldn't possibly live within the community, and Mason was already such a divisive figure that it was easy to accept the story.

There was something else too. A fact, or detail, just out of Jim's mind's eye, that caused him to waver at the time.

Something so insignificant, back then, that he'd buried it deep.

It had been bothering him since Andi arrived in town. She was eager to find some journalistic redemption, Jim thought, after her humiliation at the *Vancouver Mail*. That's why she'd taken an immediate interest in the Sarah McIntosh case. Jim had conflicting feelings. He'd said, and genuinely believed, that Joe and Sue didn't need to relive that terrible time. Why should they? Nothing would bring Sarah back. And he still thought Mason had something to do with it, even though a police investigation turned up nothing. Who else could it be? Nothing would be gained by Andi raking up all those painful memories, to stir up the gossip and rumour-mongers in Coffin Cove.

Jim remembered the shock that reverberated through the community when Sarah was killed. In one way it had brought people together. Families put aside their resentments about the McIntosh forestry practices and gathered their arms around Joe and Sue. This was a tragedy that happened to one of them. It was easy to turn their collective vitriol against the outsider, he who dared to disrupt their way of life. He who was to blame for the death of their Sarah.

The town forgot that until they discovered her lifeless body washed up on the beach, Sarah herself had been an outsider. Jim couldn't recall Sarah hanging out with the other teenage girls on the boardwalk, giggling and eyeing up the gaggle of scrawny boys who preened and paraded in front of them. Sue had never brought Sarah to the Salmon Festival or the Fall Fair. Sarah dressed differently, talked differently and kept herself to herself. Even the volunteers at the hatchery thought she was odd. After the initial outpouring of grief, the less charitable rumours started.

She was rebelling, they said. *You keep too tight a rein, and they are bound to fight against it.* It was Sue's fault. She should have let Sarah live a little. No wonder she got starry-eyed about that man.

Eventually Coffin Cove moved on. The mysterious death of Sarah McIntosh became a story that was told over a beer at the Fat Chicken on a rainy evening. People nudged each other if they saw Sue in town, and they speculated about Joe's drinking, but the tragedy, for most people, wasn't real anymore. It was Coffin Cove folklore.

Andi changed all that. And although Jim outwardly objected, he knew this story needed an ending. The truth needed to be told. Maybe Andi would yet make her mark.

Jim promised Sue that he'd meet her at the hatchery the next day. There was something else he needed to check too. He reached for his phone when he was alone in his office, intending to call Andi, but he heard the office door open, and the sound of Andi's voice. She was talking on her cell phone.

"Right. I understand. Nothing on the record. I'll meet her at the coffee shop by the Fishermen's Wharf, 10 a.m. tomorrow. Yes, I understand. Tell her I promise it will be confidential."

Jim looked at Andi expectantly as she finished her call. She was damp, steam rising slightly from her hair and jacket. A plaid jacket, Jim noted with amusement.

"So?" he asked.

"So this is getting weirder by the minute," Andi said, "and scary. This morning, Gerry Roberts's body was discovered on the beach below the DFO office. The police aren't saying much at the moment, and they haven't officially identified him, but Christina, his secretary, called me." She held up her phone. "She says that Roberts was shot."

"Holy shit! Could it be suicide?"

Explains why Gavin and his crew left in such a hurry, he thought, and wished, not for the first time, that the *Gazette* could afford more than one reporter.

Andi sat down.

"It could be," she said sadly. "Oh God, I hope my visit didn't cause that. Christina said he was acting strange, stranger than usual after that. But she didn't think he was depressed. He seemed jumpy."

"The police will want to talk to you again," Jim said. "You have the knack of popping up near dead bodies."

"Goes with the job," Andi said, not breaking a smile. "Anyway, I gave that Inspector Vega everything I had: the phone, the picture Mason sent. Not my fault if he's not making the connections."

"There might not be any connections," Jim pointed out. "You're joining up a lot of dots here, without evidence."

"What are you talking about?" Andi said, clearly taken aback. "The day before Mason gets killed he sends me a picture and tells me it's the story I should be investigating, then the other guy connected to the same picture freaks out when I interview him and then ends up dead on the beach. Of course I'm joining up dots! Can't possibly be a coincidence, right?"

"Who are you meeting tomorrow?" Jim changed the subject.

"That's the other weird thing," Andi said. "That was Christina's friend on the phone, the one who was a protester. Christina gave her my number, and she called to say that Mason's wife, or partner, or whatever she is, wants to talk to me. But it has to be off the record."

Jim nodded. "Good work. You're right. Can't be coincidence." He got up and reached for his jacket. "Come on."

"Where're we going?" Andi asked, as Jim turned off the office light.

"There's one more dot to connect," he said. "Harry. He was in that picture too."

"Jim?" Something in Andi's voice made him stop and turn around.

"What?" he asked.

Andi looked serious. "Vega's team picked up Harry for questioning earlier. The gun the diver found? They think it belongs to Harry."

CHAPTER THIRTY-ONE

Brian had suffered a coughing fit that had left him convulsing in pain. When he'd managed to stifle the wheezing, he stared down at the flecks of blood and phlegm on his sleeve then wiped them on his pants.

He was hungry but too weak to move far. Yet he had to do something.

The hatchery wasn't safe anymore.

A day ago — maybe two days, he wasn't sure — he'd watched Sue enter the hut from the undergrowth. He'd left his stuff and was foraging around for something he could eat, anything to dull the hunger pains gnawing at his stomach. Otherwise Sue would have found him. Sue would turn him in for sure, Brian knew. That bitch was as bad as Tara. But maybe if she'd found him, he could have persuaded her to feed him. She was religious. She was supposed to look after the poor and needy.

He imagined Sue offering him warm soup and bread. Then, when her back was turned, he'd grab that gun and shoot the bitch in the head. Sue was how all his fucking problems started. If Joe had never seen her, never got it into his head to marry her, he wouldn't be here now. Tears welled in his eyes.

It was all Joe's fault. Why did he want to get married, anyway? Why not just fuck her?

He started coughing again.

Sue had stayed in the hut for a while. He'd stayed out of sight for hours, it felt like, even after he saw Sue leave.

She was a good hunter, Brian knew. She might have walked away from the hut in one direction, but she could double back quietly and ambush him from behind. He shivered from the damp and the mist seeping through his worn-out jacket and tried to be as quiet as possible.

When he was certain Sue had left, he hobbled back to the hut, bent over with pain in his lungs and chest.

Brian saw immediately that Sue had rummaged through his belongings. How dare she touch his stuff!

He fell to his knees, pulled apart his rucksack and emptied the tin on the ground. He carefully spread the contents on the floor and saw what was missing. Now he was afraid.

He wished he had more booze. He grabbed the empty bottle, held it upside down and shook it, hoping for a few drops. Nothing.

This was getting harder. He thought about his options. Go back to Coffin Cove and steal more food and booze? It was a risk, but he might not have any other choice. He needed alcohol. He was starving.

In his panic to get away after the killing at the fish plant he hadn't thought this through. He could see that now. He should have given himself up. What he knew must be worth something. He could have cut a deal.

Brian sat on the floor and thought for a minute.

Maybe it would be all right. Maybe it was a good thing that Sue had appeared. It gave him an idea.

Maybe it was time to make those fuckers pay. He knew stuff. He was the one with all the power. He just needed to use it.

Brian struggled to his feet. He kicked his bag and filthy rucksack out the way. He didn't need them anymore. Not where he was going.

215

CHAPTER THIRTY-TWO

Adrian hadn't slept well. He'd barely eaten anything either. After his meeting with Steve, Adrian sat in his office for two hours trying to comprehend what he'd heard. How much trouble was he in? He knew that Steve was out there, operating in the grey area of the law. Adrian admitted to himself that he'd employed him for that very reason. Steve Hilstead took risks. He was confident. Adrian worried about everything. The business was overwhelming. There was so much he didn't know. But he'd badgered Nikos to hand over the reins. He just couldn't fail. And Steve was helping. Or so he thought.

Adrian couldn't remember much of yesterday's meeting after he'd realized in horror that Steve, or someone who worked for Steve, had bashed Brenda over the head and left her in the freezer. If the supervisor hadn't come back when he did . . . Adrian held his head in his hands, feeling close to tears again.

He had cried last night when he got home. He'd left the office in a daze and driven back to his apartment. He'd paced up and down. He'd drunk far too much whiskey and gone to bed, hoping to blot out the day, but he'd been unable to sleep.

He wished his mother was still alive.

Iris made everything better. She would have listened without judging him and figured out a way to tell Nikos, making it sound like it wasn't Adrian's fault.

Except everything always was his fault. And this mess was his fault too.

Why had he got mixed up with Steve? He'd met him years ago at some party, and Steve's easy confidence and in-your-face personality had impressed him. The gangster life had always fascinated Adrian, or what he imagined that life to be. Glamorous girls, fast cars and easy cash, he'd believed, and Steve represented all of those things.

"Try this," he'd said, dropping a tablet into Adrian's hand. "It's good stuff, the best — on me, man, enjoy," and Adrian had taken the drugs, shrugging and laughing, trying to appear street savvy. Hilstead had drawn him in, just like that.

When Adrian took over Hades Fish Co., he met Steve again. He was celebrating with friends at a nightclub, and Steve just appeared. "More champagne!" Steve had said, slapping Adrian on the back, and he'd kept the booze flowing all evening. By the early morning light, Adrian had offered him a job and Steve had accepted.

It was OK at first. Steve had good ideas, encouraged Adrian to start the bistro, listened to all his big plans, and always knew someone who could help.

Then he started making suggestions.

"I have a line on some cheap salmon," he said one afternoon.

"Oh?" Adrian said, not sure what he meant.

"It's not strictly legal, I guess," Steve had laughed, "but everyone does it. Just mix in the cheap fish with the other stuff, nobody will know. Look, if you're worried, just let me take care of it."

And Adrian did just that. He stopped asking questions. He let Hilstead run the plant. Run everything, Adrian thought now. He'd been played. Steve had zeroed in on an opportunity and taken advantage of Adrian's weaknesses.

Adrian knew he was shallow, careless. He knew he didn't pay attention or work hard enough. His father had told him all these things — not cruelly, but sadly. He hadn't wanted to put Adrian in charge. But when Iris passed away, something in Nikos died too. His drive, his purpose, his fierce energy was extinguished. Adrian saw his chance and hounded Nikos until the old man gave in.

Adrian had wanted to make Nikos proud. He boasted to his father how he would build an empire, take the small company and transform it into a massive corporation. Nikos had listened to his son and patted his hand.

"I believe you, son," he'd said. "I believe you."

Adrian looked around at his tastefully decorated office. It was all he was good at — the image. And he'd been content to turn a blind eye to whatever Steve was up to and be the face of the business, whatever that meant. Adrian wanted to pound his fists on the desk. He'd known that Steve was trouble. He knew right from the start when he hadn't wanted to tell Nikos he'd employed him. He'd just hoped it would all work out. But he'd allowed Steve to cheat his customers and fire the loyal staff who'd worked for Nikos for years.

They'd even paid that environmentalist to fuck up the herring fishery, so they could leverage the fishermen and push down prices. The only person who questioned any of it was Brenda.

And look what happened to her.

Another thought passed through Adrian's mind. Steve had left her in the freezer. He didn't deny it. What else had he done?

"Adrian? Are you OK?"

He looked up. It was Amy.

"Of course." He mustered a smile and sat up straight, trying to look professional.

"It's just that we heard you and Steve arguing yesterday, and then you left . . ."

"Just business, Amy, it's all good . . . What do you have there?"

218

She was holding an envelope.

"I think it's from Brenda. You were waiting for it?"

Adrian remembered. Yesterday he was worried about Brenda suing them. Now he wished that he'd listened to her.

"Thanks. I'll take that."

He opened the letter and saw Brenda's signature on the paper. He looked at it for a long time. A few hours ago, he'd have been relieved.

He stared at the paper in his hand and he remembered something else Steve had told him.

He looked up at Amy, who was still at the door and waiting for him to say something.

"Awesome!" he said with a big smile. "Just what I've been waiting for!"

Amy smiled back at him. "You want to go over this week's social media?"

"Not at the moment, Amy, I'm taking an hour or so to visit my father." And he got up and put on his suit jacket. "I probably won't be back this afternoon, OK?"

"Not a problem," she smiled, and trotted back to her desk.

Adrian got into his car when he left the office and turned left out of the parking lot, as if he were leaving Steveston Village.

I don't know where all the cameras are hidden, he thought as he took a left onto Moncton Street, almost doubling back on himself. *And I don't know if Steve is listening in to conversations.*

He knew, from now on, he'd have to be careful.

CHAPTER THIRTY-THREE

Brenda wandered around Steveston. After morning rain, the skies cleared, and it was good to feel the sun on her face. She was tired of sitting in her apartment. *No use feeling sorry for yourself,* she scolded her reflection in the bathroom mirror.

She tried to feel optimistic. Now she could do all those things she hadn't had time for. Reading, travelling — maybe she'd buy a little camper van and drive the Oregon Coast and visit those little fishing towns she'd heard so much about.

She started by taking a walk around the town she'd lived in for her whole adult life. So many changes, she marvelled, and she'd barely noticed any of them, she'd been so focused on her work.

Brenda wandered in and out of boutique stores on Moncton Street. It was strange not to be hurrying.

Not many fishing stores left now, Brenda thought sadly. The Commercial Marine Store had closed down. The windows were boarded up, and a notice told her that a developer was planning smart new condos.

Brenda found herself at the Steveston Hotel. She was drawn to the familiar, she supposed. The café had updated the flooring to smart new tiles and painted the walls — to clean up the nicotine stains, Brenda thought, remembering that breakfast time with the fishermen was always accompanied by billows of cigarette smoke — but the black-and-white photographs of fishing days gone by on the walls were still the same.

Brenda ordered coffee. There was a time when she couldn't come in for a coffee without bumping into someone she knew. She looked round the café. Nobody. She'd walked through town from her apartment, and nobody had nodded or waved, or called out her name. She was anonymous now.

Brenda stared out the window and her attention was caught by several large trucks parked on the street, and men shouting and waving. A movie crew was spraying foam on the sidewalk and hanging Christmas lights and wreaths around one of the storefronts.

This is the new Steveston, Brenda thought. *Smart apartments, art stores and movie stars. I don't belong here anymore. I've just been clinging to the past.*

Brenda remembered the last time she was in the café and flushed with embarrassment at the memory. *Maybe I belong in the movies*, she thought, *making up all that drama.*

So what if Adrian was running the business differently? What business was it of hers? But she had to make a big fuss and even to go and phone Harry. What was she thinking, that Harry would rekindle their relationship?

She felt tears coming.

"A top-up?" A waitress was standing beside her with a pot of coffee.

"No thanks." Brenda forced a smile.

She finished her cup and paid the waitress.

The sky was a brilliant blue. Brenda heard the cry of gulls and the clink of boats moored by the cannery. Usually, she would walk beside the river and spend a few moments absorbing the sights and sounds that were the hallmarks of her life.

Today, she retraced her steps through the town, not wanting to pass the bistro and her old workplace. She also had a stop to make.

I'm a silly old woman, she thought. *Harry and Nikos were just being kind. Humouring me. I have to move on.*

Brenda entered the real estate office, a block from her condo. An elegant young woman sitting at the reception desk smiled in welcome.

A few minutes later, Brenda had a sheaf of papers, real estate statistics, legal information and a booklet, *How to Stage Your Home for Sale*.

She felt happier than she had for weeks, and was looking forward to the future, as she let herself into her apartment block. The real estate lady had been impressed when Brenda told her how much she had paid for her home.

"Oh, what an investment!" she gushed. Brenda nearly fell over when the lady told her the selling price she could expect now.

Maybe I don't have to work, Brenda thought as she exited the elevator at her floor and reached for her door keys in her purse. *Maybe I can just downsize somewhere cheaper and travel more . . .*

"Hello, Brenda."

She stopped still. Standing outside her apartment door, shifting nervously and not wanting to meet her eyes, was Adrian Palmer.

CHAPTER THIRTY-FOUR

Jim and Andi found Harry at the Fat Chicken. He wasn't sitting on his usual bar stool but was hidden from view in a booth.

Walter pointed him out and took Jim's order. Andi slid into the booth opposite Harry.

"Just what I need," Harry said sarcastically, taking a mouthful of beer. "Another reporter looking for a story."

"I'm not looking anymore," Andi retorted. "I already have a story. And you're the main feature."

"OK, that's enough, you two," Jim said, placing a glass of wine in front of Andi and taking a seat beside her. "We need to talk to you, Harry, and I think you need to listen."

Harry was silent. Andi took that as his assent.

She pushed a copy of Mason's picture across the table.

"Pierre Mason sent this to me before he was killed."

Harry picked up the picture and studied it. "So?"

"He called it 'The Bigger Picture'. And before that he talked to me — he sat right here, in fact — and told me his main concern was protecting the ocean from poachers and illegal—"

Harry stopped her. "That's my boat, obviously. But I never poached, and I don't commercially fish now either, so I don't see how I can be part of his 'Bigger Picture'." He pushed the paper back towards Andi.

Jim took the paper and placed it in front of Harry, slapping his hand impatiently on the table. "Look again, man. You see that boat there? That's a DFO boat, and the guy running it, as of this morning, is dead."

Andi saw confusion spread over Harry's face. Then he ran his hand through his hair. *A sign of frustration?* Andi thought.

"What was his name?" he asked.

"Captain Gerry—" Andi started.

"Roberts," Harry finished for her.

"You knew him?" Andi said, surprised.

"No," Harry said, his voice worried now. "But Sergeant Fowler asked me the same question this afternoon. Except she didn't mention he was dead."

"That was your gun they found?" Jim asked quietly.

"Yes," Harry said. "But I didn't throw it overboard, and I didn't use it to kill Mason." Harry looked directly at Jim. "I didn't like him. You know we had a run-in years ago, he was in that Greenpeace boat and just about rammed me. I did lose my temper, and I did threaten him, but he put me and my crew in danger."

"But you think he killed Sarah McIntosh, right?" Andi couldn't help but interrupt. She wanted to push Harry. It was time he told his story. Two more people were dead.

"I blame him for Sarah's death. I blame him for causing all the shit in this town that led up to her death, if that's what you mean. But I don't know if he killed her." Harry's voice was getting louder, and Andi saw that Walter was looking in their direction.

She tried another angle. "What about this boat? Jim thinks it's a packer."

Harry looked at it. "It is. It's the *King of Cash*." He looked at Andi. "You said that Mason told you this was the 'Bigger Picture'? And that he was investigating poaching?"

Andi nodded.

"Shit!" Harry looked at both of them. "Look, I'll be back in a minute. I need to make a phone call, but I will be back. I think I know what Mason meant."

Jim and Andi looked at each other, as Harry disappeared out of the pub.

CHAPTER THIRTY-FIVE

"What will they find when they search your boat?" Jim asked Harry on his return. Andi was surprised that Jim was so direct. Harry was already agitated, but he answered Jim calmly.

"The fingerprints of whoever stole my gun, I hope," he said. "Maybe Hilstead. But he's cunning, he might have paid someone to do that."

"Slippery Steve," Andi murmured.

Harry looked at her and nodded. "That's what Hephzibah calls him."

"Sounds like a job Brian McIntosh would volunteer for," Jim said. "Steal your gun to order. And he's still a person of interest."

The three of them talked until after closing time at the Fat Chicken. Walter wiped down the bar and asked them to lock the door on the way out.

Harry told them what he knew about Steve Hilstead and the phone conversation he'd just had with a woman called Brenda.

Andi was wary. "How reliable is this Brenda lady?" It was a little unkind, she knew, especially as Harry was distraught. Andi could feel Jim looking at her in surprise.

"Sorry," she said defensively, "but I've been burned by sources before."

Harry didn't appear to notice. "She's reliable," he said. "Brenda is very down-to-earth. And Adrian must be worried if he's gone to Brenda for help." He explained their history.

"Well, the problem is that we've only got a second- or third-hand story," Andi said. "We have a picture from Mason, sent with a cryptic message, we have a tenuous connection with Hades, a feeling that something illegal is going on from a lady who could be considered a disgruntled ex-employee, and an angry reaction from a pompous DFO bureaucrat . . ."

"And two dead bodies, and one head injury that landed Brenda in hospital," Harry said angrily. "You came to me, remember?"

"I'm just trying to put this into perspective," Andi said as patiently as she could. "I lost a career because I didn't have proof. All I had was a made-up story from an unreliable source. Right now we have innuendo and speculation."

"She's right," Jim said. "We need more information before we can write a story or get the police involved. And if we do this half-cocked, go to the police or publish something now without concrete facts, we could put Brenda in more danger. We'll let Hilstead know we're investigating. If he did kill Gerry Roberts and Mason, he must have been feeling cornered. We don't want to make that worse."

Harry was silent.

"Hilstead talked to Adrian Palmer, right?" Andi said. "Told him enough for Palmer to get worried. What we need is Hilstead to talk again. To say enough to tie him to Mason and Roberts. Get him on the record."

"How do we do that?" Harry asked.

"I have an idea," Andi said. "Now *I* need to make a phone call."

Soon it was all settled. Harry would catch the morning flight to Vancouver. He couldn't take his boat. It would take too long, and besides, Vega's team wanted to search it.

* * *

227

Andi chose a table at the back of the Java Time Café. The last time she was here, she'd sat at the window overlooking the waterfront. But this time she thought her interviewee would prefer somewhere more discreet.

Andi ordered coffee and a scone and took a seat at the table where she had a good view of the entrance.

It was mid-morning, and the café was quiet. The sea walk in Nanaimo was deserted, too late for morning dog walkers and joggers, and too early for the lunchtime crowd.

Andi hadn't brought her laptop. She had promised that the interview would be entirely off the record, so she wanted this meeting to be relaxed. She wondered how Mason's wife was dealing with her recent bereavement. The police had omitted her from any press statement, and although Andi had scoured all the online search records and press archives that mentioned Mason, she hadn't found a single mention of a wife.

It must be hard, she thought, to lose your husband and have to grieve in secret.

Andi sipped her coffee and ate the scone, letting her thoughts wander over the events of the last weeks. She'd never worked as hard on a story before. In the city, she had always found people with information who were willing to hand it over to the press. Usually, they had an angle or were looking for some kind of payout. Politicians and their aides leaked selectively, spinning information to distract or distort facts, other people traded information for cash or benefits in kind, or used their secrets for leverage. Information was currency.

Here on the island it was different. There was no shortage of gossip and drama. Andi had seen how Coffin Cove came alive with morbid fascination after Mason's death. But there were secrets in that town. Someone knew something about Sarah McIntosh's murder. Someone knew who killed Mason. And Andi still believed that the two deaths were connected. And she hoped that Mason's wife could shed some light on this story.

Andi got the first text from Terry Pederson the photographer as she ordered her second coffee. He'd picked up Harry from the airport, and they were on their way to meet Adrian Palmer and Brenda, just as they had discussed on the phone the night before.

I'll keep my ears and eyes open, Terry texted, showing that he understood that Andi wasn't entirely sure about Harry.

Andi hoped that Jim was right about Harry. She had conflicting feelings about the man. Something about the way Harry talked about Brenda gave Andi the feeling that they were close. For some reason, this realization had disappointed her. Harry had been abrupt with her — unpleasant, almost — and Andi still suspected that he knew more than he was saying.

Harry was connected to everyone in this story — Mason, Gerry Roberts, Steve Hilstead, Hades Fish Co. and Joe McIntosh. His gun was the murder weapon in one of the homicides.

So why was she dismayed at the thought of Harry in a relationship?

Andi pushed her confusion to one side. She didn't have time for this, and she certainly didn't have the appetite for a relationship, not after Gavin, she told herself. And anyway, Harry wasn't her type at all. He was older, for a start, and they had nothing in common.

Jim had been evasive about what he was doing today. He'd asked for one of his old boxes of files back and told Andi he had an appointment. She was surprised but didn't press him. Jim would tell her when he was ready.

She hoped that Terry would come through for her. He'd never let her down in the past. He was a first-rate photographer and knew how to work a crime scene. He liked mystery and intrigue, and Andi had employed him for surveillance and undercover work before. His services came with a high price tag, something that she didn't mention to Jim, but she knew his work was worth it. Although he was always ready with an off-colour joke and the latest conspiracy theory, he was a professional. He also had many useful contacts on both sides of the law.

The second text she received from Terry directed her to her emails.

As the café filled up with passengers who had just disembarked from the floatplane, Andi checked her inbox.

> *Hilstead investigated by DFO last year re: poaching abalone. Big operation, went to court. Hilstead got off on a technicality. Investigators suspected he was a small fish, part of a bigger operation. His lawyers were Dunn and Grant Associates. They also represent Paul Nguyen — organized crime, named in casino scandal, so far coming up clean. Might be looking for a new retail outlet?*
>
> *Talk later,*
>
> *Terry.*

That would make sense, Andi thought. The recent casino scandal on the mainland involved a massive money-laundering scheme. Organized crime gangs were washing their cash through government-regulated casinos and gambling outlets. Terry was right, Andi thought, now the scheme was out in the open, those gangs would look for new ways to launder cash. Legitimate businesses like Hades Fish Co. would work. But the theory didn't explain everything.

It was possible that Gerry Roberts, if he was turning a blind eye to Hilstead's *King of Cash* drug boat, was also involved in tipping off Hilstead about the DFO investigation. Maybe Captain Roberts knew too much? Or maybe he took his own life because he'd been caught and couldn't stand the scandal? None of this explained Mason's involvement.

"Is this seat taken?" a woman's voice asked.

Andi paused midway through typing a reply to Terry. She looked up and recognized the thin, grey-haired woman with dark eyes who was standing beside her, holding a cup of coffee. She was dressed in faded jeans and a long baggy sweater and had a patchwork cloth bag slung over her shoulder. She was the woman Andi had seen in the abandoned Ocean Protection Society office. Andi realized that she must have come in with the passengers from the floatplane and wondered if she had flown in from Vancouver.

"Please, sit down." Andi smiled warmly at the woman, hoping to put her at ease.

It didn't work. The woman sat down and held on to her coffee with both hands. She didn't smile. There was an air of sorrow about her. She bent her head as if it was too much of an effort to hold it straight.

Of course she's sad, Andi thought, *she's just lost her husband.*

"Thank you for coming," Andi started, as gently as possible. "What's your name?"

"Carol Morin," the woman stated. Like Mason, she had the trace of a French accent, and Andi guessed she was from Quebec.

"You are Pierre Mason's wife?" Andi asked.

Carol Morin took a sip of her coffee before answering in an emotionless voice.

"We had a complicated relationship," she said. "We weren't legally married, but it was easier, sometimes, to say we were."

"OK," Andi said, not wanting to push it. "Have the police spoken to you since your . . . Pierre was . . . ?"

"Murdered," Carol finished for her in the same tone. "Yes. I told them what I will tell you. I know very little about his operations. I helped with his publicity campaigns."

"Yet you visited Captain Gerry Roberts?" Andi asked. "Why did you do that?"

For the first time, Carol Morin's voice shook a little. "I found notes about Captain Roberts in a file, and I . . . I wanted to follow up."

Andi sighed. "Carol, I understand that you are distrustful of the press. Maybe the police. But all I want to do is find out the truth. Years ago, your husband was accused of being involved in the death of a young girl. He was cleared, but the case was never solved. The community . . . well, many of the people in the community still suspect him. The 'no smoke without fire' kind of mentality, you know what I mean?" She looked at Carol, who nodded, and then carried on. "So it seems strange that your husband would come back to Coffin Cove, unless there was an important reason. Then he got killed. But the day before he died, he sent me this picture." Andi showed Carol a copy of the picture. "He implied that this was the important story. He called it 'The Bigger Picture'. Have you seen this before? Do you know what he was talking about?"

Carol took a long minute to look at the picture before she nodded.

"Yes. It was in his file."

"Same file with the notes about Gerry Roberts?"

"Yes." She pointed to the image of the DFO vessel. "Gerry Roberts was on this boat, and this boat here?" She pointed to the packer. "This boat was called the *King of Cash*. It was run by a man called Stan Hilstead."

"Steve Hilstead's father," Andi said. So that matched with Harry's story, she thought, and was surprised to feel some relief.

"Why was Pierre so interested in the Hilsteads?" she asked Carol.

"He wasn't particularly, not back then," Carol answered. "He was protesting against overfishing and the mismanagement of the fish stocks. He heard rumours that this boat, and the Hilsteads," she said, pointing at the packer in the picture, "were forging their tally slips, and paying off someone in the DFO to turn a blind eye."

"Tally slips?" Andi was confused.

"The record of the fish purchased from the fishermen. The fishermen keep a record of fish caught, and the packer keeps a record of the fish purchased, and then there's another record of fish sold on to the processors. All the records are supposed to match. This is how the DFO can control the fishery, make sure that there's no illegal poaching. Back then it was all recorded by hand. It was easy to forge, as long as everyone in the chain was in on it. Now it's done by cameras and computer."

"I see . . . I heard," Andi said, choosing her words carefully, "that the Hilsteads were paying the fishermen with cocaine."

Carol Morin gave a short laugh. "No doubt. But Pierre didn't care about that. He only cared about the poaching and holding the DFO to account."

"Did he ever prove it?" Andi asked.

"No. He was close, but he was only one person. He was working for Greenpeace, and they moved to other . . . priorities."

Andi decided not to probe this, so she moved on.

"Was the name 'Harry Brown' in his file?"

Carol frowned. "No, who is he?"

Andi pointed to the picture. "The other boat in this picture. The *Pipe Dream*. Harry Brown owns it."

Carol shook her head. "No, but this was a long time ago. There might be stuff missing from back then."

It wasn't entirely an exoneration, Andi thought.

"So why was Pierre in Coffin Cove?"

"Hades Fish Co. employed him to protest," Carol said simply.

"What?" Andi was stunned. "Isn't he . . . wasn't he on the other side? Wasn't he against the fishing industry?"

Carol looked at her, almost with amusement, Andi thought.

"Pierre didn't care about sides. He cared about the environment. Our oceans, our forests, our rivers. He knew how it worked. Some so-called environmental organizations are worse than big corporations. They exist only to make money from the bleeding-hearts who don't do their research. Or they work for competitors of certain corporations. They don't care about the cause. They care about the profit to be made. Environmentalism is big business now."

"So why was Pierre part of that?" Andi asked.

"Pierre worked for anyone who wanted the same result," Carol said. "Hades wanted the herring fishery disrupted so they could drive down prices and control the fishermen. Pierre wanted to stop the fishery because the stocks are depleted. The fishery is unsustainable."

Carol leaned across the table. "Miss Silvers, Pierre was a pragmatist. He did what he needed to do. He understood that sometimes you need to lie down with the Devil to do God's work."

Andi was beginning to understand.

"And Hilstead?" she asked. "Was he the Devil?"

Carol leaned back and shrugged. "I don't know. Pierre said that Hilstead was involved in a bigger poaching operation. He was working for someone else, and Pierre thought he was being helped — or at least not hindered — by someone in the DFO."

"Gerry Roberts?"

Carol nodded. "Pierre tried to talk to him. And so did I. I thought I could at least get something from him that would help find who killed my husband."

"But he wouldn't talk to you?"

"No. I guess he was afraid. And now it seems he was right to be."

"That night, Carol, why was Pierre at the fish plant? Did he tell you anything?"

"I told all this to the police. All Pierre told me was he was meeting someone who had information about illegal poaching. Someone he knew from his past."

She finished her coffee, then pulled two files out of her bag and handed them to Andi.

"You can have these. I didn't give them to the police. They are Pierre's. Everything I know is in there."

Andi flipped through the files and looked up at Carol. "This one is marked 'War in the Woods'. You're saying that Pierre's death was connected to those protests?"

Carol Morin pushed her chair back and stood up. "I'm not saying anything. But Pierre died in Coffin Cove. And his connection with that place went back to the War in the Woods."

"Carol, I have one more question. And then you'll never hear from me again," Andi said quickly. It was delicate, but she needed to ask. "Sarah McIntosh. Did Pierre . . . I mean, was Pierre . . ."

"Having an affair with a little girl?" Carol finished, her voice hard. "No, Miss Silvers, he wasn't screwing a little girl, and he didn't kill her either."

"So why do you think they suspected him?" Andi could sense Carol's anger, but she pushed for an answer anyway.

"Because he was an outsider," Carol said. "Coffin Cove doesn't like outsiders. Even though most of the community supported the protests, they still sided against him, rather than believe that one of their own could kill that child."

"Pierre thought someone in Coffin Cove killed Sarah?"

"It's all in the files." Carol Morin reached out to shake Andi's hand. "Be careful, Miss Silvers. You are an outsider too."

"Thank you," Andi said. Then she pointed at the file. "Why didn't you hand these over to IHIT?" she asked curiously.

Carol smiled for the first time. "Old habits die hard," she said. "Pierre and I got arrested many times. He was very proud of that."

Andi laughed. "I really appreciate it. I am so sorry about Pierre." She meant it sincerely.

Carol's self-control cracked for the first time. "Thank you," she said, her voice breaking with tears.

CHAPTER THIRTY-SIX

"Where's Nikos?" Harry asked as Brenda showed him and Terry into her small living room.

Terry nodded at Brenda and dumped a briefcase on her coffee table.

"I don't want him to know anything about this," a tall dark-haired man said. Harry assumed he was Adrian. He had Iris's delicate features and he was dressed in an expensive suit, far too fancy for Nikos, but there was something about his nervous energy that reminded Harry of his old boss.

"Adrian, this is Harry," Brenda introduced them.

Adrian smiled briefly, before his expression settled back into an anxious frown.

"I remember you," he said to Harry. "My father left me with you on your boat one day. He was supposed to be looking after me, but he was too busy."

"That happened a lot," Harry interrupted. "I remember. I was busy too, and pissed off at your old man, but you didn't make a fuss. You asked me a whole bunch of questions about fishing and didn't get in the way."

"Well, thanks anyway," Adrian muttered awkwardly.

Harry remembered the serious seven-year-old. They dressed him in expensive clothes then as well, too nice for a fishing boat, and the boy hung his head when Nikos left him on the wharf and drove off. Harry felt sorry for that kid back then.

He wasn't sure about now.

Adrian looked stressed. Every so often, he brushed his dark hair out of his eyes, paced over to the living room window and stared intently at the view, as if he could find answers to his troubles in the scenery.

Harry introduced Terry.

"So this is the problem we have," Harry started, and recounted the conversation that he, Jim and Andi had the previous night. "We don't have any proof that Hilstead hurt you," he said to Brenda, "and he could very well make it seem like you're nothing more than an unhappy employee, just pissed off that you're not as important to the company as you once were — you know what I mean, right?"

"Ex-employee," Brenda said, agreeing. "It was a mistake to resign, I suppose. Played right into Hilstead's hands."

"Not a mistake," Harry reassured her. "You did the right thing. You already put yourself in harm's way. Took a risk for the company." He looked at Adrian, hoping that his expression conveyed his disgust. "Anyway," he carried on, noting with satisfaction that Adrian hung his head, looking much like the young boy Harry remembered. "Here's the plan. And this is where Terry comes in."

* * *

"You're sure this will work?" Harry asked Terry. They were sitting in Terry's beaten-up Chevy van, parked across from Hades Fish Co.

"Course," said Terry, grinning. "Relax man, I'm a pro. All Adrian needs to do is get Hilstead talking. All we need is him on the record. Once we have that, we're golden."

Harry still doubted it. He'd cleared off discarded coffee cups, unopened mail and fast food wrappers from the passenger seat, and now sat with the window down, trying to air out the stale smell of grease and old running shoes.

He wondered how Andi had met this guy. He wore a woollen hat pulled down over his ears and big metal-rim tinted glasses, making him look like a seventies throwback.

He seemed to know what he was doing, Harry supposed. At Brenda's, he'd been serious and reassuring. He'd shown Adrian what he needed to wear and how it worked.

"It's not like the movies," he'd said. "This is a tiny camera that transmits audio and pictures to my phone. It's probably just like the system that Hilstead says he has in your offices."

Adrian nodded. "What do I say? What do we need him to say?"

"Much the same as he did before. If you can get him to admit that Brenda was attacked, that he's been trafficking drugs or any connection to Nguyen, if that's who he's working for — the more the better. But don't push it. Just have the conversation, take the transfer papers and tell him you'll talk to your father. We'll see what we get. Hopefully, it'll be enough."

Now, Terry and Harry waited for Hilstead to show up. Adrian was waiting in his office. They could hear him talking to his staff.

"That's really clear," Harry said. "I can hear every word. Where'd you get all this stuff? Some kind of spy store?"

"Amazon," Terry answered. "So, that Brenda — you banging her?" he asked matter-of-factly.

"No, I'm not!" Harry said, disgusted at Terry's disrespect.

"What about Andi? Because I'd like . . . hang on, is that Hilstead?"

CHAPTER THIRTY-SEVEN

Steve Hilstead slapped his steering wheel as he waited for the traffic light to go green. He was fuming. Mad at himself. He'd fucked up. He'd meant to leave the gun with Captain Roberts's body on the beach. Make it look like a suicide. The man was sad enough, would've made sense that he'd wanted to blow his pathetic fucking brains out.

But Steve had been so hyped up, so stoked to get an opportunity to do the job at the beach, instead of in Roberts's apartment like he'd planned, that he had totally forgotten to wipe down the gun and put it in the captain's dead hand.

Now there was another murder for police to investigate. And he couldn't be sure if Roberts had kept any documents or anything that connected them both. And there was that reporter. Would Roberts have been stupid enough to say anything? How had she found him?

Someone in a car behind him honked a horn. He looked up to see the light had changed.

"Fuck you," he said out loud, and hit the accelerator.

Steve's adrenaline was flowing. He needed to calm down, think clearly.

"Prioritize," he said to himself.

Paul Nguyen was his main problem. Dunn had made it clear that Steve had to deliver Hades Fish Co. in a few days. If that didn't happen, Steve knew that nothing else would matter, it would all be over. Nguyen didn't fuck around.

Steve pulled into a parking spot outside the offices of Dunn and Grant Associates. He ignored the parking meter, and went straight in. Before he could introduce himself, and explain why he was there, the receptionist handed him an envelope.

"Your documents, Mr Hilstead," she said, and for some reason, it unnerved him.

He tried not to think about it and drove straight to Adrian's office.

The atmosphere at Hades Fish Co. seemed subdued. Amy and her new colleague barely looked up when Steve came in.

Adrian's fucking sulking, he thought. After their last meeting, he must have had a tantrum and upset the girls. Steve hoped that Adrian hadn't been blabbing. This needed to go smoothly.

Adrian was in a belligerent mood. Argumentative. He scowled at Steve when he sauntered in and shouted for coffee.

"Shut the door," Adrian said rudely to Amy when she brought Steve his coffee. Amy practically ran out and slammed the door.

"What's the matter with you?" Steve said, easing back into the armchair.

"I got the letter back from Brenda," Adrian said. He was still sitting behind his desk, Steve noticed, twirling a pen nervously in his hand.

"Oh yes?" Steve said, not taking his eyes off the pen. "Did she sign it?"

"Yes, but what if she saw more than you think? Where was she when you . . . well, when it happened? What if she remembers all this?"

"If she signed the letter, you needn't worry about any of that," Steve said calmly. "She's gone now. We have something more important to do."

He threw the envelope on the table. "Here are the documents you need to get Nikos to sign."

"How am I going to get him to do that?" Adrian asked. "What should I say? 'Hey, don't worry, Dad, I'm going into business with a drug dealer who tried to kill your secretary'?"

Steve looked at Adrian curiously. Something was off.

He smiled. "I'll make it easy for you, Adrian. We'll talk to Nikos together. Let's go right now," and he watched Adrian's expression change. And he knew.

CHAPTER THIRTY-EIGHT

Vega made Andi wait.

He was tired of reporters. For days now, the media had been camped outside the Department of Fisheries and Oceans and in the parking lot of the Nanaimo RCMP detachment. They were rude, shouted questions in his officers' faces and jostled his team.

Like a pack of fucking wolves feasting on a dead man.

As far as he was concerned, Andi was one of them and she could damn well wait.

Earlier Vega had spoken with Superintendent Sinclair.

"Any connection between the two murders yet?" she asked.

"Not yet," he'd admitted.

"Put someone else in charge, Andrew," she said. "Get back to Coffin Cove. I don't want to be accused of not allocating enough manpower to the island."

All about appearances, Vega thought at the time. But now he was back in Coffin Cove, he realized she was right. He would be spread thin if he tried to run both investigations. Captain Gerry Roberts and his family deserved the full attention of a dedicated team. The best that the Integrated Homicide Investigation Team had to offer.

Not that there were many people grieving Gerry Roberts, Vega thought. One ex-wife who dabbed dry eyes and waited exactly fifteen minutes before asking about life insurance. Two daughters who hadn't seen their father in months. Colleagues who had little praise for Captain Roberts, just innuendos about a possible alcohol problem. A quick look at his finances revealed he was drowning in debts, and a search of his shabby rented basement suite confirmed the boozing.

On the surface of things, a man who had little to live for, Vega thought. Standing at the ocean, wondering what it was all for, and blowing his brains out. Wouldn't be the first time. But no gun at the scene. No possibility of it being washed away with the tide — Roberts was lying too far up the beach. So, at this point, they had to rule out suicide.

Oh well, not my problem now, he thought.

He called in Sergeant Fowler.

"That reporter is still outside, sir."

"She can wait," Vega said. "Maybe if we leave her there long enough, she'll go away. Tell me about Brown."

Fowler ran down her notes.

"So far, nothing much to tell, sir. Forensics lifted prints from the boat, and we're running them now. There are no cameras or anything at the dock to prove or disprove his story. We asked around, and he's well-liked and respected. A couple of people said he had a hot temper when he was younger, but apart from that one incident with Mason, he's never been in any trouble. Private, no girlfriend, his sister owns the café, mother dead, father lives in the trailer park — an alcoholic, but harmless. Several people saw Brown in the Fat Chicken the night Mason was killed, but he only stayed for an hour or so. Nobody saw anyone get on or off the *Pipe Dream*, but there's one name that keeps coming up, sir."

"Brian McIntosh?" Vega asked, knowing the answer.

Sergeant Fowler nodded. "No trace of him yet, sir. We're still looking."

"OK." Vega gave a half smile. "That's all we can do, Sergeant. Keep looking."

Vega followed Sergeant Fowler out of the office. He was hungry. He thought briefly of going to the pub. It was the only place to get good food in Coffin Cove when the café was closed, and he didn't want to drive all the way back to Nanaimo. But he knew that he'd be the centre of attention at the Fat Chicken, and he just wanted to be left alone.

"Miss Silvers, you're still here," Vega said unenthusiastically. "What can I do for you?"

"I have some information, Inspector Vega. About Mason."

Vega saw she was holding files. "Can it wait until tomorrow, Miss Silvers? I've had a long day."

She shook her head. So Vega stood back and gestured to the office. "Better come in then."

* * *

Hilstead? Vega was angry. Why hadn't that name come up before? How come the *Coffin Cove Gazette* had made all these connections and his own team hadn't? Time for that later, he thought, and pushed his anger aside as he listened to Andi.

Twice he interrupted her with a question.

When Andi mentioned Paul Nguyen, he stopped her.

"Wait there," he said and went to make a phone call.

"Andi, where is Hilstead now? Do you know?" he asked when he got back to the office. He noticed that Andi looked as exhausted as he felt. He also found himself thinking how attractive she was, with her glasses pushed back on her forehead, unaware that she had pen smudges on her cheek.

A second later he forgot those thoughts.

Andi's phone rang. She took the call and listened for a few seconds.

"Hang on," she said, taking the phone away from her ear. "I'm with Inspector Vega now. You're on loudspeaker. Tell him what you told me."

"Are you fucking kidding me?" Vega exploded, after listening to the call. "Have you any idea how dangerous that is? Tell me exactly where they are, right now."

CHAPTER THIRTY-NINE

"Shit!" Terry said, as he and Harry listened to Hilstead and Adrian. "What do we do now?"

"No idea. The plan was to get Hilstead on the record, nothing more."

"Should we just let Adrian take him to Nikos?" Terry asked. "Try something else?"

"Hilstead's already tried to kill Brenda, and he's a dangerous drug dealer. No fucking way we're letting him near Nikos. Hang on . . ." Harry dialled Brenda's number.

He told her briefly what they had just heard. "Text me Nikos' address. They're headed there now. Then call Nikos and tell him as much as you can. Tell him he *must* go along with Adrian. Tell him to tell Hilstead he needs to talk to his lawyer or something. Enough to get Hilstead out of there without anyone getting hurt."

Terry and Harry waited. They watched Adrian get in Hilstead's truck and pull out of the parking lot. They listened, hoping that Adrian wouldn't open his mouth and put them all in danger. But neither Hilstead nor Adrian said much. Adrian, sensing that Hilstead was on to him, maybe, hadn't argued.

Harry's phone pinged.

"Dyke Road," he said to Terry, "just near the private marina at the end. I know where it is. Don't follow the truck, go this way."

Harry recognized the house as soon as he saw it. Nikos and Iris had invited him once to an end-of-fishing-season barbeque. Nikos had proudly shown Harry around. It was a big, sprawling building with countless bedrooms. Nikos and Iris had wanted more children and eventually grandchildren. It wasn't to be. Iris died far too soon, and Adrian hadn't even married, let alone presented any grandchildren to proudly carry on the Palmer name.

Set back from the road, their large stuccoed rancher had a partial faux-rock facade that had seen better days. It was set on three acres, and Harry remembered that the back yard extended down to the Fraser River. Iris had kept a meticulous garden, but judging from the overgrown driveway, Nikos had let all that go after her death.

"Have you been here before?" Terry asked, as they parked away from the driveway entrance, their presence obscured by large rhododendron bushes and the fading evening light. They could see Hilstead's truck in the driveway.

"I've been here once, years ago," Harry said.

"Where in the house would they go?" Terry asked. "Left or right side?"

"Left," Harry said, trying to remember the layout. "Left, as we are facing it from here. I think the bedrooms are on the right. When you walk in through the front door — yes, I remember now — there's an open-plan living room on the left-hand side. Does that microphone thing still work?"

"Yeah, think so," Terry said. "Look, if this all goes to shit, we should try to get Nikos and Adrian out. Do you think there's a way in round the back?"

Harry nodded. "Just thinking the same. You see if you can listen in, text me 'GO' if I need to break in, right? Get my number punched in and ready."

"I'm phoning Andi now," Terry said. "I think we should notify the police. But it's her call. She's paying."

* * *

Harry got out of the car and Terry watched his bulky figure disappear around the corner until he was consumed by shadows. He made a call to Andi. Then he reset the audio app. He waited, and with relief he heard Adrian's voice.

"So, Dad, Steve and I would like to run something by you . . ."

Good, Terry thought, *they only just got here. Now, if Adrian can keep it together and just leave the documents with Nikos and get them out of there . . .*

He heard an older man speak. Nikos, he guessed.

"You want tea? Adrian, I make you and your friend Steve some tea, yes?"

"No, Dad . . ."

"I make tea. It's no trouble. Sit down, make yourself at home."

The audio was breaking up a bit. Terry needed to be a little nearer for his phone to pick up the signal. He leaned into the back seat of his car and pulled out his camera.

You never know, he thought.

He got out of the car and already could hear Nikos's voice much more clearly.

"The kettle is on. Now, what is all this about?"

"Dad, Steve and I have a new plan for the business . . ."

Adrian sounded calm, Terry thought, as he listened to him lay out a plan for transferring Nikos's interest in the company to Adrian.

Then he heard Hilstead.

"Actually, Mr Palmer, Adrian has it wrong. You have to transfer the shares to me. Right now. Sign the papers." He sounded desperate, Terry thought.

He edged nearer the house and could see Adrian and Hilstead sitting with their backs to the window. He wondered where Harry was.

"Wait a minute, Mr Hilstead." Nikos' voice was firm. "First, we will have tea."

What's going on? Terry thought. *Has the old guy lost his marbles or something?*

"Oh, fuck," he said out loud a moment later. He simultaneously watched and listened as Nikos came back into the living room, not carrying tea, but a handgun.

"You'll not be taking my business, Mr Hilstead. And you are not blackmailing my son. I know all about you and your illegal fish and your drugs. You've manipulated my son, but you'll not outsmart me."

There was a moment of silence and Terry thought he'd lost the audio. Then he heard Hilstead chuckle.

"Oh, I see now. Brenda was spying for you. I thought she was just a nosy old bat. Well, here's the deal, old man. You're going to sign over your shares to me. Otherwise, Adrian here will be in a world of trouble."

"I don't think so, Mr Hilstead. Adrian will explain everything to the authorities. He's made mistakes, but he'll be fine. Now I'd like you to leave."

Through the window, Terry saw Hilstead stand up and lean over Nikos.

"You don't fucking understand. Adrian won't be around to explain to the *authorities*. Now, sign the fucking papers or I'll fucking kill you myself."

Terry watched in horror as Hilstead grabbed Nikos around his throat. Terry grabbed his phone and texted '*GO GO GO*' to Harry, as Nikos struggled and Adrian tried to pull Hilstead off his father.

Terry heard some glass shatter on the audio. *Harry*.

Hilstead must have heard it too, because he hesitated for a split second. "What the fu—?" Terry heard, and then Harry was barrelling into the room, shouting at the top of his lungs, "GET THE FUCK OUT OF HERE!" and then Hilstead was running for the front door.

Terry dropped his phone. In the distance he heard sirens. He only had a few seconds. His camera was slung around his shoulder. He popped off the lens cap and aimed it at Hilstead as he ran out of the house.

FLASH. The camera's automatic flash illuminated Hilstead, and he came to a full stop, shielding his eyes, like

248

a deer in headlights. He was holding a gun, and aimed it wildly, before staggering forward, momentarily blinded. Terry kept his finger pressed down, so his high-speed camera took multiple shots of Hilstead as he made it to his truck. Red-faced, he pulled himself in and accelerated backwards down the driveway, swerving over the lawn and crunching through undergrowth, before he spun the truck round on the road and squealed away.

"Everyone OK?" Terry asked as Harry ran out to join him.

"All fine. Hilstead's got the gun, though."

"Ah. It's out of our hands now," Terry said as the sound of sirens got nearer, and they could see blue and red lights flashing in the distance. "Did someone mention tea?"

CHAPTER FORTY

"Not too early?" Jim asked.

"No," Andi said, "come in," and she stood back to let Jim into her apartment, glad to see he was balancing two coffees on top of a box.

"Where are the muffins?" she asked.

"We're economizing," Jim said, placing the box down. He looked at Andi. "You look tired."

"I was up late writing my article. Terry turned over all the audio he got yesterday to Vega's team, and they have enough to charge Hilstead. He didn't actually admit to attempting to kill Brenda, but he threatened to kill Nikos and Adrian, and that's plenty. Terry sent me a copy. Plus, I got the files from Carol Morin. I wanted to make a start."

"You ready to publish?" Jim asked.

Andi shook her head, feeling sheepish. "No, I, er . . . promised Vega I'd hold off until he gives me the go-ahead."

"Really?" Jim raised his eyebrows and said with mock seriousness, "How very responsible of you."

"Actually, he promised me an exclusive, if I waited." Andi couldn't help smiling smugly. "Lucky, really, because he was pretty mad about the surveillance."

"It could have gone very wrong," Jim said. "Lucky that Hilstead escaped without anyone getting really hurt. Can I read your draft?"

Andi handed Jim a copy of her article.

Jim sat down, and they both drank coffee in silence while Jim read through Andi's work.

"This is good," he said finally, looking up.

"It's just the start," Andi said. "Nguyen's tentacles stretch further than just the fishing industry. He's the real story. Mason knew it too — Hilstead's just a thug. Unfortunately for Mason, he didn't know how far Hilstead would go. My guess is that he confronted Hilstead and threatened to expose him, and, well . . . we know the rest."

"Any word on Hilstead now?"

"Not yet. Vega has a full-on manhunt underway. If they get Hilstead, they'll get Nguyen."

Jim put his coffee down and walked over to Andi's story wall. Andi watched him. She sensed he had something to say.

Finally, with his back to Andi, he said, "So you were wrong about the connection between the two murders."

Andi sighed. "OK, I made assumptions. It just seemed too much of a coincidence. But I was wrong. Mason's murder had nothing to do with Sarah McIntosh."

Jim turned round to face Andi. "Come here, I want to show you something."

Andi stood beside Jim as he unpinned and rearranged the documents on the wall.

"See?" he said when he was finished. "There is a connection. But not the one you thought."

Andi looked at Jim in amazement. "Are you sure? I mean, is this just a theory or . . . ?"

"It's not just a theory," Jim said. And he explained to Andi what he had discovered.

"Why didn't anyone figure this out back then?" Andi asked.

"Mason's wife was right," Jim said sadly. "It was easier to think an outsider would do this terrible thing. Even me. I thought I was being objective. I thought I was following the facts, but I was told a story I wanted to believe. And I destroyed a man's reputation."

Andi was quiet. She carried that burden herself.

Jim carried on. "You see, everyone knows everyone else's business in Coffin Cove. I was just choosing to ignore it."

* * *

"Do you think they'll get him?"

Harry patted Brenda on the shoulder.

"Don't worry. He can't get far. The police are looking everywhere for him.

Brenda nodded. "I know. I just want this over with."

She wasn't worried. A police cruiser was stationed outside her apartment block and Adrian had offered to pay for her to go to a hotel. But all she wanted was some peace.

"What will you do now? Will you go back to work for Hades?"

Brenda looked up at Harry. She let her eyes rest for a moment on his familiar weather-beaten face.

"No. It's not the same. I'm too set in my ways for Adrian. He needs some young blood. I think I'll go out east and stay with my sister. Take some time out. I'll rent out my apartment, and who knows? Maybe I'll start a new life in Ontario."

"That's good," Harry answered. "We all need a fresh start now and again, right?"

Brenda pressed her lips together and willed back tears. What had she expected? For Harry to beg her to stay?

She managed a smile. "That sounds like your plane." She reached out and rubbed his arm. "Thank you for everything, Harry. You take care of yourself, OK?"

Harry gave Brenda a hug, and she pushed him away quickly, not wanting to cry.

The floatplane chugged to the dock, and Harry picked up his bag.

"Keep in touch, Bren," he said over his shoulder as he walked away.

Brenda nodded and held her hand up to wave. "Sure, I will."

But as she watched Harry climb into the aircraft, smiling and laughing with the pilot, she knew it was time to let the past go forever.

CHAPTER FORTY-ONE

Harry drove. Jim sat beside him in the passenger seat. Neither of them said much, and Andi let her mind drift a little as the truck left the tarmac road and turned onto the gravel track that led up to the McIntosh house. As they climbed higher, the trees thinned out and Andi saw the view of the town and the ocean that had drawn Joe to build his house far up here on a rocky outcrop.

In the soft light that transitions day to night, Andi looked down on the lights of Coffin Cove. It looked so peaceful, she thought. Idyllic, almost. It was calm in the cove. The ocean stretched out like dark velvet, with just the occasional flash of light from a can buoy, warning vessels to keep clear of shallow waters.

Andi had submitted her first article to print. Terry sent pictures, including one of the startled, half-blinded Hilstead. Andi checked with Inspector Vega before publishing. She didn't want to compromise the police investigation, which was now officially a manhunt.

Vega thanked her for her cooperation and promised an exclusive when the time came.

Andi wondered if she should have given Vega a heads-up about their new suspicions about Brian McIntosh. But right now, she reasoned, they knew nothing. They just had a tiny silver necklace and Sue's grief-stricken theories. It wasn't even a story yet.

She gazed down at Coffin Cove. At night-time the shadows hid the dilapidated buildings and potholed streets. For a town where everyone knew everyone else's business, Andi thought, it kept its darkest secrets well.

Would she stay? She didn't know. Jim had been skirting around this question, probably wanting to ask, but not sure how. The *Gazette* had increased circulation a little, and was attracting new advertising — even businesses from Nanaimo were buying space — but the newspaper was far from being a viable business. Jim was paying Andi out of his own pocket, Andi suspected. She could probably get hired by one of the big media companies now, maybe on the East Coast.

She sighed. *Focus on one story at a time*, she thought. *Worry about the future later.*

"What's up?" Jim asked from the front seat.

"Just thinking about when I first got here," Andi said truthfully. "I thought I'd be spending the rest of my career reporting on community bake sales."

Jim said nothing, but Andi imagined his smile.

"OK, we're here," Harry said gruffly. He parked the truck in the driveway, and a motion light illuminated the yard. Andi could see a hunched figure sitting on the deck, a thin plume of smoke rising from a cigarette.

Harry twisted round in his seat to face Andi.

"He's in bad shape, Andi. I don't know if he'll be sober. If he gets really agitated, we might have to leave it, OK?"

Andi nodded.

The three of them got out of the truck, and Harry led them up the steps to the deck.

"Harry? Is that you?" Andi heard a woman's voice coming from inside the house. Tara, she presumed.

"Yes, it's Harry."

A woman with short grey hair and large glasses that framed kind blue eyes came out to the deck. "You've brought visitors," she said, sounding confused. "Here, wait a minute."

She stepped back into the house, and in a moment, the deck was flooded with light.

Andi blinked and refocused her eyes. Joe McIntosh was a shrunken, withered figure. He reminded Andi for a fleeting moment of Fred Harding, his father-in-law. But Fred had a life force, Andi decided, even if it was rage that still burned within him. This man was almost lifeless. The smell of alcohol was strong, and Andi realized that Joe was dousing the last embers of his humanity with booze. His life was over. He was just waiting for physical death to catch up with reality.

"What do you want, Harry?" Tara's voice was anxious. "Why is Jim with you? Who is this?"

Harry introduced Andi.

"Sorry to come unannounced, Tara. But we — well Sue, actually, she found something and it might mean something . . ." Harry's voice faltered a little, Andi noticed with surprise — she had never encountered gentleness from this man before.

"Mean something? I don't understand. What did Sue find?" Tara demanded. "That woman's not right in the head, Harry. You know that. I feel sorry for her, but we have enough on our plate." She gestured to Joe. "I don't think we can take much more, not after all this business with Mason."

At the mention of Mason, Joe reacted for the first time. He lifted his head and stared at Harry with watery eyes.

"What did Sue find, Harry?" His voice was strong, but he sounded disinterested, almost, Andi thought, resigned to whatever news might be coming.

"This." Jim stepped forward, opened his hand, and let the tiny silver necklace and cross spill onto the metal table next to Joe.

Joe stared at it for a moment and then turned his eyes away.

"What is it?" Tara pushed forward. "A necklace?" She picked it up and held it up to the light. "You think this is

Sarah's?" she asked incredulously, understanding now what Harry meant. "That's crazy, Harry. There must be a thousand silver crosses out there. Sue told you she found it? Where?" she demanded. "You know that Sue thought she saw Sarah in town months after she died? She needs help, Harry, not encouragement!" Tara dropped the necklace. "Enough of this nonsense!" she almost shouted.

"Wait!" Joe said and turned in his seat to face Jim. "Where did Sue find it? What did she say?"

"Joe—" Tara stood between Joe and Jim.

"Out of the way, woman!" Joe's bellow made Andi jump and Tara turn round in shock. Wordlessly, she stepped out of the way.

"Can I have a seat, Tara?" Jim asked calmly, and the tension eased slightly. Tara dragged over a chair, and Jim sat down, facing Joe directly.

"Sue found the necklace in one of the old buildings at the hatchery," he started. "She found it in a bundle of old belongings that she described to me. She hunts out there most days, and she said that lately, she felt that someone was watching her. We — Sue and I — went out to check, but the hut was empty. However, Andi saw Brian just before he disappeared, and from Sue's description, it sounded a lot like the bundle of belongings he was carrying." Jim hesitated. "Sue is sure that this necklace is Sarah's. It wasn't on her body when she was found, and Sue said that she wore it all the time. She never took it off. You gave it to her, didn't you, Joe?"

Joe nodded. He hadn't taken his eyes off Jim.

"Sue thought the necklace must have been lost in the water. She said it fell out of an old tin box of trinkets." Jim reached out and took Joe's wrist.

"Harry and I and lots of other people in town have seen Brian with a tin box just like the one Sue found. So the thing is, Joe," Jim moved in a little closer, "how did Brian get Sarah's necklace? And what does he know about her death?"

"That doesn't mean—" Tara interrupted, but Jim held up his hand to silence her.

"Brian was the witness who put Sarah with Mason just before her death. He was the one who intimated that Sarah and Mason were . . . close." Jim chose his words carefully. "He knew that rumours are like a virus in this town, and the gossips would do a great job of turning a hint of a salacious story into fact. And the sad thing is, Joe, we all bit. Even after the police cleared Mason, we all still believed that it must have been an outsider who took Sarah from us."

Andi could see that Harry and Tara were riveted. She felt in her jacket for her phone. She stepped back into the shadows, opened the voice record app, and replaced her phone carefully back in her pocket.

"Sue never believed that Sarah had any kind of relationship with Mason. Neither did Hephzibah. But the rest of us . . . well, it seemed to make sense. A girl with a strict religious upbringing, a broken home — we all figured that she must have fallen for Mason and the excitement of the protests. After all, how many parents really know what their kids are doing? Especially when they're teenagers."

Joe was still.

"Mason wasn't interested in Sarah. We know that because Andi met his wife recently."

That made Joe flinch for the first time. Jim carried on.

"In fact, he didn't really know who Sarah was. His real interest was stopping the clear-cutting. And someone was helping him, by feeding him information about your talks with the First Nation and your lawyers. But he wasn't getting the real story, was he, Joe? Somebody was feeding him bullshit, wasn't that right?"

Joe bent his head, and for a moment, Andi thought he was wheezing, not able to catch his breath. Tara must have thought so too, because she knelt by Joe and held his hand.

"Joe, calm down," she implored him.

Andi realized that Joe was sobbing. He was bent forward, his shoulders shuddering.

"That's enough, Jim!" Tara shouted. "Leave it be!" She wrapped her arms around Joe, shushing him.

"No, Joe. For years a man had his reputation smeared. I helped do that because I didn't do my job properly. Your daughter's name was dragged through the mud too. Her mother deserves the truth. Sue deserves to know how her daughter died, and she needs to restore Sarah's memory." Jim spoke forcefully, and Andi saw his cheek glisten.

"C'mon man," Harry said. "Tell us the truth!"

They waited until Joe's sobs subsided. Then he began to speak.

"I wanted to sell. It was getting harder to make a profit. The environmental regulations, the First Nation claims, everything was working against me. I was paying more than any other outfit, and everybody expected me to take them on. Good old Joe, he'll give you a job, even Ed," he said bitterly, looking up at Harry. "Every fucking drunk and layabout in Coffin Cove thought I should give them a job, even if they couldn't swing a fucking axe. It was killing my business."

Harry said nothing, his expression blank.

"The Americans made me an offer. And then the protesters showed up. At first, I thought it would kill the offer, and I was running around trying to figure it out, having meetings, making promises, anything to get rid of Mason and his fucking hippies." Joe paused and seemed to lapse into his memories for a moment.

"Then, I figured this could work for me. The Americans were already complaining about my payroll costs — they said the workforce was bloated and overpaid. I knew if I laid off workers, or cut wages, then my name would be mud around here. Most people were already jealous." He looked at Jim. "You have no idea how many people knocked on my door wanting money. 'You're so lucky,' they said. 'You should remember where you came from,' they said." He pulled his hand back from Jim, who had been holding his wrist.

"Everyone forgot all about those long hours I worked. They just knew I had money and thought I should give it out."

"Tell us what happened, Joe," Harry said quietly. Andi knew him well enough to know that he was getting angry.

"During the protests, nobody was getting paid. I had some logs stockpiled, so I kept selling. I thought if I could keep the protests going long enough, either people would find other jobs, or I could claim bankruptcy or something. The Americans offered me a bonus if I could get rid of two-thirds of the payroll. So I started feeding Mason information. I would have him believe that I was going to log in different areas and give him time to get his barricades in place. It was working too."

"How did you get the information to him?" Jim asked.

Joe dropped his head. "I paid someone."

"Brian?" Jim asked, although Andi knew that Jim was leading Joe through a story he had already figured out.

"Yes."

"Joe!" Tara let go of the arm she'd been rubbing and stood up. "Why does this matter now? Stop, Joe," she said urgently.

He waved his hand. "It doesn't matter now, Tara. Can't you see that? I have no life. *You* have no life, just watching me piss the rest of mine away. I'm tired. I want this to be over. I want to see my Sarah again." He started to weep.

"Joe," Jim said impatiently. "What happened? What happened to Sarah?"

Joe wiped his eyes with the back of his hand.

"She was so mad with me about the hatchery. I was doing it for her, I was selling because of her! I thought she would take my money if I was out of the logging business and go to university! Get out of Coffin Cove and make something of her life. I didn't even care when she joined the protest. But one evening she overheard me talking to Brian. She heard everything." Joe buried his head in his hands.

"She said I was destroying the town. She said . . . she said . . ." he faltered. "She said many terrible things to me. Brian was mocking her. He always hated Sarah, he was jealous. I was furious, and I'd been drinking . . ." He stopped and his breathing quickened.

"Go on, Joe." Jim's voice was soft. "Get it out, man, you've been carrying this too long."

"I don't remember exactly what happened." Joe's voice was almost a whisper, and Andi moved nearer to catch everything he was saying.

"I know that Sarah screamed at Brian and threw something, I think. She said that she had suspected all along and would tell Mason and everyone. Brian just lost it. He grabbed hold of her, and I tried to pull them apart . . . I don't know, I don't know." Joe's voice rose and he cried, "I pushed her, I pushed her so hard and she fell, and . . . and . . ." He collapsed in sobs again.

Andi closed her eyes, feeling her emotions well up, as Joe cried like a baby.

"It was an accident, Joe. You didn't mean it," Harry said, his voice thick, and Andi could tell he was grief-stricken.

"Brian said he could sort it. He would put her in the hatchery, everyone would think it was an accident. And it was an accident," he said fiercely. "I didn't know . . . I didn't know . . . she was still alive . . ." He was forcing each word out now. "Not until they found her all tied up. They said she drowned!" he wailed. "My little girl, she must have been so frightened . . ."

"Why didn't you go to the police?" Harry asked in disbelief. "Why didn't you turn that fucker in? Why did you protect him all these years?"

"He'd already told some story about Sarah and Mason to the police. He told me that Mason was suspicious, and that he did it to help me. He threatened me too. Said that if he went down, so would I. I threw him off the property, told him that if I ever saw him again, I'd turn him in, I didn't care anymore."

"You let us all feel so fucking sorry for you." Harry practically spat the words out. "We searched for your little girl. My sister cried tears for you. You even told us that Sue was a madwoman." Harry shook his head. "You're pathetic, Joe. Pathetic. I looked up to you, man." He turned away in disgust. "I've heard enough — let's go to Vega, Jim. He needs to hear this."

Joe rocked back and forth, crying. Tara stood by his side, with a hand on his shoulder. She didn't protest.

Jim sighed. "I'm sorry, Joe . . ."

"Hey!" Harry shouted suddenly. At the same time, Andi saw a movement in the undergrowth near the deck. Harry ran, taking the steps off the deck in one bound, and dove into the shadows. A moment later and he dragged Brian McIntosh into the light.

"He's been here all the time?" Harry shouted angrily at Joe. "You're still protecting this shit? What's the matter with you, man?"

"It's all fucking lies," Brian whined. "Joe killed her, not me. I was just tryin' to help my bro, it's not fuckin' fair."

Harry shook him. "Shut the fuck up."

In the distance, Andi heard a truck rumbling up the track. She could see the headlights glinting through the trees.

"Is that Vega?" she asked Jim. "Did you call him?"

"I—" Jim started to say, but at that moment, Brian McIntosh twisted out of Harry's grasp and took off running into the dark. Harry ran after him, and as the truck rounded the corner into the yard, Andi saw Harry tackle Brian McIntosh to the ground and pin him there easily.

The headlights of the truck blinded her. She expected Vega to call out, to have brought his officers, but only one figure got out of the truck. The engine was still running, and the lights were on full beam. Andi shielded her eyes.

"Inspector?" she called above the growl of the diesel engine.

The figure didn't answer. Instead, he held his arm out straight. A gun, Andi thought, not comprehending, and at the same moment she realized it wasn't Vega, the man pulled the trigger and fired at Harry and McIntosh.

"Harry!" Andi screamed.

"Get down!" Jim dragged her onto the deck and pushed Tara back into the house. "Turn the light off!" The deck plunged into darkness.

"What the fuck?!" Andi heard Harry's voice in the darkness and nearly cried with relief.

"Well, thanks for doing all the work, Harry," the figure said. "You seem to be turning up everywhere. Hand him over. I don't want to hurt you. I just want Brian."

Hilstead, Andi thought.

To her surprise, Harry laughed.

"You've killed two people already, Hilstead. You'll kill me in a heartbeat. You want McIntosh? Come and fucking get him."

"What is he doing?" Andi said frantically. "He'll get himself killed!"

"Shut up," Jim muttered to her. "He knows what he's doing."

Hilstead strode away from the truck. Andi's eyes readjusted to the dark. From where she was lying, stomach down on the deck, she could make out the outline of Harry's bulk. She could hear Harry grunting and guessed that he was dragging McIntosh with him. She hoped that Tara was calling the police.

Hilstead was advancing slowly, his gun — Nikos's gun, Andi thought — held in a firing position. He stopped. Andi guessed that he was listening, trying to hear movement. Harry must have stopped still, because she couldn't see him anymore.

Andi heard a click, followed by a loud quick flash of light. In that second, she saw Harry holding on to Brian, right in the line of fire. She heard Hilstead laugh, and before he could fire again, she pushed herself to her feet and started running towards Hilstead.

"Stop firing, you fucker!" she screamed.

"Andi!" she heard Jim shout behind her, but she kept running.

She heard another click, and she swerved to her right, as the gun flashed in front of her and the sudden loud noise made her ears ring. But then one leg crumpled under her.

I've tripped, Andi thought, as she fell — in slow motion, it seemed — to the ground. But her leg didn't move with her body and she felt a searing pain in her thigh.

Oh, Andi thought to herself, as her head hit the ground, *I've been shot.*

A dark shadow loomed over her.

Hilstead, Andi thought. *He's going to kill me. I hope my phone is still recording.* And for some reason, that thought made her giggle.

She heard another click over the buzzing in her ears.

He must be near.

This is it.

In the distance, Andi heard gunfire. But she felt nothing, except the burning in her left thigh.

She felt the ground vibrate beside her. The movement made her leg hurt more, and although she just wanted to close her eyes, she put her hand down and pressed hard. Somewhere she'd read that this was the right thing to do.

Her hand was wet.

There were shadows above her. They faded in and out of sight.

Andi was getting cold.

And then lots of shouting. Was that a truck? Was Hilstead getting away? Andi tried to turn her head. She felt a presence beside her. *Harry?*

"Are you OK?" a voice asked her.

Andi recognized the voice, but it wasn't Harry. It was a woman.

"Sue?" Andi said. "I think I've been shot."

Sue's face came into view. "Stay still. You'll be fine. Help is on the way."

"What are you doing here?" Andi wondered, her voice sounding like it was coming from far away.

"Settling a debt," Sue said.

"Oh. OK. I see," Andi said, although she didn't.

And then it all went very quiet.

CHAPTER FORTY-TWO

Andi was surprised to receive flowers at the hospital.

Hope you get back to writing soon, best wishes for a speedy recovery, Andrew Vega, the card read.

He'd been as good as his word too. He'd visited Andi and allowed her to ask as many questions as she wanted, with the one stipulation that he got to read the story before it went to print.

Vega's team had Hilstead in custody. He'd been charged with the murder of Pierre Mason and Captain Gerry Roberts. He'd first hired Dunn and Grant Associates as his lawyers, but had possibly been persuaded, as Vega put it, that if he cooperated and handed them some decent information on Paul Nguyen, he might not serve life in prison. His decision was still pending. Nguyen's influence was everywhere. Even in prison, Vega explained to Andi.

Brian McIntosh had been charged with Sarah's murder. He'd known she was alive when he tied her up and left her to drown in one of the abandoned, flooded hatchery buildings. He was also charged with stealing Harry's gun. McIntosh was busy trying to blame his brother, Vega said, sadly.

"And Joe?" Andi had asked.

Vega shook his head. "No charges. Joe has liver cancer. He only has weeks, maybe days to live. His life has been a torment, a living punishment. I can't imagine. Punishment harsher than the court system can hand out, I think."

"What about Hades?"

"We've left that up to the DFO. But I think after the embarrassment with Captain Roberts, they'll not pursue charges. I think Nikos Palmer is going back to help his son."

"And you'll be glad to hear that I'm not charging you with anything," he'd said with a smile that Andi found quite charming.

"That's because I didn't do anything," she had replied.

"Really? How about impeding an investigation, conducting unlawful surveillance, being a pain in the ass?" He'd laughed. "When you come to Vancouver, I'll buy you lunch."

Andi had agreed. She liked him. He had a dry sense of humour and he wasn't bad-looking when he smiled, she thought.

Jim hadn't been enthusiastic about Andi going to Vancouver.

"Is that a date?" he asked suspiciously. "Haven't you had enough of Vancouver men? Can't you find a date on the island?"

"Sure," Andi said sarcastically. "I'll learn to fish and skin squirrels, OK? Then I'll have to beat off Coffin Cove men with a stick."

Jim laughed. "C'mon, we're not that bad."

He didn't want her to leave, Andi knew that. She wasn't sure what she wanted to do. The gunshot wound was healing, but she'd had a long time to think about her future while she lay in that hospital bed.

"I can't promise anything long-term," Andi said to Jim when he visited, "but I'll stay until the *Gazette* is on its feet. But we have to make some changes if it's going to work."

Jim listened to her. "I can't make promises either," he said. "We're . . . well, I'm practically broke. We'll try what you suggest and see what happens. Let's say we give it a year. Let's reassess where we are then. Does that work?"

"It's a deal," Andi said, glad to kick this decision down the road. And it was settled.

* * *

It was her last day in hospital. Andi was surprised to see Harry.

He looked uncomfortable, sitting in the small metal visitors' chair with his arms crossed.

"Are those from that newspaper guy?" Harry asked, nodding his head at the flowers by Andi's bedside. "Your old boyfriend?"

"No," Andi said, and smiled at Harry. She wondered why he had come. Just to make nosy comments about her flowers and sit there looking grumpy?

"How's your girlfriend?" Andi asked, breaking the awkward silence.

"Who?" Harry said, looking startled.

"Brenda," Andi said, "I thought you and she . . ."

"No, no . . . well, not now. Once upon a time we . . . well, that was years ago," Harry said, stumbling over his words. "She's leaving Steveston and moving out east to live with her sister. She's renting out her apartment and might even sell up. Says she needs a fresh start."

"Oh, I see," Andi said, amused to see him so flustered. "So, did you bring me some of Hephzibah's muffins?"

"Er, no, I . . ."

"No flowers, no muffins, why exactly are you here?" Andi said, wanting to laugh, but frowning at him.

"OK, I wanted to say something," Harry said. He looked serious and Andi wished she hadn't teased him.

"That night, when you got shot, you were running towards me and Hilstead, do you remember?" He leaned forward and took Andi's hand.

She nodded slowly. "Yes, I remember."

"What I wanted to say . . . well . . . Andi," he looked at her, and said slowly, "that was the most unbelievably fucking stupid thing I've ever seen in my life."

TWO MONTHS LATER

"You know, there's one thing I never did find out," Andi said as she accepted a mug of coffee from Harry.

"Oh? What's that?" Harry sat on his faded canvas chair and looked at Andi perched on an old upside-down fish container, her arm resting on her crutches.

He handed her one of Hephzibah's Morning Glory muffins, still warm.

Andi accepted it. Her appetite was coming back. She was sleeping better and had stopped drinking wine. Well, not so much anyway. Her leg was healing slowly, and she'd managed to clamber onto the deck of the *Pipe Dream* that morning without help from Harry.

He'd been surprised to see her.

Andi had been planning the visit. She needed an answer to a question that had been niggling her for a while.

"I never found out who shot the sea lions."

Harry took a moment before he answered.

"Maybe Mason shot them himself?" he suggested.

Andi considered for a minute.

"I guess that's possible. He wanted to create some drama so he could whip up some outrage."

"Wouldn't be the first time," Harry replied.

"Hmm." Andi wasn't convinced.

They both sat for a moment in the morning sun.

"The DFO have announced a study," Harry said, breaking the silence. "To find out if there is any evidence that the sea lions are depleting fish stocks." He rolled his eyes. "I could have saved them the cash."

Andi laughed and winced a bit. "I suppose that's a start."

"After all the publicity about Mason and Gerry Roberts, I guess they thought they'd better do something. At least they are listening to our side this time."

Andi looked at Harry.

"You should thank that person who shot those sea lions then," she said, her gaze steady. "In a way, he started all this."

He turned his head to look at her.

"I suppose he did," he said, and smiled.

THE END

ACKNOWLEDGEMENTS

This book and the Coffin Cove series would not exist without the encouragement and support of my family, especially my husband, Bob.

Thanks also to my husband and other people in the commercial fishing and forestry industries who have corrected my terminology, explained processes and generally added to the authenticity of the story. Any errors that exist are mine alone.

AUTHOR'S NOTE

The War in the Woods as referred to in this book is a fictional event. The real War in the Woods, also known as the Clayoquot protests, took place in 1993 on Vancouver Island.